I0718061

DARING

Lipstick and Lead Book 4

BY SYLVIA MCDANIEL

Books by Sylvia McDaniel

Contemporary Romance

Standalones
The Reluctant Santa
My Sister's Boyfriend
The Wanted Bride
The Relationship Coach
Her Christmas Lie
Secrets, Lies, and Online Dating
Paying for the Past
Cupid's Revenge

Anthologies
Kisses, Laughter & Love
Christmas with you

Collaborative Series

Magic, New Mexico
Touch of Decadence

Western Historicals

Standalones
A Hero's Heart
A Scarlet Bride
Second Chance Cowboy

The Cuvier Women
Wronged
Betrayed
Beguiled

Lipstick and Lead
Desperate
Deadly
Dangerous
Daring
Determined
Deceived

Scandalous Suffragettes
Abigail
Bella
Callie
Faith

The Burnett Brides
The Rancher Takes a Bride
The Outlaw Takes a Bride
The Marshal Takes a Bride
The Christmas Bride

Anthologies
Wild Western Women
Courting the West
Wild Western Women Ride Again

Collaborative Series

The Surprise Brides
Ethan

American Mail Order Brides
Katie

Daring

Published by Virtual Bookseller

Cover Design by Lyndsey Lewellen
https://lyndseylewellen.wordpress.com/

Edited by Andrea Dickinson
http://www.qualitybookservices.com/

Formatted by Laurelle Procter
laurelleprocter@gmail.com

Copyright © 2016 by Sylvia McDaniel
This book and parts thereof may not be reproduced in any form, stored in a retrieval system, or transmitted in any form by any means—electronic, mechanical, photocopying, or otherwise—without prior written permission of the author and publisher, except as provided by the United States of America copyright law. The only exception is by a reviewer who may quote short excerpts in a review.

Short Description: Ruby McKenzie works with a man she once loved to bring in her father's killer.

ISBN: 978-1-942608-56-1 (paperback)
ISBN: 978-1-942608-00-4 (e-book)

{Historical Western Romance – Fiction}

www.SylviaMcDaniel.com

Synopsis

Ruby McKenzie loves being a bounty hunter in west Texas. She loves chasing bad guys and bringing them to justice using her beauty and wiles to catch criminals. But her sisters refused to let her hunt alone and now they're married, no longer interested in seeking outlaws. When Ruby takes her cousin Caroline out on a hunt, they stumble upon the handsome cowboy who broke Ruby's heart. Deke Culver. The only man who has ever resisted her charm.

Deke Culver is shocked when Ruby McKenzie rides into his camp and steals his bounty. Ruby was the girl who got away, the woman he sometimes dreams of and knows he can never marry. When the two decide to work together to bring in her father's killer, neither one is prepared for the feelings that are reawakened. But Deke has a secret that will keep him from ever committing himself to a woman. Can Ruby heal his heart and open it to love once again?

Table of Contents

Chapter One

Ruby McKenzie knelt beside her cousin Caroline McKenzie in the Texas dirt and gazed down at the campsite. The fire barely glowed in the pre-dawn light. She loved her life. She loved what she did for a living. And she loved her independence.

"Were you nervous the first time?" Caroline asked her voice soft and trembling.

God, sometimes she just wanted to shake the girl. How could she ever expect men to respect her with a voice more suited for the bedroom? "No. I couldn't wait. I wanted my first man so bad, I was almost giddy."

Ruby's occupation was a lonely, dangerous one. One she'd learned after her father had died, saddling her and her beloved sisters with a bank note on their farm and no skills to earn a living. So they'd become bounty hunters. Hunting criminals for cash.

And they were good at catching outlaws.

"The man lying in front of the fire is the man on the wanted poster," Caroline said, gazing at the camp below them. "But I don't recognize the other man."

Ruby glanced over at Caroline, her cousin's black as midnight hair was braided down her back, making her look almost like an Indian squaw with her dark coloring. She was beautiful and sophisticated and much too soft for the job. This was her first hunt and Ruby worried. Was she ready for the action? The possibility of having to use her gun? Could she protect Ruby in a gunfight?

She sighed and peered down in the darkness trying to discern the features of the unknown man. "There's no way of knowing who that second man is until we get down there. He could be a bounty we hadn't planned on collecting."

"Or not," Caroline whispered.

"Relax," Ruby said squirming, an itchiness to get started making it hard for her to sit still. She couldn't wait to spring into action and snap up another criminal. Maybe even two.

"How are we going to do this?" Caroline asked licking her lips nervously. "It's almost morning. The sun should soon be rising."

"Once we catch them, we're two hours from town. We'll turn them into the sheriff in Dyersville and be on our way," Ruby said, pushing back her blonde curls away from her face. Excitement pulsed through her veins as she prepared herself mentally for the capture. She could hardly wait to slap the rope around their wrists, but maybe that part of the abduction would be better for Caroline to handle. "Let's go over the plan."

Caroline bobbed her head, her eyes large in the moonlight. "What do I do?"

"We're going to walk into their camp with our guns drawn. You tie them up while I hold my gun on them. You've got to be quick before they start to think we're just a couple of women and try to disarm us. I don't want to shoot our guy, but I will if I have to."

"What kind of knots do I tie? A bow or a square knot? How tight around their wrists? I don't want to hurt them."

The words sent uneasiness flowing through Ruby. Why had her sister, Meg decided now was the time to fall in love and marry the Sheriff of Zenith? They were great partners and she'd left Ruby stuck with a novice like Caroline. "Tie a knot that keeps them from getting loose. I'll double check that they're secure once you're done."

"Oh," Caroline said biting her lip. "So, we burst into their camp with our guns drawn and tell them, we're bringing them to justice. Then I approach the men and pull their hands behind their back and tie a rope around their wrists?"

"Stop thinking so hard and just react. Are you sure you can handle tying them up?"

What if Caroline froze in the middle of the capture? How would Ruby be able to save both of them if her cousin became scared?

Caroline inhaled enough air for a battalion of soldiers. "I think so. But what if they grab me? What if they pull their guns on us? What if they shoot at us?"

"Calm down, Caroline. I don't need you passing out on me."

Ruby watched as Caroline sucked in air more leisurely and released it slowly. She practiced slow breathing several times. "Better. When we charge into camp I will tell them to throw down their weapons. I'll collect the guns while you keep your six-shooter trained on them. Once I have their guns, then I will hold them at gunpoint while you secure them with rope."

Caroline shook her head. "No. I don't like this. I'll hold the gun on them, while you collect their guns and tie them up. I'm afraid to get too close."

"All right," Ruby said her tone clearly frustrated. But she had to make certain whatever job she gave Caroline the tenderfoot could handle. Right now she wasn't certain Caroline wouldn't get them both killed. "You're as nervous as a prostitute in church."

Caroline jumped up. Her body stiffened, as she placed her hands on her hips and gave Ruby a haughty glare. "Now, Ruby there's no need to get nasty. Don't be using prostitute and church in the same sentence. That's just not nice."

Ruby wanted to roll her eyes, but refrained. Caroline had always been a little uppity. Well in this business, there was no place for airs. Working alone had to be simpler than training this greenhorn. "Concentrate on us getting the bounty."

"Okay," she said taking a deep breath. "I'll keep my gun trained on the bad guys while you pick up their guns and tie them up."

"Correct. Now let's get going before it gets any lighter."

Ruby pulled out her little pot of lipstick that Meg had taught her how to use. They'd made a ritual of putting color on their lips before each job, almost like putting on their war paint.

"Why are you putting on lipstick? These men won't see it in the dark."

"No, but it's a habit Meg started. Put on your lipstick and then go after your bad guy. It gives me strength."

Caroline shook her head, like she thought it was nonsense. "Give me some."

Smiling Ruby handed her the little pot. "Just smooth a little on your lips." She watched her cousin put on her paint. "Now we're ready."

"Just let me get my horse."

"No, we're walking."

"But what about my mare?" Caroline said, her eyes widening like she'd lost her best friend.

Really? She thought they were going to walk all the way to Dyersville? That she would leave their horses behind? The next time she saw Meg, she was going to tell her marriage and motherhood better be well worth the sacrifice.

"You'll come back for the horses."

"Oh. Okay." Caroline glanced around almost like she wanted to run. Like anything would be better than capturing this bounty.

"Come on, after this first time, it'll be a piece of cake. You'll wonder why you were so nervous."

"I hope so. Because right now that pig farmer mother wanted me to marry, is starting to look a little better."

"Soon you'll start to enjoy the chase. The rush of excitement you get every time after you catch one of these guys and the sense of gratification when you collect the money. Before long you'll love this life as much as I do."

Of course, Annabelle, Ruby's other sister had hated being a bounty hunter. And after she'd chased Beau, her husband only to learn he wasn't a wanted man, she'd given up the profession. Now, she was expecting her first child.

What was it with her sisters? They went bounty hunting, came home married and shortly were pregnant. That would never happen to Ruby.

Ruby watched Caroline shaking her head. "I don't know. Maybe I should have stayed in Zenith and married that pig farmer. At least I wasn't risking life and limb."

"You think not? You would have slowly died from boredom. I'm waiting for the day my sisters come to me and tell me they are bored out of their minds. Men do that to you. Crawl inside your skin and mesmerize you with their soft words and silky lies. I'm not going to fall for sweet promises."

Ruby couldn't believe her two sisters were married and both expecting babies. Marriage and men. She wanted absolutely nothing to do with either. The taste of men she'd experienced was enough to swear off of them forever. Men were easily deceived, would pay for kisses, assumed the worst about a girl, and couldn't be trusted. Nope she wanted nothing to do with the opposite sex, except to bring them to justice and collect the bounty. And she'd do the same if a woman had a price on her head.

"Are you ready," Ruby said rising from the ground. It was time.

She dusted off the split skirt Meg had fashioned for her. She loved how she could ride like a man, but it looked like she was wearing a skirt.

"Yes," Caroline said pulling back her shoulders, lifting

her head. "I'm going to earn a living on my own without the aid of a husband."

"That's the spirit," Ruby said. "You're going to become an independent woman."

"Yes," Caroline said her voice whispery soft.

God, if only she could toughen up this woman's image. She talked like she was about to attend a tea party, not haul in a wanted criminal.

~

Deke Culver was lying in his sleeping roll thinking he needed to get up, trying to will away the dream that had awakened him. He'd dreamed of Laura. She'd been so beautiful and happy and he'd followed her, knowing it would end badly, expecting the worst. And when the screaming started…he'd forced himself to waken.

Now he lay here pushing the darkness down into the recesses of his mind, willing himself to rise and face yet another day. A day he didn't deserve to live.

The snap of a twig, alerted him. Angry whispers started like the wind rustling in the trees, but at a higher pitch. What the hell was going on?

Two women burst into their camp, brandishing six-shooters. He rose and reached for his gun.

"Throw down you weapons and raise your arms," a girl screamed. Something about that voice was familiar.

Slowly he stood. The man tied up on the ground next to him, his prisoner, was unable to stand.

"Get up," the woman yelled at his bounty.

"He can't get up," Deke said calmly.

"Why not?" she barked.

"He's tied up."

"Oh," she said standing on the edge of the firelight, her features dark. "Where's your weapon?"

"It's in my blankets," he said not willing to help her

out.

He stared at the two women fear of one of their weapons discharging keeping him still. He wondered what they wanted. Were they looking for the man? Were they family members who'd come to rescue his criminal or what? The dark haired girl's hand was shaking so bad that it was a wonder she didn't drop her weapon, but the blonde...the blonde she knew exactly what she was searching for. She found his weapon and when she turned to face him, to his shock he recognized her.

"Ruby McKenzie," he said, unable to stop the grin that creased his face. The memory of their last meeting was a pleasant one except for her firing bullets at him while he rode off.

"Deke," she said her smile forced her voice tight. "Still kissing girls and making them cry?"

"Not since you," he said. He dropped his hands. "What are you doing out here?"

She jabbed him in the ribs with her six-shooter. "Oh no, put those hands back where I can see them. Caroline watch him closely. He's a sly one."

"Yes, ma'am," the girl said, her hands shaking like a rattler with a chill. She was more ornamental than useful.

"What are you doing Ruby, girl?"

"This man is wanted. I'm taking your bounty, Deke. Call it payment for the kiss you stole from an innocent."

He started laughing. "I didn't steal a kiss from you. You were begging me to take that kiss and more. Out of respect for your Pa, I walked away from you that day. Or I would have accepted your offer of more."

"That was a young and foolish girl," she said grabbing his hands and pulling them down. She began to wrap rope around his wrists.

"So to repay me you're going to take my bounty and leave me tied up here in the wilderness?"

Part of him was frustrated she thought she had the right to his bounty, but another part felt guilty for how things had ended between them. That seemed to be his lot in life when it came to women. He was a sucker to help pretty girls and then he let them rip his guts out.

She finished tying the rope around his hands and tied it off. "Sweetie, you just made my job easier. You caught him for me and now I'm hauling him in."

"Isn't that stealing?" he asked.

She stood right in front of him and leaned in close. "Your kiss was the icing on the cake of the worst day of my life. I really don't have fond memories of us. In fact, I pretty much hate men now because of you and Clay Mullens. You taught me what a worthless lot all of you are."

He took a step closer to her and felt her six-shooter up against his ribs, his chest against her chest, his hands tied behind his back. "That's a real shame. Because I have very fond memories of that kiss. A young, innocent girl who was hurt. If I'd been the cad you're making me out, I would have taken advantage of everything you offered that day. But I didn't want memories of Clay tainting me and you. If you'd been older, and not healing from an attempted rape, I'd have been all over you."

Ruby licked her lips and stared at him. "Too bad. You missed your chance."

He shook his head. "Oh no. We've got now. We've got right this moment. Untie my hands and we can finish what we started."

She laughed and glanced at him like he'd had too much loco water to drink. "Sorry, not interested. I've got a bounty I need to turn in."

A gunshot went off behind them and Deke knocked her to the ground, covering her body with his. At this moment, he knew he could have gotten out of his ropes and taken her gun away, but he didn't. It wasn't like there was a lot of money riding on this guy and he'd never forgotten how poor the McKenzie sisters had been after their father died. Deke didn't need the money, maybe she did.

"Get off me." She pushed him away and then whirled around. "What's wrong, Caroline?"

Trembling she stared at Ruby, tears filling her eyes. "Oh my God, I could have killed you. I was shaking so hard, I accidentally pulled the trigger."

"Ohhhh," Ruby groaned. "Just guard our bounty."

Rising she stood and watched as Deke rose. "That's some partner you got there."

"She's okay."

He chuckled. "I'd heard stories about women bounty hunters but never thought it was you."

Ruby dusted the dirt from her skirt. "I wish I had time to tell you all about it, but unfortunately, we need to be going. I'm sure you'll eventually get out of your ropes, but we'll be long gone."

"Thanks. Glad I could do the work for you."

"We appreciate it," Ruby said. "Grab our horses, Caroline. Let's ride."

"Me?" she squeaked. "But?"

"Just do it."

Caroline tried to shove her gun back in her holster, but it became stuck and for a moment Deke feared she'd shoot her foot into next week. Finally she got the gun back in the holder.

Watching her walk away, Deke couldn't help but laugh. "She's a real greenhorn. I don't think they get much greener than that girl."

"She's doing okay."

"Yeah, you keep telling yourself that, right up until the day you get shot because of her."

In a few moments, Caroline brought their horses into

camp. She halted them in front of Ruby.

"So long Deke and I'm so sorry we couldn't just pick things up where they were," she said in a sarcastic snit.

"Don't worry we will," he said confidently. Knowing he'd be behind her just as soon as he could get the ropes around his wrist untied. They had unfinished business.

"When pigs fly," she said, and grabbed the prisoner by the arm, yanking him to his feet. Quickly she untied his feet, so he could ride. "Come on you're going with us."

She pulled him toward his horse. The man stiffened resisting Ruby. "I'm not getting on this horse. No way, I'm riding with a couple of women."

"Suit yourself. But if I have to make you get on that horse, you'll go with a bullet in your man parts. Get my drift?"

"For a pretty woman, you're a mean bitch."

She glanced back over at Deke and smiled.

"That I am." She pointed her six-shooter towards his crotch. "Now are you going to climb on your horse or do I have to put you there?"

He crawled up on his horse. She and Caroline climbed on their horses and Ruby turned to wave goodbye to Deke. She should feel bad for taking his bounty, but she didn't.

As they rode out, Caroline sighed. "I've captured my first bounty. I'm a real woman bounty hunter."

Ruby almost choked trying to keep from laughing out loud. What could she say? That her cousin was a buffoon who had almost gotten them both killed? That if it hadn't been Deke Culver, they would have faced a much tougher resistance? As it was, she couldn't believe he just let her take his bounty.

She took a deep breath and released it slowly. Caroline had to get better if she wanted to keep from dying. "Yes, Caroline you are an official bounty hunter."

"Better than a pig farmer's wife."

Ruby laughed. "Most definitely better than a pig farmer's wife."

As she turned her horse towards town, she glanced back at Deke. He was standing in the center of camp, working the knots on the ropes. He'd soon be loose.

Once again, the man she'd fought Annabelle over, flirted outrageously with, who she'd begged to take her virginity had shown up in her life. And this time she was older, wiser and frankly had no desire to ever see that jackass again.

When she'd needed him most, he'd turned her down. And while now she could see he was right, that didn't ease the embarrassment or the shame at how she'd handled his rejection.

In fact, even taking his bounty hadn't eased the pain of him declining to take her virginity. Since the day of his dismissal, she'd believed that men were ignorant beasts.

No man had changed her mind, yet.

~

Deke Culver leaned against the wall just outside the sheriff's office. He was too late to take his bounty back. Ruby's horse and her cousin Caroline's were tied to the hitching post outside the lawman's office. And while he could go in and protest, he really didn't want to create the scene he knew Ruby would stage and become the star in.

No, he was better off letting the bounty go, though he wasn't ready to let the woman go. She was still a sassy little thing he couldn't resist and felt attracted to. Before she'd been way too young and out of respect for her father, he'd refused to participate in any deflowering no matter how much she begged.

Because then he'd have felt honor bound to marry the girl.

After realizing she was one of the bounty hunter

women he'd heard about that were collecting rewards on criminals, he realized someone else had probably already done the deed and he could just be there to sample the wares. If she'd let him get close enough. It had been a long time since he'd experienced a woman. And he was more than ready.

The door opened and the two women walked out unaware he leaned against the wall behind them. The dark haired woman was a beauty, but she lacked that fiery spirit that he found so appealing in Ruby. Her I-dare-you-to-come-and-get-it attitude was like an aphrodisiac to him, drawing him to the blonde bounty hunter.

So unlike Laura.

"Wow, I can't believe we made twenty-five dollars a piece," the soft spoken woman said. "I'm going to go check in at the hotel, take a bath and rest up. What are you going to do?"

Deke walked up behind them. "She's going to buy me lunch, since she has my bounty money."

Ruby whirled around and faced him, her blue eyes flashing. "Last I heard, hell hasn't frozen over yet, so I don't think so."

He smiled. "Now Ruby we don't know that. It's have lunch with me or I march in there and tell the Sheriff you stole my bounty. Your choice."

It was an empty threat. He knew it, but he wanted to spend more time with her. He needed to know the McKenzie girls were doing okay. They'd been nice and their father had been the man he looked up to. Who'd taught him what he knew about the profession.

"It's your word against mine and after I'm done with him, the Sheriff is going to choose the side of the lady bounty hunter."

"But the prisoner knows better," he said smugly, leaning back and crossing his arms over his chest.

A frown appeared on her forehead as she considered his words.

"Why would I want to dine with you? What is there to talk about?"

"For starters you can tell me how your sisters are doing. How the three of you got into the business of bounty hunting. Why aren't you at home in Zenith working on the farm? We have a lot to discuss."

"What about you? What are you going to tell me about you?"

There was so much he could tell her had happened in the almost three years since he'd seen her, but most of it, he refused to talk about.

He shrugged his shoulders. "Not much to tell. I've been working, dreaming of getting out of the business."

One brow rose. "If I have this lunch with you, will you disappear and never come around again? Never lay claim to the bounty I just turned in?"

"The bounty is yours," he said, knowing he was *not* agreeing to the disappearing and never coming round again. "You can even invite your friend as long as she doesn't bring her gun."

"Meet my cousin, Caroline," Ruby said and then smiled. "Afraid you'll have a meeting with her bullet?"

"Nice to meet you. But you're a loose cannon with a pistol."

"Hrmph," Caroline said, in that soft whispery voice that grated on Ruby's last nerve. "You sir are no gentleman for pointing out my faults."

"You're right," Deke said with a grin. "I've never claimed to be a gentleman."

"Caroline I'll meet you back at the hotel. You go ahead and get some rest."

"Are you sure," she said.

"Yes, I'll see you later and make certain the horses are

taken care of," Ruby said, and turned towards Deke.

The mare neighed and he felt drawn to the animal. He walked over and rubbed his hands over the mare's ears and then down her side gently. He walked back to her muzzle and petted her again. "Have them give her an extra ration of oats. Ruby's mustang has been stealing her food. Have the stable separate them."

Ruby's mouth dropped open and she stared at him. "Sure, she just whispered in your ear and said 'give me more feed'."

He smiled. "Yes, she told me. But if you look at the horse's sides, it's pretty obvious. Your horse is either bloated or a little heavy. Either one is not good and both could be caused from eating too much."

Her brows drew together in a frown and she shook her head. "Let's go and get this lovely dining experience over."

He held out his arm. "I can hardly wait."...

Chapter Two

Ruby wanted to scream in frustration when she saw Deke standing there, waiting for them, outside the sheriff's office. The man was tempting as the devil and yet she wanted nothing to do with him.

Sure she'd taken his bounty from him, but he needed to consider payment due. She'd collected. Now he could go away. Still, part of her kind of enjoyed gazing at him, his dark green eyes and black hair, his strong manly physique was something that she could stare at all day long, as long.

"You're choice of restaurants, since you're buying," he told her. "With my money."

"You promised you wouldn't lay claim," she said, flipping back a blonde curl that had blown in her face. "You didn't bring him in."

"I was in the process. I had him tied up and was on my way to town."

"Snooze and lose," she replied.

He chuckled. "Still that same flippant, sassy miss looking out for her own interest."

"I'm the only one who ever will."

With her sisters married, she felt more alone than ever before. Sure, they loved her, but they were living their own lives. Happy newlyweds who gazed at their husbands like he was the only man in the west and they couldn't wait to close their bedroom doors.

Determination pulsed through her veins. Once she'd been a prissy girl who dreamed of a husband and kids. Now she was a prissy woman who dreamed of bringing men to justice.

"When did you become a bounty hunter?"

They walked along the wooden sidewalk, the two of them side by side in the bright sunshine. It was going to be a warm fall day. Summer refused to end and the heat continued on even in late October.

"Right after you left. We were all fired from our jobs. Tired of working hard for minimal wage and being disrespected, it was either get married or starve or do something that would bring us cash and respect. We became bounty hunters," she said her head held high. She loved her job. She would take a bullet before she would ever get back down on her hands and knees scrubbing floors for the rich.

"So all three of you are bounty hunters?" he asked his eyes widening in amazement.

They stepped into the restaurant and found a table. Once they were seated, she turned to him. "Meg and I did most of the hunting until Meg married the sheriff. Annabelle stayed home and took care of the farm, until she decided to go hunting alone and met her new husband Beau. Which left only me. I've been training Caroline."

Unfortunately, from what Ruby could see, the girl needed more lessons. She was certain Deke would tell her what a novice Caroline was.

He laughed. "That woman is a danger to herself."

Ruby shook her head. "I know. She still hasn't quite gotten the hang of it, but I'm confident she will."

"Have you been successful?"

A smile spread across her face. They'd made more money than she'd dreamed possible. Annabelle had brought in the most when she'd followed the Harris gang. But soon Ruby would out collect her and then she would have contributed the most to the family operation.

"We paid off the farm and now we have some operating cash. So yeah, we've been very successful."

He frowned for a moment. "Then why haven't you given up this life? I can't imagine anyone wanting to continue, especially a woman."

She could feel herself bristle. "Oh no, I enjoy the chase.

The thrill of catching the criminal and then bringing him into the sheriff. I don't want to quit. I like what I do for a living."

People were sitting at the tables around them, deep in conversation, not paying attention to the two of them. But she had already checked out every person in the restaurant. Searching for anyone who she thought looked suspicious. She was always on the lookout for her next bounty.

Shaking his head, he stared at her. "How many men have you brought in?"

"Counting your man, twenty."

Throwing his hands up in the air, he chuckled. "The new hasn't worn off yet. Just wait until you capture almost a hundred. You get sick of it. Especially when you bring a man in more than once. You start to question our justice system."

She stared at him. He seemed different. The Deke she remembered had been more lighthearted, not nearly as serious as he seemed now. An ache built inside her chest as she remembered that afternoon when he'd kissed her. It'd been the best kiss of her life and the worst kiss at the same time.

"I guess I can understand why you'd feel that way, but it's a lot better than scrubbing floors," she said. "What would you do if you weren't a bounty hunter?"

"I love horses. I'd raise horses and train them. I understand the animals," he said. His face brightened and it was the first and only time he appeared relaxed and happy. She could tell this was his passion. Not being a bounty hunter like herself. Odd that during the years, they had reversed their roles.

She nodded. "So why aren't you doing that now?"

A frown flittered across his face and then he shrugged his shoulders, like it was nothing and smiled. Why did she feel like there was something he wasn't sharing? "I guess life has gotten in the way. What would you do if you weren't a bounty hunter?"

Shaking her head, she knew right away the answer to that question. "Nothing interests me. I love my life the way it is right now."

Out on the hunt for the first time in months, she felt at peace with herself. Working at the farm with her sisters and their husbands she'd felt like the spoke of a broken wagon wheel. She'd been the odd man out and while they did their best to include her, she'd been ready to hit the trail, earn some money and find her own way in life. All that love floating around the farm house was enough to nauseate her.

"What happened to that flirty, crazy girl I met? That girl that wanted to get married?" he leaned in close. "The girl who wanted me to make her into a woman?"

"She grew up. She realized that the only person she could depend on was herself. Not a man, not her family, no one. She's alone in the world and has to take care of herself." She leaned in close. "She's independent and doesn't need men."

Their waitress poured them each a cup of coffee and they ordered the special of the day. For a moment there was silence between them. He gazed at her his warm green eyes and she remembered how her and Annabelle had fought over this man. She'd wanted to marry him, have babies with him and settle down in a comfortable little house. All the dreams of a love-starved fifteen year old. Now almost no man since Deke had gotten close to her. And she doubted that anyone ever would.

She didn't want or need a man. Not even Deke. She'd had all the experience she wanted with men and decided it was so much better to be independent and self-sufficient. Deke was prettier than any man she'd ever met, but the only driver in her wagon was herself and she aimed to keep it that way.

He stared at her. "I hope I didn't make you hate men?"

She steeled herself against the memory of the humiliation she'd felt the day Deke had ridden out of her life. She'd been knocked to her knees and slammed into the ground by his refusal to make her into a woman. Now she was grateful they'd never been together, though she'd never admit he'd been right.

"You could have been my first." As soon as the words slipped from her mouth, she knew that was the reason for the tension that flowed like a river between them. Only now there was nothing to worry about. She no longer wanted Deke.

"I was not going to disrespect your Papa by having a quick tousle in the hay with you. I wouldn't do that to the man who taught me everything I know. I wouldn't have ridden off and left you then. "

"Well aren't you an honorable cowboy," she said swallowing the lump that filled her throat thinking about that day so many years ago, when she'd been young and naive. In the space of two hours, two men had upended her beliefs on love and changed the innocent, young girl forever. If only she'd never been forced into the closet with Clay, then she would never have begged Deke. And her pride would not have smarted so bad that she felt the need to chase him down and fire her pistol at him.

"I do my best," he said smugly.

She wanted the attention off of the past. She didn't want to remember how she'd begged Deke or what had happened that day with Clay Mullins. She'd done her best to put that part of her life behind her, forever.

"Both of your sisters are expecting?"

"Yes, Annabelle is eight months along and Meg is three months. And Meg has a dress shop now. She no longer wears pants, but dresses like a lady. She's beautiful."

"And you are now the more masculine one in the

group."

For a moment, Ruby felt shocked that he would say that, but then she realized he was right. Oh, she didn't wear pants, but still she rode like a man, shot like a man and had a profession that was more masculine than feminine. And she loved her life. There was nothing she'd change.

"That I am," she said proudly. If he didn't like it, what did she care?

"What about you? What's happened to you in the last three years?"

"Not much."

He said the words so quick, without giving any thought to her question. As she stared at him a shadow passed over his face, his eyes darkened and his jaw tightened.

"So you've been chasing bad guys and bringing in bounties?"

"That's it," he said.

"You should be a rich man then." Though her and her sisters were not rich, they were well on their way for their farm to be self-sufficient. It felt good not to owe anyone.

He chuckled. "Hardly."

"So how many bounties have you brought in since I last saw you?"

"That's a little nosy."

"Hey, just trying to pass the time and talk shop. You're the one who wanted to go to lunch and catch up." Sure she'd been curious about him, but that was all in the past.

He leaned in closer to her, his voice low and deep. "Just because I said no, didn't mean that I didn't enjoy being with you, Ruby. I just wasn't going to take advantage of a young girl whose father had been my mentor."

Her pulse pounded in her ears, she raised her chin and looked him square in the eyes. "And I'm no longer that young girl."

"No, now you're one strikingly beautiful woman who I

wouldn't think twice about seducing."

She couldn't believe he'd just said those words. "I'm going to pretend that I didn't hear you say that. I'm not interested."

"Oh, that sounds like a challenge."

"No. It's a woman who knows what she wants or better yet, what she doesn't want."

"Oh honey, maybe we should test that theory just to see if you're really certain of what you want."

"No need," she said. "I have no doubts whatsoever. I'm a bounty hunter looking for my next payday."

The sheriff walked up to their table. "There you are."

Ruby glanced up at the man wearing the badge. "What do you need sheriff?"

"I just received a telegram from Sheriff Taylor that outlaw John Jones is in Dyersville. They fear he's going to rob the bank. They're asking for assistance in catching him. There's a five hundred dollar bounty. Are you interested?"

"Yes," Deke said.

"He didn't ask you," Ruby replied. "The sheriff is talking to me."

"Why don't you both go?" the sheriff asked. "He's too dangerous for one person and needs to be caught."

"I don't need Deke's help," Ruby said thinking how inept Caroline had proven. She was so green she glowed with lack of confidence and Deke…had learned from her father.

"Oh yeah, your current helper, will certainly keep you safe," Deke said laughing.

"She's learning. Give her a chance. This is her first outing."

This man knew just how to touch on all of her fears. She wasn't worried about her own personal safety so much as she was about Caroline. What if the woman froze or even worse repeated what she'd done today and accidentally pulled the trigger?

"I hope she lives through the next shootout."

The sheriff laughed. "It's a good thing you two aren't married. You'd kill each other."

Ruby spun around to him. "I'll take care of it sheriff. As soon as I finish my lunch, I'll head over there."

Deke threw his napkin down. "I'm finished. I'm on my way."

Ruby grabbed her water glass, gulped down a sip, threw down her napkin and stood. "I've had enough. I'm on it sheriff."

The man with the star laughed. "This criminal is in so much trouble. Don't kill each other on the way."

"He is. See ya," Deke said and started walking towards the door.

"Deke Culver, don't you dare go after my bounty," she called rushing out the door after Deke, her legs moving as fast as she could in her boots. She probably owed him a bounty, but she wasn't one to give up, especially to a man who'd hurt her.

"Don't forget to pay the bill." He held up his hand and waved. "First man, woman there, gets the bounty."

~

As Deke walked down the wooden sidewalk towards his horse, he heard someone running behind him. It had to be Ruby. She was either going to run past him or she was going to stop and negotiate a joint effort.

"What if we work together?" she called out to him.

He stopped and turned to face her. Her blue eyes flashed with anger. She really didn't want to work with him. He could see it in her expression and the way she stood there with her arms crossed a frown gracing that full mouth that he longed to kiss. "Why should we?"

"Because three against one is better than one against

one and we don't want him to get away," she admitted, her lips turned down in a pout. The woman had a face that could awaken a dead man. "I expect at least a third of the bounty."

"Understood."

"We do things my way," he said knowing he was pushing things, but trying to get his way.

"We do things the way that works best," she countered.

Oh, she would be a handful. But he needed something to make this job more interesting. He needed some excitement to keep from shriveling up inside. The last few years had not been easy. They'd been damn hard. He could use some entertainment right now. And these two women would keep him on his toes.

"How long will it take you to get Caroline?"

"About five minutes. How far is it to Dyersville?"

"A day's ride. If we leave now, we'll arrive this evening."

"We could have this all wrapped up by tomorrow morning," she said.

"And then you could go home in time for the birth of Annabelle's baby."

"And you could go do whatever it is you do when you're not bounty hunting."

The image of Laura washed over him and he hurriedly pushed the thought away. He didn't want to go back. He couldn't go back. "Let's go."

~

The next day, Deke watched as Ruby talked to the hotel desk clerk where their outlaw had been staying. She smiled at the man, leaned over the counter and chatted with him like he was the most important person she'd spoken to today. Envy flowed through Deke's veins as he watched her laughing with the clerk, her manner easy and outgoing.

Years ago, she'd responded to him that way, but not anymore. Not since the day he'd kissed her until desire surged through both of their veins like fire water, scorching them with its power. God, he'd wanted her so badly that day, but he'd walked away. And regretted it ever since.

"She's good at getting the information she needs, isn't she?" Caroline said walking up to stand beside Deke.

"Yes," he said. "Is this how she found out where my bounty had gone?"

Caroline laughed. "All we knew was that he'd been seen leaving town, riding north. We didn't know that you had captured the man."

At least they hadn't deliberately followed and taken his bounty, though somehow if Ruby had known it was him, she might have done the same.

"Good, that makes me feel better. I feared that she'd done this on purpose."

"We didn't know who was with him until we rode into your camp last night."

Deke turned and gazed at Caroline. This woman was so far out of her element. She sounded like she should be serving tea to the ladies auxiliary or something more feminine. Outlaws were not going to take her seriously and when her hand shook so badly holding her gun, she was a danger.

He turned back to see Ruby laughing with the desk clerk. She shrugged her shoulder and flirted outrageously with the man and jealousy spiraled through Deke surprising him.

There was no reason for him to be envious of this man, yet he did. What would he feel if Ruby gazed at him the way she looked at that clerk?

His dick hardened at the idea of her flirting with him. No, Ruby and any other woman were completely off limits. There was no room in his life for a woman. None.

"How often does she interview people like this?"

Caroline shrugged. "I don't know. This is my second hunt with her. But I know Meg, says that she's way too good at being a bounty hunter. Meg fears for her safety and wants her to quit, but she refuses."

That was information he doubted that Ruby would appreciate Caroline sharing. "Did she say why?"

"They don't need the money any longer and it's a dangerous way to make a living."

"What did she think of you going out with Ruby?"

"She wasn't happy at all. No one was pleased that the two of us were going hunting together. Not Meg, Annabelle or my mother. No one."

Deke laughed and then glanced back at Ruby. "Here she comes with the information."

"Let's go," she said, as she walked past them and through the lobby of the hotel.

They stepped outside into the bright sunlight.

"What did you learn," Caroline asked.

"The desk clerk is single. He's the son of the hotel owner. He wants to have dinner Friday night and the man we're looking for checked out this morning."

The urge to go back inside the hotel and punch that little dandy in the nose was overwhelming, but Deke gritted his teeth and resisted. Why should he care that this man had invited Ruby to dinner? That she'd flirted outrageously with him? It didn't matter. She was just a girl that he'd kissed when she was younger.

"Darn it we're too late," Caroline said with a soft sigh. "I was looking forward to us rounding up another outlaw."

Somehow, Deke didn't believe her. Caroline felt relieved and thought the chase was over, but it had just begun.

Ruby smiled. "Our man told the hotel clerk that he had some errands to run and then he'd be leaving town."

Deke held his breath. "He's going to buy supplies and then rob the bank. Come on we've got to hurry."

"Exactly," Ruby said. "Wait. Caroline check your weapon. Do you have bullets in the chamber?"

Deke thought he was going to bust a gut either laughing or screaming. He didn't know which one. But for Ruby to remind Caroline to check her gun was like the cowpuncher asking the cow to let him put his rope around his neck.

"Yes," she said swirling the tumbler with her finger. "I'm all set. What about you?"

Ruby smiled at her. "My gun is always loaded with a bullet in every chamber."

"Deke?" Caroline asked.

He shook his head. "Don't worry about me. I'm always prepared."

"Oh," she said dejectedly. "I'm prepared as well. Let's go."

Ruby started walking towards the mercantile and Deke followed. When they reached the store, he placed his hand on her arm.

"What's the plan?"

"I'm going to scout out the store, talk to the clerk and see if he's in here. Then I'll come out and let you know. If he's in there, I'll signal from the window. You wait out here with Caroline."

He frowned. "Okay, but I don't like this plan."

She smiled at him sweetly. "You don't like being told what to do by a woman."

"That too."

What could he say? He'd never taken orders from a woman before and no, it didn't sit well. But then again Ruby likes to think she was in control. And he'd let her, though he knew the truth.

Turning on her heel, she strolled into the mercantile like she didn't have a care in the world. Like she was invincible, but he knew differently. He'd seen her hurt.

He glanced in the window and saw her talking to the man behind the counter. He hated standing around and waiting. Maybe that was one of the reasons why he no longer loved his job. It seemed like all he did was wait on criminals. Wait on getting paid and wait on the next one. It was like a constant round-robin. Wait. Wait. Wait.

Nothing appeared to move inside the mercantile. He turned and glanced around the street and spotted their prey.

John was walking towards the bank.

"Damn, there he is." Deke started hurrying towards the man.

"Wait," Caroline said. "I'll go with you."

Oh, that was so not what he needed. He didn't need a greenhorn that couldn't shoot getting in the way or even possibly shooting himself.

"No," he said and turned around. "Get Ruby. Then you two meet me in the alley of the bank. I'm going in."

He'd give them a job to keep them busy and out of his way, while he captured their criminal. Then he would ride off without them and with the bounty. All in all a good days work.

Chapter Three

Ruby was talking to the mercantile owner when Caroline came running into the store. "Ruby, come quick. Deke spotted the outlaw and has gone after him."

Her feet didn't want to move fast enough as she hurried out the door. Stepping outside into the bright sunshine, she glanced up and down the street looking for Deke. "Where? Where did they go?"

Caroline stopped beside her, her eyes large. "He was headed towards the bank and Deke was going to stop him."

Fear trickled down her spine like a wild river current and she took a deep breath. She didn't want to feel anything for this man. She didn't want to care that he might be in danger, but damn it, she did.

"Why can't that man wait," she said walking towards the Texas Bank and Loan, her steps sure.

"I tried to tell him," Caroline said, all but running to keep pace with Ruby.

The bank sat on the corner of First and Main Street, glass windows framed the front of the building. She could see customers milling about inside. Suddenly screams were heard coming from inside the building. Her heart leaped like a Mexican jumping bean inside her chest.

Deke was inside.

Ruby ran to the side of the building and peered around the corner into the glass windows. There was her outlaw, with a gun in his hand waving it wildly his arm wrapped around Deke's neck. He put his gun up to Deke's skull and yelled at the people inside, trying to herd them all onto one side of the room. Fear rose like bile inside her throat, almost choking her.

Deke. She had to save Deke.

"What do you want me to do?" Caroline asked, peering over Ruby's shoulder.

"Pull your gun out and stay close."

She watched as the gunman yanked Deke's gun out of its holster and shoved him aside. The clerk handed a sack full of money to the gunman. He backed slowly towards the door his pistol trained on Deke.

As much as the handsome cowboy frustrated her, she didn't want to see him die. No matter what had happened between them in the past, she'd do everything she could to save him and keep the criminal from walking out of the bank with the money.

"Caroline, go behind the building and come up on the other side of the door. Be ready. When he comes out we'll each be on one side of the door. We can stop him."

"What do I do?"

Those were not the kind of questions, she should be asking. They were in a situation and she should know instinctively to do everything to protect Deke. Caroline needed lots more instruction.

"You train your weapon on our bad guy and tell him to stop or you're going to shoot." Ruby shook her head. "Never mind. Just have your weapon ready. I'll do all the talking."

Ruby observed her cousin as she disappeared around the back of the bank. She showed up on the other side of the door, opposite of the way he was coming out. Ruby would have to remain hidden until he emerged from the building so that he couldn't see her in the window. But then she'd be ready for him.

She waited, the seconds ticking slower than honey dripping on a biscuit. Unbelieving, she watched as Caroline struggled to get her six-shooter out of her holster. When she finally had the gun out, Ruby could see her hands visibly shaking like a limb blowing in the wind. The weapon pointed in the direction of Ruby. If the bank robber didn't kill her there was a good chance Caroline would.

The door opened slowly as the outlaw eased out waving his guns in both directions, toward the bank and the street, the money bag in one hand, his hat low as he scanned the street. Deke was nowhere in sight.

Ruby starred in horror as Caroline stepped out from behind the door, her gun quivering. In a weak, wobbly voice, she said, "Stop. Put down your weapon. You're under arrest."

Startled, the outlaw jumped, starring at Caroline. Tilting his head, his eyes gazed at Caroline and he began to laugh. "Lady, get out of my way or I'm going to kill you."

Before Ruby could get to her, Caroline pointed her pistol at the man's chest and fired. The bullet hit him in the foot.

Oh my God, this was quickly spinning out of control like a Texas tornado churning up the prairie. Ruby had never been more frightened for her cousin. If the gunman turned his gun on her, she was dead. Swallowing her fear, Ruby ran.

"Dang it, I closed my eyes," Caroline said, raising her pistol to fire again.

"My foot," the man screamed hopping on one leg trying to maintain possession of the money and his fire arms.

Ruby rushed at the bank robber just as Deke busted through the door. They tackled the man, sending him sprawling into the dusty street. Ruby took his left hand and Deke his right. They wrestled the guns from him while he screeched in agony.

"You bitch. You bitch, you shot me," he cried.

"You're lucky it was just your foot and not your head," Ruby told him.

"Get me a doctor. And get that damn woman away from me," he yelled.

Caroline looked down at him in the street, a frown on her beautiful face, her gun still dangling from her fingers.

"I'm sorry," she said in her whispery, soft voice. She heaved a big sigh. "You scared me. All you had to do was drop your guns. But you threatened to kill me. That's not nice."

Deke yanked the man up and Ruby quickly tied a rope around his wrists. They half-carried, half-walked him the short distance to the sheriff's office.

"That woman is dangerous," the man said, his brow sweating from the pain. "I can't believe she shot me in the foot. She looked like a nice miss!"

"She's a bounty hunter," Ruby informed him.

"Yeah, I am," Caroline said in that soft voice that sounded more like an invitation to tea.

Though technically Caroline had yet to learn the trade. In fact, she was just a bit too reckless and scary enough with that pistol that Ruby knew she had to go home. It was that or watch Caroline be killed and she wasn't going to be responsible for the death of her cousin.

"We're collecting on you," Deke told the man.

He groaned as they walked him into the jail.

"Why don't you find us a hotel room, while we take care of Mr. Jones," Ruby told the girl just wanting her to get off the street before someone else decided to test her gun skills.

"All right," she said, jamming her gun back into her holster. "I'll meet you there."

Half an hour later Deke and Ruby strolled outside the sheriff's office together into the bright Texas sunshine. The town had resumed its normal activities and the street was once again teeming with wagons and horses and people hurrying along the wooden sidewalk.

Deke separated out the money and handed her and Caroline's share to her. "You know it's a wonder one of us didn't get killed by that bullet of Caroline's."

While she knew that he was only saying what she

already understood, she wanted to tell him to mind his own business, but she didn't. This was Deke. The man who had unbeknownst to him gave the girls a lot of pointers about being a bounty hunter over supper one night years ago.

"Yeah, I know," Ruby sighed and hung her head. "I'm sending her back to Zenith. From here on I think its best I go it alone."

"That's dangerous," he said. "Why don't you back with her?"

She turned and glared at him. Since Annabelle's disappearance and then subsequent marriage, Ruby had been at home. Sitting and waiting and sitting and waiting until she'd been about to go crazy with the need to chase bad men again. "Because I hate farming. I hate chickens. And I get bored sitting around staring at the four walls. I'm not exactly into needlepoint."

He laughed. "No, I guess you're not."

"And if I take Caroline home, then my sisters are going to insist I stay. This way I can continue doing what I want. But you're right, Caroline needs to return to Zenith before she shoots someone that's not a criminal or gets shot."

Deke took Ruby by the arm as they crossed the street to the other side. "You know I'm impressed with how you've caught these last two criminals. You're good. We even work pretty well together."

She turned to face him and was struck by how his dark hair and emerald eyes could send a girls pulse to racing. Even hers, though she wasn't interested in pursuing that chase that would only end up with her heart aching once again. "Thank you."

She halted on the wooden sidewalk and stared at him. For a moment, she considered asking him to join forces with her, but then realized that would never work. He'd want to take control. "You're good too. I'm sure we'll run into each other again."

"Maybe," he said. "I want to get out of this business. Soon. Before someone shoots me. You need to be thinking about what you want to do besides bounty hunting. Eventually you realize you're going to die if you keep chasing outlaws."

Even her own father had died at the hands of a criminal. But a man could expire sitting around watching cattle munch grass.

"Take care," he said. He turned and she watched as he walked away, his boots echoing on the planks of the sidewalk.

If she'd been interested in attaching herself to a man, he would still be her first choice. But she had plans. Regardless of what Deke said, she loved her job and had more bounties to catch and a cousin to send packing.

~

Later that evening, sitting in their hotel room, she counted out Caroline's portion of the money. She handed it to her.

The young woman's eyes grew wide and she stared at the stack of cash. "In the last two days I've made more money than I would have made all month working a job. I like being a bounty hunter."

Ruby sighed, bit her lip and gazed at her cousin. "Caroline, this isn't working. I should never have brought you out on this hunt. You're not ready."

She watched as Caroline absorbed the news that she was sending her home. Her face tightened and her eyes widened.

"But, we've captured two criminals," Caroline said, defiantly. "This last one, I caught by myself."

Ruby didn't want to make her cousin feel bad, but she feared for her life. She didn't want to take her body home. "You did catch him, but your shot was way off thank goodness. But what if you'd killed him? How would you have felt? Or what if you'd shot me?" She licked her lips. "I know you want to do this, but I think its best that you go home and practice your shooting skills. Then you can rejoin me once you're better."

Though that time period would be several months down the road. Time enough for Caroline to develop her gun skills. And while maybe Ruby should take Caroline home, she knew better than to try to leave the farm without someone with her. There was no way her sisters would knowingly let her hunt alone.

Caroline hung her head, her voice that whispery soft caress. "I know I've had two shots misfire. But I don't want to be forced to marry that horrible, stinky, pig farmer."

She crossed her arms across her chest, big tears forming in her eyes, making Ruby feel guilty as sin. She didn't want to hurt Caroline. She only wanted to protect her until she was ready.

"Then don't get married. Go home. Practice your skills and when I come back for the birth of Annabelle's baby, then you can go out with me again. This is not you can never go bounty hunting again with me. Practice and get better, then we'll go together. I just don't want to be responsible for you getting killed."

Ruby could see the determination in Caroline. She knew she wanted to do better and the woman had a very good reason. When a girl approached the old age of twenty, mothers began to get nervous and tried to force their daughters to accept any proposal. That's what Caroline's mother was doing. She wanted her daughter to marry the pig farmer. It was a marriage proposal. Accept it, her mother had insisted, like Caroline should settle for less than what she wanted.

Drawing her shoulders back stiffly, Caroline sighed,

and lifted her head. "Okay, you're right. I wasn't ready. But when you return home, I'm going to be so dang good at shooting that I can knock all the cans off the fence without closing my eyes or my hand shaking."

Caroline scooped up her share of the bounty and stuffed it in her skirt pocket. "This is a start. Now I know what I'm getting into and I know the kind of money I can make. Now I have a goal to work towards. A goal where I can go alone. A goal where I'm a good bounty hunter."

If only there was a way to make her sound tough. Right now she still talked like she was soft as cotton, and not as durable. There wasn't a criminal alive that was going to tremble in his boots at her gentle, mellifluous voice.

"Please don't go out on your own. You're not ready yet," Ruby said, gazing at her cousin, hoping she would listen to reason. She wanted her to like being a bounty hunter, but she didn't see her get hurt.

"I won't. I'll wait for you, unless you do something stupid like get killed or married," Caroline promised.

Ruby started laughing. "You don't have to worry about that. I'm careful. I'm not worried about getting killed. And I'm never getting married."

"Yeah, well you better tell that to Deke. That man looks at you like he'd enjoy nothing better than a good roll between the sheets with you."

"You don't have to get married for that."

"Ruby. You need to save your virginity for your husband," Caroline insisted.

"I'm not getting married. And I'm not having sex with Deke Culver. I once asked him to bed me and he refused."

"Ruby!" Caroline exclaimed. "What were you thinking?"

How could she explain to Caroline or anyone the complete loss of power a woman feels when a man forces himself upon you and treats you like a whore? How could she explain the loathing that sweeps through your body and how she'd shriveled up inside to escape the revulsion that permeated from every pore?

"I was thinking I wanted a man to erase all the bad memories of Clay Mullins attack. Deke refused and said I wasn't old enough."

"Well, you were just a girl."

Yes, she'd been young, but she had friends who were married and expecting their first baby by that age. Then to erase the bad memories and the need to understand why a man would overpower a woman just to have sex she'd gone to the one man she'd had such a compelling attraction to. And when he'd turned her down it had been crushing. Totally defeating.

Now she was cured. No need for an escort, a husband or a man in her life. She could live independent and alone.

"I was old enough. And I'd just buried my Papa. I was ready to learn what it's all about. Now, I just don't care."

"At this moment it seems he's ready and you're not."

"Deke Culver is the past. Bounty hunting is the future. No man tells me what to do. I'm an independent woman. "

~

The next day she walked down to the Sheriff's office before the scheduled time to put Caroline on the stagecoach to Zenith. She'd be home in two days with an adventure to talk about. She'd promised to let Ruby's sisters know that she was all right, though Ruby knew they would be angry that she was bounty hunting alone. Thank God, they were both pregnant or else, they'd come looking for her insisting that she come home and Ruby wasn't ready to settle down with a husband and babies. She enjoyed this life, though she was about to experience her first hunt without anyone's help.

Strolling down the wooden sidewalk she meandered

towards the sheriff's office. She wanted to take a look at the latest wanted posters and see if she could make some quick money, before she had to return home and help Annabelle and Meg.

Pausing outside the jail, she gazed at the posters that were hanging on the outside wall. There were rustlers, bank robbers, thieves and wayward women. There were drawings of people who were missing. As she stared at the posters, Deke strolled up beside her.

He chuckled. "Looking for a new bounty to hunt?"

She gave him a sideways glance.

"You can say that? I bet you're doing the same."

Of all the people to run into today, she'd hoped to get out of town before seeing him again. They'd caught up, had a little fun catching a criminal, and now she was ready to move on. Though she had enjoyed gazing at his dark hair, muscled chest, full lips and emerald eyes once again, that's all she could do was look. Someday a woman would capture his wayward spirit and enjoy every inch of Deke. Just not Ruby.

"Need a new outlaw to chase," Deke said softly. "Where's Caroline?"

"Packing. I'm taking her to catch the stagecoach at noon" She replied.

Turning towards her, he raised his brows and stared.

"She agreed that she needs more practice."

He sighed. "Thank God, we'll all be a little safer now. After the second time her gun misfired, I knew we were in danger."

"She told me she closed her eyes and squeezed the trigger."

"It's a wonder you weren't hit," he said not looking at her, but staring at the notices on the wall. "Who are you going after next?"

Like she would share that information with him. Did he

think she was that much of a greenhorn? She darted him a quick glance and frowned. "Now why would I tell you? You'd race after them and steal my bounty. I'm not disclosing anything to you."

Besides, she wanted to put as much distance between her and Deke Culver as she could. Few men made her feel safe, but with Deke she felt sheltered and secure. She didn't understand why, but with Deke she almost felt protected. Still she wasn't willing to stick around and find out why. She didn't have time to explore the baser feelings in life.

He grinned and continued studying the public notices.

Suddenly the door to the sheriff's office opened and the lawman stepped out. "Saw you two out here looking at the posters and realized I had a new set that just came in. Thought you might be interested in them."

He took a hammer and nail and pounded the first one up on the wall. Then he hammered the nail into a second sign, stepped back and smiled. "Keep up the good work."

Disappearing back into the office, both Ruby and Deke stepped up to see the new bills. He tried to block her way and she walked underneath his arm and came up between him and the notices.

"Get out of my way," she said pushing him back. "I was here first."

Deke chuckled and pulled her snug up against his chest, her head fit perfectly below his chin. "I think there are plenty of outlaws here for both of us."

"Maybe, but I'm wanting the ones that are local and will be quick and easy."

"Huh, that's the ones I want as well."

"Imagine that," she said in a drawl.

She took a deep breath realizing being this close to the man had her body tingling with nerves. Why with Deke did her body light up like a prairie fire? The heat rapid and fast acting.

"Who are the new criminals?" he asked, looking again at the posters.

"John Leverton, Billy Clanton and James Rivera…the man who killed Papa." her voice trailed off.

"What?" Deke asked, looking back at the posters.

"I thought you turned him in," she said rounding on Deke, her fists clenched and her heart pounded inside her chest like a hammer and an anvil.

Deke's green eyes flashed with hatred. "I did. I took him to jail, turned him in and collected the bounty. Remember I brought half the money I collected to you and your sisters."

"But he's out. He's running free while my father is six feet under," she said raising her voice at Deke. All the anger and frustration from her father's death spilled into her blood, slamming her like herd of cattle gone wild.

"He must have escaped or someone rescued him."

She tore the poster down off the wall.

"What the hell are you doing?" he asked.

The sheriff stepped out. "What's all the commotion out here?"

She raised the notice in her clenched fists. Fighting back the angry tears that threatened to spill. No crying woman ever received respect. She could not let her emotions get the best of her.

"How did he get loose? He killed my father. He should be hanging."

Raising his hand, the sheriff ran his fingers through his hair. "Some of his friends rescued him. I'm surprised you didn't hear about it. Sheriff Jim Handley was killed in the escape."

Agony of the loss of her father knifed her, sending pain radiating through her. Her lungs refused to expand and she feared she was going to faint. Rivera had killed again. Another family was enduring loss because of this man.

That was it. Now she knew exactly who her next bounty was. Now she had a purpose. "No, I hadn't heard. I'm sorry to hear about the sheriff. Any news on Rivera's location now?"

"No, but he's got family in Hide Town, near Fort Griffin. But I'd be very careful. That town is known for harboring outlaws and their families. The law is not reliable if you get my drift."

A crooked town and sheriff, she could deal with. She couldn't abide the idea of her father's killer running free. Rivera must be caught. She walked down the steps of the office. "Thanks Sheriff."

Deke grabbed the bridle of her horse. "Just where are you going?"

"I'm going after Rivera. This time he's not going to get out so easily. This time he's dead. I'll kill him myself."

"You're not going alone."

"You're not going with me."

"Why?" he asked staring at her. "I know what he looks like. All you've got is a poster. I know his habits, what he likes. I've chased and caught him before," he said, gazing at her, staring at her with those eyes that had drawn her the first day she met him. That day when he'd brought home her gravely wounded father.

"I work alone."

"And you're going to die alone. Don't do this Ruby," he said softly. "I know you're still angry with me over the past, but we could do this much quicker together. You need to think about Annabelle. She's going to need you at home."

She thought about it for a moment. She really didn't want to hunt by herself. And more important than anything was catching the man who'd killed her father. Deke knew things about Rivera that she didn't. He could make this job go quicker, so that she'd be home by the time Annabelle's baby was due.

The only real problem she could see about riding with Deke was being with him. She enjoyed looking at him, she even kind of wanted to kiss those full lips that beckoned to her, but she'd never forgiven him for the past and now her purpose in life was to live as an independent woman without a man.

She'd better make some rules quick. "As long as you don't come near me, we're good."

He frowned at her. "I'm not making any promises I can't keep. There's always been this pull between us. Only now you're older."

Yes, there was this enticing lure that she felt whenever he was around. But she wasn't going to act on it.

"And I'm wiser," she said. "We'll work together to find this outlaw, but afterwards we go our separate ways. You don't kill a McKenzie and get away with it."

Chapter Four

Caroline rode her horse to the farm to let Ruby's sisters know how she was doing. As she entered the yard, Beau, Annabelle's husband came out to greet her.

"Good morning, Caroline. Good to see you. Where's Ruby?"

"That's why I'm here," she said alighting from her horse and stepping down on the ground.

"Oh no. She's okay?" Beau asked.

"She was fine the last time I saw her," Caroline said.

Leaving Ruby had been difficult, no one like to come home in defeat. For a moment, she felt a twinge of shame. She'd been a hindrance and unable to help Ruby. And she was going to change that. The next time she went bounty hunting she'd be prepared.

"Meg is visiting Annabelle, so you picked a good time to drop by the house. Let me know if you need some support in there. Together the sisters can be a little intimidating," he said smiling.

Intimidating? No, the sisters were going to grill her like a confederate spy in a Yankee prison.

Caroline nodded as she walked into the house. Might as well get this over with, so she could get home and face her mother. That would be the biggest challenge of the day. When she entered, Meg stood. "Caroline! Where's Ruby?"

Annabelle walked to her and hugged Caroline, her belly protruding. "Good to see you. Sit down. Where is our wayward sister?"

Sitting in the rocking chair across from Meg and Annabelle, Caroline's stomach clenched with nerves. The two of them waited patiently and she knew they were not going to be happy with the news.

"Ruby sent me home."

"What?" Meg said. "What is that girl thinking?"

"She said that I'm not ready and she was right." As much as Caroline hated to admit it, Ruby was legitimate to send her home.

"Well, then she should have come home with you," Annabelle said fury in her gaze as she stared at Caroline. "If I wasn't eight months pregnant, I'd be climbing on my horse and going after that girl."

"What happened?" Meg asked. "Maybe we need to send our husbands after her."

Caroline told them how they had brought in the two bounties and how Ruby had introduced her to Deke Culver. "When I left Ruby her and Deke had just learned that James Rivera was loose. He broke out of jail. They were going after him together."

"James Rivera is out?" Meg asked her voice rising. She stood and her dress showed the faint outline of her pregnancy. "We should go help them bring that outlaw in. He needs to hang."

Annabelle patiently looked at her like she was crazy. "Meg, you're expecting. I'm too far along to ride a horse. Ruby is the only one of us who can bring him to justice. And my husband is not going anywhere until after this baby is born."

Meg sighed and sat back down. "You're right, but that doesn't mean I wouldn't have wanted to go after that outlaw."

Until recently, Caroline had not realized how much of a hothead, Meg could be. But after learning that she tied up her husband and left him naked in the middle of Main Street, she was careful of Meg. No need to rile her up and receive some of that redheaded spitefulness.

"I know. But this will be good for Ruby and maybe Deke can talk some sense into her. Maybe he can help her realize that she has no business hunting alone. Ruby has always been sweet on Deke," Annabelle said. "This might be good."

"You're right. But I worry about her. Since that Mullins kid attacked her, she's never been the same."

"Agreed. Deke is a good man. Maybe he can find out what caused her to react in such a strong manner. Plus, she'll be safe with him. I trust him."

Caroline had admired Meg for years. She'd watched her as a child, taking care of her sisters. She'd been envious of the three girls. As an only child, she thought the sisters were so close and for many years longed for a brother or sister that she could share adventures with. Now, she knew that Meg was the visible, strength of the girls, while Annabelle was the strong, quiet glue that held them together.

"I hope so," Meg said. "I worry about her."

The McKenzie girls had their share of heartache as well. Losing first their mother and then their father and almost their farm.

But now they were happy. Everyone at least except Ruby, who didn't realize that the people who loved her knew something, was wrong. Even Caroline could see that Ruby was no longer that flirtatious, happy, fun girl. Now a strong-willed, determined woman to make bad men pay for their crimes had taken her place.

"Deke cares about Ruby. She'll be fine," Caroline said remembering how the man had watched Ruby's every move. She wanted a man to look at her like that.

"So are you going to marry the pig farmer, Caroline?" Annabelle asked, changing the subject, her blue eyes laughing with merriment.

Caroline dreaded going home and facing the wrath of her mother for leaving and not accepting the pig farmer's proposal of marriage. Sure, she wanted to marry and have a family, but she wanted a husband she could feel proud of. Someone who when she looked at him, butterflies took over her organs in a good way. Not her nose twitching from the odor of the man.

"When pigs fly is when I'll marry that man."

~

The state of Texas was so big that in some parts, God must have been tired when he created the state. He'd left out a few important details like grass and trees. While there were plenty of mesquite trees in the area, there were very few good solid oaks and no pinewood. Deke liked grass and seedlings, something besides prairie. Riding to Hide Town, Texas a person could get lost and ride in circles for days on end, seeing the same scenery over and over. And now that winter was approaching, everything looked more like saplings or nothing at all.

They had ridden all day and said very little to one another. Deke had no doubts she was an experienced horse woman or that she knew how to find a criminal or even how to fire a weapon. He wasn't worried about her skills, he was concerned about her.

She was no longer the carefree girl he'd met almost three years ago who had begged him to make her into a woman. To show her what happened between a man and a woman. And while he'd ridden away that day hard with the desire to fulfill her every wish, he knew he couldn't have taken her virginity and disrespected the man who had taught him the profession that had gotten him out of poverty.

Even now they were ridding to avenge the man he esteemed, whose loss had been such a waste. And Deke knew from firsthand experience that death often came when you least expected it and was unprepared.

It was the main reason he wanted to settle into a different kind of life. One where he wasn't chasing the worst of humanity. One where he spent his time doing what he loved.

"Find a good spot off the trail and let's make camp for the night," he said not looking at Ruby fearing she would see the desire he felt for her in his eyes. Truly he was trying to hide it as much as possible, but still it was there.

The bleak landscape around them with rolling hills and few trees would soon be dark and he had no desire to risk their lives or the life of their horses. As much as he dreaded this first night, it was time to stop and make camp.

"No, we should keep going as long as we can."

"We're still a full day's ride from Fort Griffin. There's no sense in taking a chance and risking we hurt one of the horses. Let's stop and get a fresh start early in the morning," he said trying to talk some sense into this stubborn woman. She just didn't give up. Or was she just as nervous as he was of being alone on the trail?

"If we kill ourselves, then he'll get away with murder," Deke said.

She flashed him a hostile glare, but pulled her horse up. "All right. There appears to be a grove of mesquite trees over there. Let's make camp beneath them."

In less than thirty minutes, she had a fire started and was frying up some trail hash while he took care of their horses.

"That smells awfully good," he said as he walked back into the area after ground tethering their animals for the night. He'd rubbed both animals down, fed, watered them and then spent some time just doing what he loved. Since the time he was a young boy, he discovered he had a special way of communicating with horses. His mother had called it his sixth sense and he couldn't really explain it, but he understood the animals.

Spreading out his bedroll he glanced over at Ruby. She was watching him suspiciously, like she feared he would try something. Why she was so distrustful he didn't understand, but before they could begin to catch this outlaw, he had to gain her trust.

"So when is Annabelle's baby due?"

"Next month," she said dishing up their supper into metal bowls.

Pain speared through him and the memory of his son's face swam before his eyes. In the last eighteen months he'd tried very hard to forget his image. Most days he was able to block it out of his mind, but there were days when his son's face swam before his eyes.

"Are you ready to be an aunt?"

"What kind of question is that? I don't really have any choice in the matter. If it was up to me, both of my sisters would not have married and would still be hunting."

"Are they happy?"

He hadn't been ready to give up his life and get married, but Laura had needed his help. And he couldn't say no. Not to his mother and not to Laura.

"Yes," she said with a resigned sigh.

"Then why can't you be glad they're settled and content."

His mother had been thrilled when he'd married Laura. She'd told him of Laura's situation and he couldn't refuse to help her. Though he'd given her his name, he'd never given her his heart.

"Because we had a great life. Catching bounties, making money. I miss them being on the trail with me."

When Laura told him about the baby, he'd been thrilled. They'd been newlyweds and every day she'd spent working on their home, preparing for the baby's arrival. Closing his eyes, he blocked the memories.

"Things change. Life changes." Glancing over at her, he took a bite of his hash. "This is great."

"Thanks."

"You've admitted you're not really into womanly

duties, so I'm pleasantly surprised how well you can cook."

She shook her head. "That's assuming. Besides don't you remember the box of cookies I sent with you the last time you went searching for Rivera?"

He grinned. "Yes, I remember them. They were gone before I was ten miles down the road. I ate every one of them."

When he married Laura, though he cared for her and promised her forever, it had been Ruby's image that came to mind when he thought of love. His stomach clenched as anger rolled through him. Anger at the ugliness in his life over the last several years.

"I think that was the last time I baked cookies."

Stretching out his legs, he leaned back against his saddle. "So once you were all into the things that a woman normally does? But not now?"

"Kind of," she said staring out into the fire. "But now I'm into things that make me money. That are exciting and fun and not boring like deciding on what to fix for dinner."

"Someday you'll get tired of this life."

Deke was weary from the trail, the sleeping out in the weather, chasing after men that would just as soon kill you as to let you take them into the law. He wanted to settle down and do what he loved. Raise horses.

"I've been a bounty hunter now for almost three years. I wouldn't say there have been times I've been glad to get home," she said tossing the rest of her supper in the fire. "I hate it when the weather turns nasty. God, I hated it when we were trying to find Annabelle. I wanted to kill Beau, her husband, but she wouldn't let me."

Silent they sat around the fire, sated and watched the flames leap into the air. The night was cool, but it wasn't cold and winter had yet to arrive. Actually, it was the perfect time of year for being outdoors. Deke hated the hottest months of the year and his memories haunted him during the cooler months when he'd married Laura.

"How come we always talk about me, but never about you?" she asked. "What have you been doing in the years since we last saw you? You're pretty vague about it."

"That's kind of my life in a description. Vague," he said standing up. He scrapped his bowl out, took a little water from his canteen and washed it out. On the trail, that was about as clean as it got.

She stood and did the same to her utensils. Then cleaned out the frying pan. He took the heavy utensil from her and was drying it with a dish cloth she had laid out. Ruby might not be in a house, but she was still doing things on the trail, a man would never do. And he kind of liked that. It was nice having a companion. The loneliness that gripped him receded, leaving only an empty ache. He could deal with the pain that throbbed with each heartbeat.

They bumped into each other and she stared up at him, her blue eyes glinted at him daring, almost challenging, and he was stunned. Every time he touched her – she seemed skittish.

"Ruby, you jumped like a roadrunner on a rattler. I'm not going to hurt you." He licked his lips staring down at her soft, full tempting mouth. He so wanted to taste her again. He remembered how they'd kissed and he'd almost broken his promise to himself. He'd almost relented that day and taken her right there on the spot.

Thank goodness, he hadn't.

"Men like you have a way of making a woman nervous."

"Do you think I'm bad?"

"No, Deke. I know you're a good man. But we're not starting back where we left off. We have a past, which I don't want to repeat."

For some reason he didn't like being told no. Not that he wanted to stir things up between the two of them again, but it didn't feel right for her to tell him no.

Years had passed since their kiss, but in his loneliest moments it was her mouth he remembered, not Laura's. Sometimes he just wanted to erase the memories of how she tasted.

"Okay, but I think we should kiss just to prove to each other that we're not serious about starting things up again. You think I want to and I think you're the one wanting me." Even he would admit it was a stupid argument, but maybe it would cure him once and for all. Maybe he would think of Laura's kisses instead of Ruby's.

"What? Are you crazy? I don't want to kiss you or any other man."

"Oh come on, Ruby. The woman I use to know was the biggest flirt and tease in the state of Texas."

The first time he met her, she was the sassiest little vixen he'd ever met and it had taken all of his respect for her father to keep him from acting on the urges that she incited.

"And what did that get her?" she asked. "Nothing but trouble. Now I know that I don't need a man. I don't need any one."

"Then that's why you won't mind me kissing you. We'll just get this out of the way and that way both of us will know it was in the past."

She stared at him like he'd been drinking loco juice. And all he could do was gaze at the shape of her mouth. How her lips were full and curvaceous and when she wore that red stuff on her mouth, reminded him of ripe cherry, his for the picking.

"You're crazy. You're just trying to kiss me."

Nobody could accuse her of being dumb. Yes, he wanted to taste her once again, but he truly hoped that once they touched lips, they would know this attraction he felt was in the past. They were no longer affected by whatever feelings they'd once possessed for each other. He'd quit thinking about Ruby and remember his wife, Laura, once again.

"No, I'm trying to cure this awkwardness between us so we can move forward to capture this guy without us worrying about the other person. This way we'll know it's behind us."

God, maybe he was the stupid one. Here he was talking to a woman about kissing. A woman whose kisses he often dreamed about.

"I don't see how this is going to help," she said. "We just need to focus on our goal."

She was gazing at him and for just a minute, he thought he saw a spark of something that looked like desire, but then it was gone.

"You're right. We do," he said as his hand brushed hers sending a tingle of awareness through him like a lightning bolt. The surge of hunger was enough to clear his mind of only one thing. "Oh hell."

He grabbed her and pulled her into his arms and layered his mouth over hers. She tasted of heat and passion and longing, leaving him aching with the need for more. Just another taste of how she would feel in his arms, in his bed, and crying his name. Ruby filled him with a hunger that couldn't be quenched and that couldn't be good. Like a stampede of cattle charging towards him, all those hidden feelings for her from years ago poured over him, filling him with an urgency to throw her onto the ground and…

…And that was how babies were made. The thought made him go cold inside, while his body glowed with a sexual heat that wanted fulfillment. He wrangled with the thought of where this could lead. Ruby moaned deep in her throat and he realized he was the crazy one. They couldn't do this. He couldn't do this.

He pulled back. "We can't."

Slowly she opened her eyes and he could see the desire lingering there.

"Haven't I heard those words before? Don't you like to start something and then get cold feet? What's your excuse this time?"

"I'm married."

~

Ruby pushed out of his arms. For the first time in years, she'd relaxed and felt safe in a man's arms. Once again, she'd let herself go, thinking that maybe they should see if there was anything left between them before they found themselves in a dangerous situation. And once again, Deke Culver had proven just what a snake in the grass he could be.

He was married! As in holy matrimony. He had a wife. And he'd kissed Ruby.

If she caught one of her brother-in-laws kissing someone other than her sisters, they'd find a bullet hole in a very important male part of their anatomy.

Without thinking she reached up and walloped him upside the head. "Why the hell were you talking about kissing when you're married? That ceremony means one woman—one man. No one else. Understand?"

"Ouch. You didn't have to hit me."

"The hell I didn't. I'm not smooching a wedded man."

"You just did."

"I didn't know. You're lucky I'm not putting a bullet in you." She turned and glared at him over the fire and then moved her bedroll as far from his as she could get. "This is why you didn't want to tell me what happened to you in the last three years. This is why nothing much is going on in your life. You're married."

Ruby couldn't sit still. He was hitched as in a wife, ring and vows of till death do us part. The shock of those words had not worn off. Revulsion swept through her like a band of Indians chasing the cavalry.

And to think he had a wife sitting at home waiting on him. Poor unknowing woman. Ungrateful bastard.

"When did you meet her?"

"I've known her all my life."

"Oh, so even before you puckered up with me that very first time, she was in your life. Maybe I should do this woman a favor and make her a widow."

How could he have betrayed the woman he was going to marry by kissing her? He couldn't be the man she believed if he had knowingly smacked his lips with hers all those years ago and then gone home to stand before a preacher man.

"No, I didn't know we were going to marry. It wasn't planned. I didn't tie the knot with her until six months after I left your place."

Ruby sighed. Thank goodness he'd never taken her up on her offer. But still the man was attached with a ring and a vow, he shouldn't be smacking lips with her now.

"Maybe it's time we caught some shut eye," she said.

She climbed into her bedroll, still smarting from the fact that for once she'd felt safe in a man's arms. She'd enjoyed his touch and hadn't cringed until after the kiss when she'd learned he was married.

Listening, she heard him rustling around getting into his bedroll. Finally he settled down and she began to relax.

"Just like your father dying unexpectantly, sometimes things happen to people and they have no control. I hadn't planned on marrying Laura," he said from across the fire in the darkness.

Years ago, she'd been so angry when he'd ridden off that afternoon after telling her no, she'd even pulled out her gun and fired at him. Then he'd gone home and married another woman. If this didn't prove to her that men were simple minded creatures who didn't know what they wanted, what did? She didn't need the heartache. Her independence was much more satisfying.

"After kissing me, you married Laura." Not that kissing was a commitment, more like a promise.

"I had no choice."

"Well, I do. Goodnight Deke. As soon as we catch Rivera we part ways forever, do you understand."

"Clearly."

Hopefully after tomorrow, they would never see each other again.

Chapter Five

As they rode into Hide Town, Ruby noticed that though the town was small, a fair amount of people bustled about. There was a small hotel, a mercantile, a saloon, the sheriff's office, a barber, livery stable, blacksmith and a church. On the outskirts of town, were several homes and then the shanties. Those tiny buildings, built of scrap, where men and women lived with barely enough room to survive.

Ruby cringed at the thought of having to live in a dwelling that was more like a cell than a home. Usually, they consisted of a kitchen and a bed. Nothing else.

"I've been thinking Ruby. Maybe we should check into the hotel and pretend we're married. That way you'll be protected," Deke said, glancing over at her.

She shot him her surliest look, her lungs freezing at the audacity of him. The man *was* married. And she wasn't sharing a hotel room with a man who had a wife. "Absolutely not."

"Why?"

"If I need to explain the reason why a single woman and a married man do not share a hotel room, then you're not the man I thought you were. In fact, I'm going to check into the Hide Town Hotel and pretend that I don't even know you. I would suggest that you do the same. This way we can both be scouting around town without anyone knowing we're connected."

Though Ruby had never lain with a man before, she knew most people assumed the worst about her. They thought that because she was strong and hunted criminals for a living that she'd probably slept with half of Texas. Well surprise, she was a virgin.

And she intended to stay one for awhile. There was no hurry or reason for her to lay with a man.

Their horses clip clopped along the street as they headed towards the livery stables. People stopped and stared at the two of them riding into town.

"We've already been spotted coming in together," Deke said.

"That doesn't mean we know each other."

"No, but they're going to wonder if we do."

So what. This was a town filled with criminals, they probably suspected everyone who rode into town. They would want to protect themselves and their families from people like her and Deke. "Well good for them."

"Ruby, don't be difficult."

"Difficult? You think I'm being difficult?" A surge of red hot anger spilled into her bloodstream and she could almost hear the sizzle, pulsing through her veins. She turned and slanted her eyes at him. "You haven't begun to see difficult. I don't kiss married men."

She wondered what his wife looked like. And if they were in love, why was he smooching with Ruby? Where did she live? There was more to this story than Deke was telling and if she ever met his spouse, she would fill the woman's ears full of information on the cad she'd tied her wagon too.

Passing through town, she ducked her head so that her hat covered her face, yet tried to peer at the people along the sidewalk. Was Rivera here? She spurred her Mustang towards the livery stable. Once she dropped him off, she'd do some exploring of the town, some investigating.

And no, Mr. Married Deke Culver was not going with her. She needed some time away from him. Some distance to clear her head and remind her body that yes, she was attracted to him, but he was strictly off limits as in wedding band restrictions.

"I'm going to check into the hotel and then I'm going exploring," she informed him as they rode down Main

Street.

"I'll go with you."

"No, I'm doing this alone," she said turning in the saddle and glaring at him. Sometimes a girl needed some solitary time. They'd been together for three days. Enough.

"Why? Why can't I go?"

"Because people don't talk to me as easy if you're around. I want them to open up and tell me what I need to know. If you're near they're uneasy, glancing over my shoulder watching you, waiting for you to pounce."

Deke could give another man a mean stare when he was looking at Ruby. Since he wasn't responsible for Ruby, he had no right and at the moment, she needed to get out and do some exploring.

"I don't know why. I'm not going to pounce on anyone," he said.

"Well, let's see. Could it be the guns on your hips or the way your black hat sits down low on your forehead or the chaps you wear on your thighs? Or the scowl on your face?" She put a finger to her mouth and pretended to concentrate. "I just don't know which one stands out more."

"Smart ass."

"Thank you. I'll take that as a compliment."

"Where are you going?"

"If I knew I wouldn't tell you, but I'm not certain." Oh, she knew exactly where she was headed but he didn't need to know. She didn't want to listen to his lecture on her personal safety.

She pulled up in front of the livery stable and slid down from her horse. She began to unfasten her saddle, pulling the straps free. An eager young man came running out. "Can I help you miss?"

"Why thank you. I need to board my horse."

"Sure. I can take care of that for you. Do you want us to

feed him?"

"No, she wants you to starve him," Deke replied.

The boy shot him a look that if it'd been a bullet he would have been dead. Just what she didn't need, for Deke to alienate the livery boy. They were some of the best resources of knowledge, knowing the comings and goings of just about everyone in town. This was why she refused to pretend that they were husband and wife. Their association had to be kept to a minimum starting right now.

"Don't mind him. He's a cranky old man I met on the trail. We're parting ways right here," she whispered to the stable boy.

"Oh," the kid said kind of surprised. "I thought you were together."

She looked at Deke. "No, I'm alone."

"Are you visiting someone in town?" the boy asked. A horse neighed in the background and she glanced over to see Deke wandering over to the animal. He put his hand on the horse's nose and stared into the animal's eyes. What he was doing?

"I do," she lied. "I'm looking for the Rivera family. I'm a distant relation and I wanted to say hello while I was in town. Don't know how long I'll be staying, but it would be nice to say hello."

"I don't know them."

"Too bad," she said, trying to pay attention to the livery kid, but also watching Deke caressing the horses face with his fingertips.

"Hey, mister, I wouldn't get too close to that horse, he's a mean one," the kid warned.

"He's not so bad. What you're feeding him is giving him gas. He's in pain."

The kid stared at Deke like he'd lost his mind and Ruby wondered how he knew these things about horses that no one else identified. After Deke had recommended that they separate Ruby and Caroline's horse at night, Caroline's mare had done better. But just watching him with the animals, she didn't know how Deke determined what the horse needed.

The livery stable boy turned back to Ruby. "Miss, I'd be happy to bring your saddle down to the hotel for you."

"Why thank you. What's your name?"

"Tim, Ma'am."

"Nice to meet you Tim. I'm Ruby Callahan," she lied not willing to give her real name. Afraid if the town had heard of Ruby McKenzie if they would indeed go after her."

An older man appeared in the doorway, his hat pushed back, his stomach hanging over his pants, with a gun slung low around his hips, staring at them. A star was pinned to his shirt. He glanced over them head to toe as if memorizing every detail.

"Who are you folks?" he asked.

"I'm Ruby Callahan," she said, stepping forward and offering him her hand. She smiled at the lawman. "I don't know the name of this gentleman. We just happened to ride into town at the same time."

"Deke Culver." Deke's voice was low and she watched the two men eyeing each other like a pair of bull fighters in a ring, circling.

"What's your business here in town?" the sheriff asked.

Boy what a friendly place this was. The welcoming committee was the local law wanting to know why you were here.

"What's your name?" Ruby asked, lifting her chin, staring him in the eyes.

"Sheriff Wyatt Thomas," he said.

"I'm looking for employment."

"At the saloon?" he queried.

"Maybe," she said not willing to say much in front of

Deke. He would only disapprove and she didn't want to hear his reasoning.

"What about you sir? What's your business in town?"

"I'm looking for my brother. I'm here to do God's work."

Ruby had to clench her jaws to keep them from popping open, leaving her mouth hanging wide. She wanted to roar with laughter, but knew that would get them a quick ride out of town. The least said the better. But Deke a man of God? Really, the man who was married and kissing a single woman?

"We got all the preacher men we need in this town," the sheriff said not welcoming. In fact, he seemed rather hostile to the fact that Deke was here. With startling clarity she remembered how the sheriff had warned them that this little country village was known for being a place where the law was corrupt and criminals openly walked the streets.

"Maybe so, but I'm also looking for my brother, Jacob Culver. Have you seen him?" Deke asked, eyeing the man more like a gunfighter than a preacher. Oh, he had just made this trip a little more exciting. The kind of excitement they didn't need. Throwing verbal spears at a crooked lawman.

"No and the name is not familiar," the lawman said, crossing his arms across his chest and staring at them.

"My brother rode with the James gang until recently, when he received the calling of Jesus Christ to be saved." Deke tensed and she knew he was poking at the lawman.

"Check with the reverend. He might have heard of him," he said with a nod. He glanced between the two of them. "How long you planning on staying in town?"

The sheriff wanted Deke gone and gone as quick as he could. Could he possibly know that Deke was a bounty hunter?

"Just long enough to find my brother."

I'll give you a few days to search around, but then you might want to move on down the road to the next town," he said. His voice held a strength in it that let you know he was used to getting his way.

Deke smiled. "Why Sheriff, I may find a few more sinners in your town to convert."

The man didn't think Deke's attempt at humor was funny. In fact he frowned, his eyes narrowing. "All the sinners have moved on. We make certain of that."

He turned his attention to Ruby. His eyes skimmed her body, sending a shiver of revulsion from her head to her toes. She swallowed trying to hold back the bile that threatened to spill.

"I'm as free as the wind, sheriff. I'm going to stay, until I get the urge to move on."

The sheriff stared at both of them. "We're a small cozy place and as sheriff I don't put up with any shenanigans. Don't make me chase you out of here..."

Ruby almost laughed. An outlaw town with a controlling lawman. Wonder which side of the law he operated on? She just bet it wasn't the side of the constitution, but rather a vigilante type of law.

"Sheriff," she said with a drawl as she flashed her lashes at him and smiled her most flirtatious. "I don't know about the gentleman but I'm here to earn some money until I get that wandering eye again."

The man laughed. "Honey, I'm not worried about you. But the preacher man here. We don't need any more gospel preached in this town. One of you guys is enough."

With all this scrutiny, they would need to find Rivera as quick as possible and get out of center of corruption. If he hadn't killed her father, she would let this one go, but he'd harmed someone she loved by causing the death of her father. For that, she would stick out this one horse borough with the crooked lawman and make certain she found Rivera.

"Oh, I'm not a preacher. I just follow the spirit and go wherever it takes me. Right now it's calling me to find my brother."

The sheriff wasn't nearly as receptive to Deke as he was to Ruby. "Just don't overstay your welcome preacher man"

The man turned and walked out of the livery stable.

"Does everyone get a welcome into town from the sheriff?" Ruby asked Tim.

"Just about. Be careful and you'll be all right."

Ruby frowned and thought of Zenith and how the law would never accost visitors unless they were causing trouble or were wanted. Somehow she got the feeling that she needed to find Rivera quickly before trouble wearing a badge found her.

~

Later that afternoon Ruby pushed through the swinging doors of the saloon, walking towards the bar. Inside the smell of whisky and smoke lingered in the dark shadowy room. A staircase led the way upstairs where she could hear women laughing and talking. Downstairs a bar ran across the back wall where the bottles of liquor were stored in cabinets. To the right were tables where card games were held. And to the left, was a stage where entertainment could perform.

A middle aged woman with dark hair and an elegant dress met her before she reached the bar.

"Can I help you?" she asked, eyeing Ruby up and down in her split skirt and fitted shirt.

"I'm looking for a job?"

The woman smiled. "I'd be happy to help you, dear. I charge one dollar for the men to sleep with my girls and you receive half. The other goes towards your room and board. Clothing is added on to your bill and taken off at the end of the month."

A shudder rippled through Ruby at the idea of unknown men touching, kissing her and trying to…there was no way she could ever work in a bordello. Never.

"No, ma'am. I respect your business, but I'm a card dealer," Ruby said hoping that they wouldn't try to force her upstairs. She'd heard horror tales of women being coerced into prostitution. She'd kill anyone who tried.

The woman didn't even try to hide her fascination with Ruby's figure. Her eyes were taking in her measurements as they stood there talking. It was the creepiest feeling Ruby had ever experienced. "Oh honey, you could be making so much more working upstairs."

Firmly, Ruby shook her head. "No, I about killed the last man who tried to sleep with me. So I don't think I'd be much good."

Maybe by telling the woman she would kill any man who tried, she'd understand that Ruby would never be a willing participant.

The lady laughed and held out her hand. "Mrs. Emily Hutchins."

"Ruby Callahan."

"Nice to meet you Ruby." She continued to stare at Ruby, her eyes traveling the length of her body, like she was assessing a piece of meat. "I've never hired a woman card dealer before. How do I know you can deal?"

Now Ruby's acting ability kicked in and she thought of the card games she once played with her sisters.

"I was a dealer at the Elephant saloon in Fort Worth for many years. I also worked in Dodge City for awhile."

"Great credentials," she replied, her eyes finally gazing into Ruby's. "While I would rather hire you upstairs, I think you will certainly draw the men into the saloon. I tell you what. I'll hire you for one night. Please the clientele and if I like what I see, we'll talk about a permanent job."

"Thank you, Ma'am." Ruby said, thinking she didn't have any quarrel with the woman owner. She didn't care that she ran a house of prostitution. But she had to find Rivera.

"Do you have something nice to wear? This is great for the road, but I'd like you to dress in a gown. If you don't have one, I think I have a dress that will fit you. Chrissy," she yelled.

A black servant girl came running.

"Run upstairs and bring down the gowns for Ruby to consider."

The young girl hurried up the stairs into the bordello. A few minutes later, she hauled down three dresses and placed them in front of Ruby. The fabric was the richest silk trimmed with lace and pearls. They were gorgeous, but they either were so low cut Ruby's breasts would be falling out or they had a slit in the front that went to the top of her thighs, almost to the juncture of her legs. An open invitation to see underneath her skirt.

Oh no, you weren't going to get her in that dress. That dress would certainly bring trouble.

"I think this one will do," Ruby said, picking up the garment that only showed half her breasts. Her sisters would have a fit if they saw her in this outfit. She would never hear the end of it and if possible they would chain her at home for the rest of her young life.

But it would certainly draw a man's attention from the cards.

"Be here at eight o'clock and prepared to work until the men go home."

"Yes, Ma'am. See you tonight."

Ruby walked out of the door, knowing that she had an in. Now she needed to learn more about where the Rivera family lived. And she hoped her father's murderer came to the saloon tonight, but she was prepared to stay until he arrived.

~

Deke heard the pounding on his hotel door and wondered what was going on. The only person who knew he was here was Ruby.

He opened the door and his vision almost exploded before his very eyes. He swallowed hard to keep from choking, feeling his manhood harden and swell. She wore a teal colored gown that made her blue eyes shine brighter than the sky. Her blonde hair was piled high on her head with curls spilling down. Curls a man would love to run his fingers through.

God, he wanted to pull her inside and strip that dress from her body and plunge himself deep within her.

The dress fit her trim curves in all the right places, with the bodice cut low in the front. If she coughed he feared she would spill out of the dress and everyone would see her gorgeous, creamy breasts. Breasts he longed to caress.

"Oh no, you're not going into the saloon dressed like that. Your Papa would come back from the dead and haunt me."

She frowned at him. "Stop. You're not talking me out of this. I need your help and I have very little time."

"I don't care. You're not going dressed like that. If you were my wife I wouldn't even let you wear that dress around the house."

"Well, I'm not your wife, so there's no need to worry."

Oh God, he really should tell her the truth. But he wasn't ready to answer her questions. There was no way to make Ruby understand his choices without telling her everything.

"I need you to play a few hands of cards with me."

"Why?"

"Because I'm the card dealer tonight and if I don't know what I'm doing, I won't get the job."

"Good. Then you'll come to your senses and see that I was right. You're taking a senseless chance."

She took a deep breath. "Deke. Play cards with me. If you don't, I might get shot."

He shook his head and motioned her inside his room. Glancing up at the ceiling, he said, "Sir, I'm sorry, I tried to talk her out of dressing this way. She's definitely your daughter because she's so damn stubborn."

He knew he couldn't stop her, but he was hoping that maybe guilt would work. But she was stubborn as they come and he didn't even faze her.

Ruby walked by and punched him in the gut. "Stop it. Let me deal the cards to you."

Sitting down on the bed, she shuffled the deck and dealt him a hand. Even her sitting on the bed was enough to send his mind spinning with what they could do on that mattress. How she would look naked against the sheets.

Focus!

"Always make certain that the cards are turned down so that the other players can't read the card that their neighbor received," he said watching her sitting on the edge of his bed, thinking that dress just begged him to remove it. To peel it slowly from her shoulders, down past her waist to her pantaloons. He'd like nothing more than to stare at all that creamy white flesh.

"Okay."

"Do you know the rules of poker," he asked, focusing his eyes on her forehead and not her chest. Man these men were going to lose tonight and the house was going to love her. They wouldn't care that she was stealing their pay bit by bit. They would be lost in her beautiful blue eyes and those breasts. The dress was a definite distraction to any man sitting at her table.

"Yes, at least the way my sisters and I use to play."

"Oh God, you're going to get killed."

"You don't know that. Annabelle could deal a mean hand of five card draw."

He glanced at her. "I'm sure Annabelle is quite the card shark."

"She is. You look at her all quiet and innocent and she will quietly strip you of your money."

Just like Ruby was going to steal these crooks blind when they lost themselves in her beauty. God, he had to be there to protect her. "What about twenty-one. Do you know the rules of that game?"

"Seems pretty simple."

"But you're the dealer. You have to know how to run the table. You have to stand on seventeen."

"Okay, I can do that. What else do I need to know?" she asked looking at him all innocent eyed and beautiful and they neither one would live through the night. He was certain he'd die in some kind of fight protecting her.

"Watch for cheats. Sometimes men have been known to hide cards that they need. So watch their hands carefully," he warned trying to focus on what she needed to know.

She shuffled and dealt another hand of five card stud.

"No, don't do that. You can't look at your cards until everyone has received their hand," he told her.

"Oh."

"Ruby, I feel really nervous about this."

"Don't worry, I'll do okay. If I can play a saloon girl, I can do a card dealer."

"Why didn't you do the saloon girl part again?" he asked wondering why she'd put herself in so much danger.

"Because the saloon girls also work upstairs, if you understand what I'm saying."

He smiled. "So you draw the line at being a whore."

"Absolutely. I could play the fancy woman for the right man, but he wouldn't remember the night."

Deke frowned. "What do you mean?"

"I mean it would be lights out for him, as soon as he walked in the door and my weapon connected with the back of his head."

He laughed and shook his head. "I don't like this. There are other ways we can get the information we need. You don't have to work in the saloon."

"Nope, this is how we're doing it."

When it came to Ruby, his negotiation skills had dried up and blow away in the Texas sand. Because he seemed to lose every round. "What time do you have to be there?"

"In about ten minutes."

"Do you have a gun on you?"

"Always."

He walked over to and stood within inches of her. At the sight of her, desire was pulsing through his blood, rushing at him like a runaway train. He stared at her lips, wanting to taste them again, wanting to put his mouth over hers and drink from her body. But knew he'd be a dead man if he tried.

The smell of roses, teased his nose and he knew her table would be crowded. He couldn't resist letting his finger trail down her chest to her exposed cleavage. "No man should be viewing these. They're exquisite."

She grabbed his hand. "Including you. You're a married man."

Her skin felt silky smooth. He was envious of the men who would be at her card table tonight, feasting their eyes on the tops of her breasts.

She opened her reticule and pulled out her pot of lipstick. Twisting the little pot open, she dipped her finger in and smeared the red paint across her lips. She dropped the little pot back into her bag. He'd watched her perform this little ritual more than once and each time he wanted to kiss her until the red was gone.

"I've got to go," she said softly.

"And I won't be far behind you," he said. "There's no way you're going over there alone, looking like this."

"Just let me do my job," she said.

She walked out the door, leaving him behind.

The scent of roses lingered in the room. He breathed deep, his body needing release.

Sooner or later he needed to tell Ruby. Yes, he considered himself married. He had a wife. A wife he'd never given his heart to. But Laura was dead and he was to blame for her death. Ruby needed to know the truth.

Chapter Six

While Ruby walked up to the table and watched as the men checked out first her displayed chest and then her eyes. If she sneezed, she could be exposing herself to the six randy cowboys who sat staring at her waiting for her to deal the cards.

"Good evening, gentlemen," she said shuffling the card deck, nerves skittering down her spine like a snake slithering across the ground. "How is everyone tonight? Anyone need a drink from the bar?"

Breathing in deep calming breaths, she squelched her nerves. She'd played cards as a kid, but never as a dealer in a local gambling establishment. While she and Meg had been in several saloons, Ruby had all but ignored the tables concentrating on locating her outlaws. So tonight was do or die by the hand of her employer.

"Just deal the cards," an old man sitting on the end said. "And make them good."

"What's your name, sir?" she asked him politely.

"Jack," he murmured.

"Would you like to cut the cards?" she said with a smile and leaned over towards him, giving him a good view of her cleavage. Yeah, if she had to, she could play a man's game with a woman's wiles. She didn't like it, but sometimes a woman had no choice and men were easy to fool with a tease and a sultry glance.

She needed this job, because if not tonight, James Rivera would soon come to the saloon and she'd be ready to haul him back to justice.

The old man's forehead drew together and his lips pursed into a frown. "I'm not going to tip you."

"Honey, I don't expect you to. The house is paying my wages." Glancing at the money on the table, she checked with her players. "Everyone has anted?"

The man on the end threw his money in the pot. She would have to watch that one. No one played for free.

"Good luck, gentleman," she said with a purr.

The man cut the deck in half and she put the cards back together and then began to deal.

She dealt the first two cards one down and one face up. The man in the middle started the betting. When all bets were in, she dealt a third card up and the same cowboy upped the betting by fifty cents.

When all five cards were dealt, the betting continued until the man who'd been rude, Jack, won the hand with three two's. He raked in the pile and she smiled at him.

Collecting the cards, she shuffled the deck once again, her heart beat slowed as she realized she hadn't been yanked out of the chair yet. As she relaxed, she felt herself smile. She'd fooled them into believing she was a card dealer.

"Ante up?" she asked checking to make sure that all the players had bet. Then she dealt the hand.

Soon she felt comfortable enough that while she dealt the cards, she could also check out the patrons. Some men just came in to drink and smoke, while other men played the different table games available. Other men were perusing the women that Mrs. Hutchins had available.

Ruby couldn't help but be curious about what would make a woman decide to become a whore? Did they choose this lifestyle or had life given them no choice? She thought back to right after her Papa had passed away and shuddered thinking that if Meg hadn't been so determined, this could have been their lifestyle.

"Miss Callahan, deal the last card," one of the men said.

"Sorry, gentlemen, I was trying to get the girl's attention to bring over a bottle of whiskey for anyone that might need a drink," she said softly as she dealt the cards.

She'd also been searching the saloon wondering if Rivera might already be among the patrons. Maybe he was here and she didn't recognize him.

"Last card, gentlemen," she said and placed the final card on the table for that hand.

Soon, she had the rhythm down and the men seemed to accept and even flirted with her. When she could, she gazed around the room and tried to find Rivera, only this time she saw Deke. Sitting alone at a bar, he nursed a drink and watched her, his brown eyes dark, his face unreadable.

She smiled at him and he nodded his head, though he didn't return her smile. In fact, he touched his hand to his gun and she knew what he was saying. He was there looking after her. She didn't need his protection, but maybe when he wasn't scowling at her, he'd spot Rivera.

After all these years, she'd never considered that he could be married. For some reason the thought just never crossed her mind. While she hadn't pined for the man, she'd often wondered about him. Mainly, if he was still kicking or if a bullet had found Deke and the grass now waved over him.

Mentally shaking the worrisome thought away, she glanced at the men around her table. Could they know anything about the location of Rivera?

"Gentlemen, I just arrived on the stage. Tell me what you like about Hide Town?"

"The law," one man said with a slur. "It's kind of relaxed."

"Shut up, Bryan," Jack told him. "The sheriff hears you and you'll be starin' at the sky and seeing nothing."

The men all looked at her with glazed eyes. Obviously, they were well into the liquor. Maybe she should ask her more serious questions earlier in the evening, before they were drunker'n than a fiddler's clerk.

"Just wondering. My last town was as wild as a corncrib rat. I was hoping for a little reprieve from the craziness."

One man laughed. "Right now there are probably ten men in this room wanted by the law. You've come to about the wildest town in west Texas. This isn't a quiet town by any means."

That was obvious with most of the businesses in town catering to a man's wilder side and filled with women of ill-repute. And Mrs. Hutchins owned many of them.

"Well gentleman, even ladies need a place to hang low for awhile."

Jack grinned at her. "Some wife chasing you for looking twice at her man?"

Ruby laughed. "Not hardly. Let's just say, my man and I had to separate to keep the law from connecting us."

So it was a lie. She had no man, not really. Sure she and Deke were working together to find Rivera, but he wasn't her man. He was married and she wasn't going to be the woman who came between him and his wife. No matter how much she enjoyed Deke – she wasn't stealing another woman's man.

A drunken cowboy sitting at her table leaned forward, his head swaying from the effects of the liquor. "You ain't Belle Starr are you?"

Ruby felt the urge to create some suspense about her identity. She bent low and whispered. "Shh…don't say that name very loud."

"Oh my gosh, it's her," he said loud enough to draw attention, yet barely sober enough to keep his head from slamming into the table.

"Now, I didn't say that I was Belle Starr did I?" she said, knowing that probably someone in town had seen the woman's poster and they didn't look a bit alike.

"No, but you're pretty enough that you could be her."

"Thank you," she said and smiled around the table at

the gentlemen, working to charm them out of their money and information. "Who hasn't anted up?"

With a drunken glare, the straggler at the end of the table, the one she had to watch, pushed his coin into the pile of bets.

After two hours, Mrs. Hutchins came over and tapped her on the shoulder. "After the next hand, meet me in the office behind the bar. We have things to discuss."

A flurry of butterflies invaded her stomach and she cringed inside. Now she'd learn if she'd successfully conned everyone into believing she'd been a dealer before tonight. If not, she could find herself with a madam threatening to run her out of town before she collected her bounty.

At the end of that hand, she looked at her patrons. "Well gentlemen, it's been a pleasure serving you tonight. I'm taking a break and George is going to take over dealing the cards. I hope you all had a good time."

"Ruby," one of the men slurred her name. "Will you marry me?"

She laughed and clucked him under the chin with her fingers. "Why thank you for the kind offer, but I'm not available."

"You married?" one of the other men asked.

"No, but I'm just not the marrying kind of woman. Excuse me, gentlemen."

Picking up her skirt, she strolled towards the office and the waiting Mrs. Hutchins. She passed Deke and didn't even give him the time of day, though his fingers reached out and brushed her hand. A spiral of warmth wound its way through her, but she continued walking.

The man was married. He was strictly off limits and no matter what, her body needed to forget how he made her feel. He had a wife waiting for him at home. And she had a bounty to catch.

Rounding the bar, she went into the office. Mrs. Hutchins sat waiting. "Sit down, Ruby."

At first Ruby felt nervous as the woman stared at her like she was suspicious. She leaned back in her chair. "You've done well. You're hired. Be here every day by eight in the evening and plan on staying until at least three am."

Ruby wanted to release a sigh of relief, but held it back not wanting the woman to see that she'd been nervous. This woman was sharper than a nail and Ruby didn't think she missed much that went on in her business. Tonight she'd watched her handling the bartender, while she paraded the girls out like property to be chosen from. The madam was a shrewd manager, Ruby would do well to keep her emotions hidden and her eyes open.

"Thank you for the job. I hope I don't disappoint."

"I have confidence that you'll be very good. And you're going to distract these men so much that they'll be losing their money all the time, unless of course you would consider working upstairs. I know we'd both make a lot of money if you were one of my girls," the woman said a smile on her face.

"No, thank you."

"You get ten percent of all your earnings," she said with a smile, like it was going to be a huge amount of money to deal cards.

The woman was trying to get her for as cheap as possible. While Ruby hoped she'd never collect a dime of her wages, she didn't like the idea of being taken.

"No, I get twenty percent," Ruby said.

The woman smiled and shook her head. "The most I can offer you is fifteen percent of all your earnings."

"That's better," Ruby said and stood.

"Of course, I'm going to charge you for the use of the clothes."

How did her whores ever get out of this business if the madam charged them for every little thing, eating up most of their wage? A shudder rippled through Ruby at the thought of being trapped in this life. She couldn't wait to catch Rivera and leave the dust of this town behind.

"I'd be shocked if you didn't."

"And if you want, I'll offer you room and board."

Oh no, that was a trap she wasn't getting caught in. She'd continue staying at the hotel.

"No, I think I'll stay where I'm at."

She shrugged. "Suit yourself." The madam stood and gave Ruby a smile that didn't quite reach her eyes. "Get busy and earn the house some money. Go help those poor men lose their coins. Do whatever it takes."

Though she would help the house win, she wasn't about to cheat no matter what the crooked woman wanted. Cheating was the way to find herself being chased out of town, by the men she'd gouged.

"I'll do my best," Ruby said, and walked out the door. She went back to her table and as she passed Deke, she winked at him.

He narrowed his eyes at her and frowned. She put a little extra twitch in her behind as she passed him. Make the man suffer a little as he watched her flirt outrageously with the men at her table. After all he'd rejected her and then gone home and gotten married.

Gazing around the saloon, she wished she would see Rivera. Acting as a card dealer was fun, doing this every night would get old. She wanted to catch their man and get out of this hell hole of a town, before they got caught. Before Annabelle had her baby. She wanted to be there when her first niece or nephew made their appearance in the world.

As she walked back to her table, a fight broke out between one of the women upstairs and a man. He was pulling the whore by the hair down the stairs and she was screaming. Mrs. Hutchins ran to the man, not exactly pulling him off the girl, but more interested in his actions.

"What's wrong?"

"I caught her stealing from me."

"I did not," the beautiful auburn haired girl said, her lips forming almost a pout. She looked young. Younger than Ruby.

"Her hands were in my pants," the man said, slapping her on the head.

"She can put her hands in my pants," a cowpoke yelled from across the room. "I can handle it."

"No, I dozed off and when I awoke, she was going through my pockets."

After the way he'd pulled the woman by the hair and was slapping her on the head, Ruby hoped she'd taken him for every dime he had. Nobody deserved to be treated the way the man was handling the woman while the madam watched.

"Is this true, Hannah?" the madam asked.

"I…I was looking for a handkerchief," the girl said, her body shaking.

The kid looked scared and it was all Ruby could do to keep from going to her and telling it was going to be okay.

"You were looking for money," the geezer who she'd been with replied.

Mrs. Hutchins took the arm of the girl and whispered in her ear. She walked away towards the office and a tear trickle down the girl's cheek.

Ruby felt her chest tighten as sympathy filled her making her stomach clench. Pity surged through her, she would hate that job. Putting up with men who abused her like this old man. The pawing, the smell, the dirty unwashed bodies, just the idea sent a shiver through Ruby.

"Sir, did she take any of your money?" Mrs. Hutchins

asked.

"No, but she would have if I hadn't woken up."

Ruby watched as the Madame soothed the man and turned his attention away to another girl.

"Hussy," one of the men at her table muttered. "She should be on her back more if she isn't happy with what she's making."

Ruby swallowed the bile that rose in her throat, anger replacing it making her hands shake as she controlled the urge to smack the ignorant fool. If she tried to help the girl, she'd be run out of town and the girl would still be enslaved to the madam. She took a deep breath and let it out slowly. "Mr. Jones, while I work in the worst saloons, I'm still a lady and I think there are more pleasant topics we could discuss."

The man just about choked on his drink. "The card dealer wants to be treated with respect."

He laughed, his voice making a mockery of the courtesy she demanded.

"Lady Luck is a lady and demands respect."

The men at the table stared at her for a moment. "Ante up, gentlemen, the next hand could be your lucky hand."

~

Deke waited in the shadows for Ruby to come out of the saloon. The moon was on the downward slope of the sky and would soon be setting. And she had yet to come out. When the whore had been reprimanded in public, he'd been afraid that Ruby was going to step in and defend her. He'd watched her, seeing the emotions on her face knowing she hated what she'd witnessed, holding his breath she wouldn't interfere. If she had, they would have been run out of town with half the men in the town chasing them, seeking vengeance.

Most people believed, whores had little value,

regardless that they were women.

Finally the doors swung open and Ruby stepped out into the street.

"About time you got out of there."

She jumped. "Good grief, you could let a girl know you're there."

"I've been waiting."

After watching her tonight dealing cards to ruthless men, he wasn't about to let her walk down the street to the hotel alone. A mere two blocks, where she could encounter all kinds of danger in the wee hours of the morning.

"Well, I just got off."

"How did it go?" he asked wondering if they'd hired her permanently. From what he could see the men were more than anxious to have a seat at her table and play cards with the woman dealer and try to beat her. They thought she was an easy target, but soon learned she could handle the cards with the best of them.

"I'm hired. What about you? Did you see Rivera tonight?" she asked.

"Nope. He wasn't there," he said, thinking of at least three other criminals he'd spotted tonight, but none of them were the man they were searching for. And while he'd tried to ask discreetly, that bar was not a place you spent time asking questions. Especially inquiring about wanted men. "He'll recognize me, so I will probably slip out if he comes in."

"You're right. You'll have to get out of there before he sees you."

Deke shook his head. He didn't like the idea of leaving her alone in a saloon filled with randy men who would like nothing better than partake of her womanly wiles.

A cool breeze blew, sending a shiver through her. Winter would soon arrive. He wanted to wrap his arms around her and warm her up, but knew that would be frowned upon. Few people were about the street, just the town drunks and several men making their way home, but still people didn't need to see them all cozy together. They might get the wrong idea.

"Aargh," she cried. "I don't know how women do this day in and day out. I could never work in a saloon for the rest of my life. And that whore. Oh my God, I walked back down to the bar to get me a drink and I saw the madam slap her. Why don't they walk out?"

"Maybe they can't. Sometimes women are sold into prostitution," he said, thinking of Laura and the reason he'd married her.

"That's wrong. Evil."

"The world treats women pretty bad," he said walking beside Ruby, his hands in his pocket, appearing relaxed, but observing the street. For some reason he felt like they were being watched, since they'd left the saloon. In this town, it wouldn't be good to draw the attention of anyone. The quicker they finished this job, the better.

A board on the wooden sidewalk creaked and he knew someone was behind them.

"Miss Callahan, I appreciate you giving me the honor of letting me walk you to the hotel. Especially since I was headed in that direction. It being late and all, I would hate for a woman like yourself to be out alone."

Her brows drew together in a frown and she gazed at him like he'd lost his mind. With his eyes, he motioned behind them and she opened her mouth in an O. She dropped her purse. "How clumsy of me."

At that point, he turned and glanced behind them while Ruby leaned down to pick up her purse.

"Evening Sheriff," he said. "What are you doing out so late?"

"Checking up on my citizens finding out what they're up to," the burly man said. "The bigger question is what are the two of you doing out?"

"I just left the saloon and I'm escorting, Miss Callahan back to her hotel."

The man frowned. "I thought you guys didn't know each other."

Ruby stood and glanced at the sheriff. She pulled her shoulders back and he could have sworn that she pushed her chest out. If she had, he was going to give her hell.

"Sheriff, so good to see you. I got the job as card dealer over at Dusty's Saloon. I just got off work and Mr. Culver graciously offered to walk me home, because you weren't there to escort me. A girl can never be too careful how she gets home."

Deke thought he was going to throw up as he watched the old man eating up everything that she said, his eyes strained on her chest like he was feasting on Christmas dinner. But the ploy was working as he didn't seem too interested in the two of them.

"You're almost back to your hotel. I'll let you folks get in. If I'm out and about late at night, I'd be proud to walk you back to your hotel," he said smiling at her.

Irritation flowed through Deke's veins like water over a dam. Could Ruby stay out of trouble? It wasn't good to play with the sheriff? After all, that could go bad in a heartbeat and they might find both of themselves in trouble.

"Good night," he said, and walked on down the sidewalk towards the jail.

"Are you crazy?" Deke asked.

"What?" she said. "He took the bait."

Yes, the old man had been devouring Ruby's exposed chest and drinking in her bubbly personality all the while she'd turned the conversation away from the two of them knowing each other.

"That bait could get you killed or jailed or even worse. Don't play with the sheriff, Ruby. He's dangerous. He could get both of us killed."

The law in this town was known for being a vigilante outfit that fashioned the law however it fit their needs. If they learned Ruby and Deke were bounty hunters, they'd soon be climbing the golden stairs on a rope.

She waved him away. "You worry too much."

"And you're going to get yourself shot."

Ruby took way too many chances and one of these days she'd roll the wrong dice and find herself in more trouble than she could handle.

They reached the hotel door. "I'm going up. I'm exhausted. Tomorrow, I'm riding out to the Rivera's homestead."

"What?"

Of all the crazy things for her to spring on him, like she was spraying him with buckshot.

"I was about to tell you. I learned tonight that the Rivera family has a homestead not too far out of town."

"Why didn't you tell me earlier?" he asked wanting to throw her across his knee and bring his hand down on her lovely bottom.

"You were too busy trying to warn me away from the sheriff."

"Woman you drive me crazy."

If only she knew, that he was a widower, she would know just how much being around her was a danger to him. A danger to the vows he'd made to himself, not Laura.

She smiled. "I don't have to. You already are."

Shaking his head, he just stared at her. Maybe she was right. He was definitely nuts to be here with her taking a risk for another bounty.

~

The next afternoon, Deke sat on his horse waiting on the side of the barn, while Ruby went to the door of the

Rivera homestead. He was hidden just enough not to be seen, but close enough he could see what was going on.

This woman didn't know the meaning of danger. At the mere mention of the word, she got excited. She loved taking chances and risking it all. That frightened him worse than a band of Comanche Indians.

Someday she was going to get hurt and he didn't want to be there to see it happen. As soon as they captured Rivera, he was gone. He wasn't sticking around to watch Ruby shot by a bounty that went wrong. Oh no, he wasn't going to witness her dying. He'd seen one woman die and never again. While he couldn't stop Ruby from her brazen actions, he didn't have to watch her get herself killed.

She knocked on the door. Finally, a man taller than herself, with a scroungy beard and dark eyes opened the door. "What do you want?"

"Is this the Rivera home?" she asked.

"What if it is?" he said not at all friendly.

Ruby shook her head. "I don't know how to say this. I'm kind of embarrassed. I met James while he was in jail. Our church group was ministering to the prisoners and well, he's just the sweetest man. I wanted to come by and tell him hello. I'm in this area for a few days and if he's here, I'd love to say howdy."

The man stared at her and shook his head. "What the hell are you talking about lady?"

"James Rivera? Is he here?"

"No, he's not here. We haven't seen him."

The man was being cagy and Deke couldn't really blame him. Some strange woman shows up at his door, he wouldn't tell her anything.

"Well darn. I was hoping we'd have time to catch up and say hello before I have to return. If he comes home, you tell him Martha paid came by to say hello. Tell him I'm praying for him."

The man started to laugh at her. "Honey, no amount of prayers is going to help my brother. But you keep up the good work." His eyes darkened and then they trailed down Ruby's body. "Would you like to come in and rest before you head back to town?"

Deke was reaching for his weapon, ready to storm in and rescue her if necessary.

"No, I've got to get back. I'm working temporarily at the saloon, Dealing cards and trying to save souls," she said with a laugh.

"What? You said you were praying for my brother and that your church group ministered to him in jail? But you work in a saloon?"

Shaking his head, Deke eased his hand away from his gun. The girl was taking crazy chances and making up stories as she went. And yet, she was damn good at getting people to talk.

"Where is the best place to reach sinners, but in a saloon? I'm a card dealer. Come see me and maybe lady luck will shine your way."

He laughed. "If James comes home, I'll definitely send him in your direction."

She smiled at him in that Ruby flirtatious way that Deke just hated unless it was aimed at him. He had no right to feel the jealousy that consumed him, but that didn't stop him.

"Thanks!"

Walking away, she stepped into the foot stirrup of her saddle and climbed on the back of her horse.

The man stood in the doorway and watched as she rode off.

Deke released the breath he'd been holding. There for a minute, he feared he was going to have to go and save her, but somehow she'd pulled it off.

And told the man she was a bible-thumping card dealer.

But the worst part was that he'd fell for it. She could probably talk a rattlesnake into being friends. She talked out of both sides of her mouth to get what she needed and people believed her.

Someday it was all going to catch up to her and he didn't want to be around to pick up the pieces whenever they fell. He wanted to be a long ways away.

Yet, he admired the girl. Her spirit was infectious and fun and damn she was the sexiest woman he'd ever met. Given the chance he'd bed her in a heartbeat if not for the consequences of his actions.

Chapter Seven

The next day Ruby walked down the street headed for the mercantile. The wooden sidewalk resounded with each step she took. A warm breeze blew, scattering the dust from Main Street into any crack, crevice or cleft. This dusty, little hell hole of a town was only three blocks long, and the people who lived and worked here were rugged hearty souls who dealt with cold winters, hot summers and dust. Lots of blowing, gritty, dust.

Often times if she befriended the owner of the local store, she could learn who had come in buying goods. It was a way to learn if the man you were looking for was in the area.

The sun beat down on the wooden sidewalk as she strolled like she didn't have a care in the world, towards the business. Dressed in her saloon outfit, she'd put a shawl over the top to cover her breasts, tying it strategically to hide her assets.

While she was at the store she intended to fill up on supplies. Her little pot of lipstick was getting low and she needed another rouge pot to give her lips that dark red color she loved.

As she hurried down the street, she saw the whore from last night that had been accused of stealing scurrying along the sidewalk. Hannah had been her name and Ruby watched as she ducked her head and slid in between two buildings. What was going on?

Ruby hastened to catch up to her. As she all but ran, she saw one of the men from the saloon, searching the street as if he were looking for someone. Soon he would be upon the alley that the woman had gone into.

She watched the man turn and sprint down the alley. Ruby glanced along the path and could not see Hannah. On a whim, she went back to the sidewalk to the next open alley and there was Hannah.

"What are you doing?" Ruby called.

The girls eyes widened and she put her finger to her lips.

Ruby waved to the girl and motioned for her to run. The girl frowned and gazed suspiciously, but dashed towards her. When she reached Ruby's side, she pulled her into the mercantile.

"What are you doing?" Ruby asked. Bruises marred her beautiful face and her emerald eyes searched frantically about the store.

"I'm trying to escape," the girl whispered. "I can't do this anymore. I just can't."

"They're hunting you. How do you plan to leave?"

"I…I was going to walk out of town," the girl said, her voice shaky, her eyes wide with horror. "You don't understand. I'm not this way. If I don't leave, I'm going to kill myself."

Shaking her head, Ruby frowned at the girl warning her. "If you try to walk out of here, they'll catch you. You think your life is bad now, they'll make it even worse. You're not prepared."

There was no way the woman had a chance of escaping today. They were already searching for her, she probably wouldn't make it out of town.

"I know. This is my third attempt. She said next time she'd kill me," Hannah said, her emerald eyes dark with despair.

Ruby sighed. She had to help the girl, there was no way she could walk away from her, especially after viewing the bruises on her face. Women needed to know how to defend themselves, how to make a living without it being on their backs. And gosh darn it, Ruby McKenzie had the secret.

"Deke is going to kill me," she said with a sigh. She gazed at Hannah. "Just play along with me for now. Do what I say."

Putting her arm through the whore's, she strolled to the window of the mercantile where they could gaze out at the town and be seen standing inside the business. "Act like we're shopping and you're having fun. And for God's sake smile. Maybe even laugh."

The girl plastered the most petrified smile she'd ever seen on a human being man or female. "You've got to do better than that. Laugh."

She laughed the sound fake and brittle.

Ruby shook her head, she was in so much trouble. She could lose her job, her status with the madam if she helped this girl, but couldn't let them find out she was trying to escape. They would find and kill her. Whores were cheaper and more accessible than a gaggle of hens and one missing would not create a shortage in this ruthless town.

"Have you tried this shade of color on your lips?" Ruby asked the girl. "It will make them stand out more."

"No…I've only used what I've been given," she said her voice trembling.

The goon entered the mercantile and Ruby continued as if she hadn't seen him walk in. "You know I think with the coloring in your cheeks, this one would make you appear perkier and happy. I bet you'd make more money using this shade."

"What about the powder?" the girl asked timidly. "Do you wear facial powder? It makes me itch."

"What the hell are you doing?" the man said, and grabbed Hannah by the arm.

"Ouch," Hannah said glancing up into his eyes, her gaze almost deadly from the way she looked at him.

Yes, Ruby had to help her. Teach and show her how she could make a decent living.

"I've been hunting for you," the man replied.

Ruby slapped his hand away. "What are you doing? Can't you see we're shopping?"

The man appeared startled.

"I'm giving her some tips on how to look more appealing to the men. Then we're going to have lunch over at the café. She's not a prisoner is she?" Ruby asked surprised. "I'll have her back at the saloon before time for her to go to work."

The man frowned and stared between the two women. "I guess she's not a prisoner. It's just she's never done this before and Mrs. Hutchins was certain she was running."

The women looked at each other and burst out laughing, their strained voices ringing in the small store.

"Like that's worked for me before."

Ruby shook her head. "Where would she go? To another whore house? How would she get there? You going to take her?"

Glancing between the two women, the man put his hands on his hips. "Mrs. Hutchins isn't going to like this, but I reckon it can't hurt. You ladies do like to shop. But I'm going to be watching you, so don't try anything funny. I'll be right outside the store, waiting to escort you back to the saloon."

"You're welcome to join us, but you have to try on a shade of this rouge pot. You might even look nice wearing this color on your lips and cheeks," Ruby said, all innocent to the man who glared like an angry bear.

"I'll be waiting outside," the man all but growled.

"Too-da-lou. Will you be joining us for lunch at the café?" Ruby called.

He shook his head and continued out the door.

After he was gone, the girl sighed with relief. "Oh my God, you were right. They saw me sneak out. Thank you for helping me. You didn't have to do that."

Ruby stared at the girl. "Why not? You were in trouble and needed help."

"It's just that I'm a whore and most women avoid me," she said softly, glancing around the small store.

The owner watched them carefully and Ruby sent him her most charming smile, hoping he couldn't overhear them.

"I'm a card dealer. I don't care about the women who avoid me," she said lifting her chin, knowing she was so much more than just a lady who dealt winning and losing hands of poker. "And neither should you."

The girl smiled. "I'm Hannah. Hannah Williams."

"Nice to meet you Hannah. I'm Ruby Callahan." She took the young girl by the arm. "Let's go have lunch. You can tell me all about why you want to run away when we get to the restaurant."

The girl stopped in the middle of the store, her big eyes filling with tears. "I never wanted to be a whore."

Ruby patted her on the arm. "It's okay. We'll talk when we get to the restaurant where it's more private."

"I don't know if they'll let me into the diner," she said, her voice breaking.

There was no way that Ruby wanted to embarrass the girl, but it was the logical place for them to go and have lunch. They could sit down and she could learn a little more about Hannah's story. "Let's try. If not, then we'll just have a picnic somewhere."

"And Madam's goon will be keeping an eye on my every move."

Glancing out the open door, she could see the man leaning against the frame of the building, waiting, watching. Mrs. Hutchins was looking after her investment like a jailer scrutinized his inmates.

"Let him," she said. "We have nothing to hide. Today is not the day you're leaving town."

They strolled out of the mercantile and down the sidewalk to the café. When Ruby asked for a table, the waitress seemed reluctant. She glanced at Hannah and then Ruby.

"We don't serve her kind here," the woman said, in a low shaky voice.

"You don't serve women?" Ruby asked feeling surly. "We don't want any trouble. We just want to sit down and have lunch."

The waitress glanced around. "Okay, but don't take too long."

Finally they were seated and Hannah peeked around the room. She shuddered.

"What's wrong?"

"I've had sexual intercourse with half the men in this room. Some of them are here with their wives."

Ruby laughed. "Don't you think they feel a little nervous right now?"

She couldn't imagine what it must be like to look around the room and see cowboys who she'd known in the most intimate manner. Scanning the restaurant, there were a lot of men in here that looked like a good bath, a shave and a haircut would clean them up, but not enough to entice her to share a bed with them.

Hannah grinned, a real smile for the first time. "Good. They should have stayed home where they belonged."

Laying her menu down, Ruby looked closely at the young woman. There was a slight bruise marring her face, she had long, dark lashes that curled around pretty green eyes. And her hair was a mixture of auburn with blonde highlights. A beautiful young girl, she couldn't have been more than eighteen.

"If you hate the job so much, why did become a whore?" Ruby asked.

The girl tensed and her emerald eyes flashed with rage. "Don't assume that I wanted this. My step-father owed the saloon a lot of money. After my mother died, he sold me to Mrs. Hutchins. If I want my freedom I have to pay off my step-father's gambling debt to the madam, which will take years."

Of all the rotten stinking things to do to a young girl. Ruby shivered at the thought of letting countless unknown men touch her because of her step-father's mistakes. No wonder the girl was filled with bitterness and rage and eager to escape.

"I was a virgin when he brought me to the madam. Told me we were going to town to pick out a tombstone for my mama's grave and he needed my help. Stared me in the eye and handed me off to Mrs. Hutchins. Bastard."

"Oh my God," Ruby said, swallowing the hate she could feel rising. "Have you seen him since?"

Hannah's eyes turned colder than a blue norther dropping ice pellets. "A couple of times he's come in, but they won't let me near him. They know I'd kill him."

Ruby jumped back. This soft-spoken quiet young girl had threatened to kill her step-father and she didn't doubt that she would. Ruby couldn't even blame her. She glanced around to make certain no one had overheard her.

They were receiving plenty of stares, but no one appeared to be eavesdropping. "I'm not going to help you kill a man, even one that deserves it. What would you do if you could get out of here?"

The girl shrugged her shoulders. "I don't know. I always thought I would get married, have some kids and settle down. You have to believe me that this is not the life I would have chosen."

Their waitress set plates of the special in front of them. Ruby watched the girl hungrily dig into the food, like she hadn't had a good meal in a long time.

Taking a deep breath, Ruby smiled at the girl. She couldn't imagine having to live this kind of life. "You're going to need some help getting away from these people. You can't do this on your own or they'll kill you," she told the girl. "One day you'll just disappear. Do you understand? You're a liability and Mrs. Hutchins will never let you leave."

The girl sighed. "It's already happened to one girl in the house. During the middle of the night she vanished, her room was cleaned out and no one asked questions."

"You could be next."

Like a refined lady, she sat down her fork and pushed her plate away. Gripping her hands in front of her, her big green eyes pleaded. "I'm not going to spend my life, having sex with strangers. One day it will kill me."

Ruby knew she was right. She had to help her and she even knew how. A sense of purpose filled Ruby and while she knew this was dangerous that part sent a thrill zipping along her spine. "Look, I can't tell you anything right now. Just do what you're told. Don't steal from anyone. Don't argue with anyone. Just pretend that you've accepted your life and you're going to make the best of it."

"And then what?" Hannah asked staring at Ruby, her face intent, like she needed something to hold on to. Something to keep her from taking her own life. "I'll never accept this life."

"That's the part I can't tell you. But I won't leave town without you. And I'll help you learn how to make a living and get your revenge."

Hanna frowned at her. "How do you know that I'm not going to go running back to Mrs. Hutchins and tell her what you said?"

The question troubled Ruby for a minute, but then she realized the girl was testing her. Trying to make certain that what Ruby offered was real and not just a lie to keep

Hannah on her back instead of running for whatever safety she could find.

"I don't. But just like you hate your step-father for what he did to you. I have someone that I hate. And I'm going to get my revenge," Ruby told her, staring into her eyes so that she understood she meant every word.

Hannah smiled. "I'm not going to tell Mrs. Hutchins. Someday I'd like to return and shut her down. Give her what she deserves."

A grin spread across Ruby's face. "Oh, your list is growing."

"First I have to get away."

They ate their food in silence, Ruby glancing around the restaurant wondering if her man was here even now. She stared at Hannah, questioning if she knew the man.

"Have you seen a man named Rivera in the saloon? I know he likes to gamble."

"Lately, he comes in about once every two weeks. One of the girls thinks he's going to whisk her away. I think she's dreaming."

Relief flooded through Ruby, almost making her giddy. She'd begun to doubt that he was in the area, but since he had a lady friend in the saloon, he should be coming in anytime and she would be ready.

The waitress came by and picked up their empty plates, a clear signal she wanted them to leave.

"I better get you back before they come busting in here trying to locate you," Ruby said.

"Promise me you won't forget me when you're ready to leave town."

"I won't," Ruby promised. "I won't. Be patient and stay out of trouble."

The door to the restaurant opened and the sheriff strolled in. He looked around the place and when he spotted Ruby, he shook his head and walked in their direction.

"Oh no," Hannah said, beneath her breath. "We're in trouble."

"Let me handle it," Ruby whispered.

The sheriff stopped at their table and stood there staring at them like they were naughty school children. If he meant to intimidate them, it wasn't working on Ruby. The man was an irritating nuisance.

"Miss Callahan, why am I not surprised that you are the one causing trouble again?" he asked her standing over their table staring down at her, his arms crossed.

"Good afternoon, Sheriff. I have two responses to your question. One how can having lunch with a lady be considered causing trouble? And two haven't you learned yet that I'm like a trouble magnet. It just seems to follow me, even when I'm good."

Shaking his head, he laughed. "I have two things to say to you. Miss Williams is not a lady, she's a whore."

"Even whores have to eat, Sheriff. They need their strength to perform their job. And girls do like to occasionally go shopping."

Placing his hands on his hips, he sighed. "Two, didn't I warn you not to cause trouble in my town or I'd send you packing?"

The man was just looking for an excuse to run her out of town. Strangers were not welcome in Hide Town until they proved themselves. And the man clearly believed this piece of land was his to protect with his style of justice.

"Yes, you did. But how can two *ladies* having lunch together be a problem."

"Miss Callahan, find more respectable ladies to dine with."

"Sorry, Sheriff, but you see the respectable ladies won't have lunch with me since I deal cards in the saloon. Surely the owner of the café didn't complain? I mean after all we're paying him for the meal. Or wait, Hannah, did you offer him a free service tonight?"

The girl shook her head, her eyes large, like she was frightened. "I did not."

"So see there, Sheriff, he's receiving money for our meal."

"Miss Callahan, you make me real tired. Let this be a warning. I don't want to receive another complaint about you."

Deke had tried to warn her that the sheriff was bad news. And she'd believed him, but that didn't mean she was afraid of the bully. More like she wanted to kick his knees out from under him and send him sprawling in his beloved dust.

"But Sheriff, who complained? The restaurant owner? Or was it Mrs. Hutchins?"

Ruby knew instinctively, that the madam had contacted the sheriff after her goon returned and told her the two of them were together. He was sent to squash whatever relationship could be brewing between her and Hannah.

"You girls should head on back to the saloon now before you get into any more trouble."

Ruby and Hannah stood and pushed their chairs under the table. Laying her hand on his arm, Ruby stared at the sheriff. "Girls do like to occasionally go shopping. How else can we stay so pretty looking for you men?"

He stared at her as if he knew what she was doing, as if he wished he were immune to her charm, but still enjoyed staring at her breasts. "I don't care. Don't let me get another complaint on you."

As she passed by the big man, Ruby winked at him. "Come play cards with me tonight, Sheriff? Lady Luck might be on your side."

"I don't gamble," he said, and walked out of the cafe.

Ruby turned to Hannah and the two of them strolled out the same doors the sheriff had gone through. "It's going to be awhile. Just keep in mind that soon this will be over. But until then don't tell a soul. And don't get into trouble."

Hannah reached out and hugged her. "Thank you. But hurry."

She separated herself from Ruby and walked towards the saloon. When Ruby whirled around towards the hotel, she caught the sheriff watching the two of them.

$$\sim$$

That night, Deke sat outside the saloon and waited for Ruby. Fall was late in arriving this year and he was enjoying the warm weather. His newfound friend nudged his cold nose against his hand and he absentmindedly petted the young dog.

While out scouting today, he'd come across the dog abandoned, miles from town. She was scrawny, flea ridden and yet Deke had been unable to walk away from the animal, knowing he'd die if left alone.

So he'd put him on his horse and rode into town with her in the crook of his arms. By the time they'd arrived back at the hotel, the puppy had imprinted his paws on his heart with his licks and whines and loving brown eyes. Deke had spent the afternoon bathing and feeding him. His intentions were to find a family who needed a dog and leave him. But right now the dog was at his heels following him wherever he went. And already Deke doubted he could leave her behind.

If the hotel caught him with a dog in the room, there would probably be hell to pay, but for the moment he just didn't care. The company only wanted food and water and an occasional belly rub. This Deke could provide.

The saloon doors swung open and Ruby strolled out. God she was stunning in that dress that showcased her feminine curves and he wasn't about to take a chance on someone taking advantage of the woman. He'd only briefly strolled through the saloon tonight, but he'd been right outside if she'd needed him.

She smiled and took him by the arm. "Good evening Deke."

"I think it's closer to morning than evening."

A laugh bubbled from her. "You're right." She glanced down at the dog that was following right behind him. "Who's this?"

"She's a stray I picked up out of town. I couldn't let her starve."

Halting, Ruby stopped and bent down to the dog, letting her smell her hand and then the puppy pounced on her almost knocking her over.

"Heel," he told the dog and she stopped, but her skin quivered with the need to jump and play, but she obediently sat. Deke reached down and patted the dog on the head. "Good dog."

"Sorry about that. We spent the afternoon, learning to heel. She gets a little excited."

"What are you going to do with a dog?" Ruby asked.

That was the question, but he couldn't let the animal suffer and he really wanted to settle down. He'd had to bring her to town. Deke had a hard time seeing anyone suffer, man, woman, child, or animal, everyone deserved a chance at life.

"I don't know. I'd like to make certain she has a good home before I leave town."

Ruby shook her head. "No you won't."

"What do you mean?"

"Look at her, she's following you. She thinks you're her mama and she's so happy you're here. I've seen you with horses and now with dogs. All that dog has to do is turn those big brown eyes on you. You'll melt like hot butter in a frying pan and the dog will have a great home by your side."

Deke took a deep breath, it was true and though he was resisting, the pup had already won a place in his heart.

"We'll see," he said thinking she could very well be right. He hadn't had a dog since he was a boy. This felt right. The dog and him.

"Something happened today that I need to talk to you about," Ruby said pulling him down to a bench right outside the door of the hotel.

The urge to put his arm around the back of the bench and pull her into his chest was strong, but they were outside in a hostile town where the sheriff believed that nothing existed between the two of them. It wouldn't do for the law to consider there was an attachment with Ruby.

"What?" he asked detecting the note of concern in her voice.

A few minutes later when she'd told him about Hannah, he couldn't believe she'd risked everything to help a girl in trouble. Especially since this bounty was her father's killer.

"You took a huge risk?"

She shrugged her shoulders, like it was nothing. "I had to help her. They would have killed Hannah."

"They may try to kill you and her if they find out you're working together."

"Let them try. I have a pistol on me all the time."

"I hope so."

Another risk. The woman took more chances than a short-tail bull in fly time.

The puppy crawled up in his lap and settled in for a nap. Absent mindedly he rubbed the dog's soft downy fur. "I haven't been completely honest with you, either."

She'd been gazing up at the stars and suddenly she whirled her head around to face him. "What do you mean?"

He licked his lips and sighed. "I *was* married, but I'm not anymore."

She frowned at him like she didn't quite understand. He really didn't want to tell her the entire story, but had a feeling she wasn't going to let him off the hook.

"Oh. Did you just take off your wedding ring and your wife disappeared?"

"No," he said quietly in the dark. He rubbed the puppy's ears. "She died."

Ruby gasped. "I'm sorry. I didn't know."

Sympathy radiated from her gaze and he hated it. He didn't want anyone feeling sorry that he was a widower. He didn't deserve their commiseration or condolences or compassion.

"I know."

"How long has it been since…"

"Eighteen months." His son would have been walking by now. He bit his lip and tried his best to block the memories of holding that tiny infant in his arms. Pain seized his chest at the memory of him so perfect, so precious, so lifeless. Until that moment he hadn't realized how much he wanted children.

"How long were you married?" Ruby asked.

"Not even a year," he said softly remembering Laura's beautiful face as she gazed at him during the wedding. Even though theirs had been a marriage of convenience, she'd been a loving person, a friend he'd cared deeply for.

Ruby stared at him, her blue eyes actually appearing sympathetic. "Tell me about her?"

Even talking about Laura was difficult. He really didn't want to, but felt that since he'd lied to Ruby, he owed her at least a token explanation. "We grew up as friends. Her brother was my best-friend and we would get together and play. We were together in school, right up until I rode off to hunt for the man who shot and killed her brother, my best-friend."

"Is he the reason you became a bounty hunter."

"Yes. I probably would have died if your father hadn't taken me in and taught me everything I know," he said, rubbing the dogs soft fur, hoping that was all the information she needed about his past.

"You were going to become a cattle rancher?"

"I was, but then I don't know, I like horses so much more," he said. "Laura convinced me that cattle were not really what I was good at."

He watched as Ruby swallowed and quickly looked away, before returning her gaze to him.

"Did you love her?"

A deep sigh escaped his lips. "I cared deeply for Laura, but I wasn't in love with her. And she knew it."

"So why did you marry Laura if you didn't love her?"

How could he explain without making Laura sound even weaker than she'd been? After all she was dead, why not just let her past die with her and not consider how frail she'd been emotionally and physically?

"Not all women are like you, Ruby."

"Thank God," she said.

"You're tough and independent and you'll always be able to take care of yourself. But not all women are capable of being strong like you."

The women were so different and yet they were the same. If Laura had the strength of will like Ruby, they could have been almost sisters.

Ruby frowned at him. "I don't know if you're giving me a compliment or being disrespectful."

"No, you're who you are. Laura was who she was. But unlike you, she wasn't strong. She lost everything and would have been forced into either prostitution or living on the streets. She had nothing. I couldn't let that happen to my best friend's sister. I saved her by marrying her."

Ruby slowly rose. She gazed down at the puppy in his lap and ran her fingers through the animal's fur. "You're like that Deke. You have a natural instinct about you that saves animals and people. Just like this puppy." She gazed at him directly in the eye. "So what happened to her? How did she die?"

He swallowed the lump that formed in his throat, blinking back the tears he felt rising in his chest.

"I killed her."

Chapter Eight

For a moment Ruby froze as Deke's words poured over her like ice water, freezing her blood and making her doubt the words she'd just heard.

"What?"

He sighed. "I think it's time we went in."

"Like hell. You just told me you killed your wife and you want to go to bed? Do you think I could sleep tonight after hearing that remark?"

He smiled, but it was more a tired grimace than a happy smile.

"Laura was a tiny woman. Small in the hips. She wasn't built to carry children."

Deke petted the dog and she could tell he wanted nothing more than to pick her up and walk away. In fact, he probably would have if she hadn't been standing in front of him, blocking his escape.

"She died during childbirth."

Ruby sighed with relief that she wasn't going to have to drag Deke down to the sheriff's office and turn him in for murder.

"I'm sorry. I don't understand why you feel responsible. What did you say to me about my sisters? Was Laura happy? Did she want the baby?"

How could a woman he married be unhappy about expecting Deke's baby? Sure Ruby wasn't wild about having babies and children, but the man she eventually fell in love with, someday she planned on having his children. Just not right away.

She watched as he closed his eyes. "She was so excited. I hadn't seen her that happy since before her brother was killed."

"Then it wasn't your fault. Women die in childbirth. You made her happy in her last days."

For the longest time he sat there, petting the puppy and staring off into space. She wondered if he was going to respond to her or if he would just sit there, staring off in the darkness.

A rumble of thunder sounded and a flash of lightening heralded an approaching storm.

"We need to go in," he finally said, not answering her comment. He stood and set the puppy on the ground. The dog stretched and then gazed up at him and whined. "You go ahead. I need to go up the back door, so the owners don't see her."

She reached out and laid her hand on Deke's arm. "You didn't kill her."

He gazed at her, his emerald eyes brimming with pain. "Good night Ruby."

Turning he walked around to the back of the hotel, leaving her on the porch alone.

~

Rain fell softly and Deke stepped into the shadows at the back of the hotel. He knew it would do no good to go to his room. His mind was racing full of images of Laura from the time they were children up to the day he'd found her in labor. He refused to think past that point. It was true, she'd been happier those eleven months they were married than she'd been in years. She'd anticipated the birth of the baby, never dreaming of anything going wrong.

Their family was past the tragedies of their youth the death of her brother, and now they would live the rest of their lives watching their children grow. She'd told him this over and over and over…until the day he'd ridden away.

He reached into his pocket for the flask he carried with him for when the pain became excruciating. When he could no longer live with the agony of what had happened, of what he'd done.

Tipping the flask to his lips, he drank deeply and stared down at the dog that once again rested beside his feet. So young. So innocent. Only needing food and companionship and giving unconditional love in return, whether or not his human was a good person or evil. Only loving the person who took care of her.

Above him a door opened and he watched in fascination as Ruby came running down the back stairs wearing a flowing white gown. For a moment he thought something was wrong, but then she laughed a delightful sound as she ran out into the cold rain in her nightgown.

Was she meeting someone in the dark? He didn't think so, but still what would send her flying out of the hotel in her night clothes?

Frowning he looked around to make sure that no one else could see this fair-haired beauty that had suddenly appeared. She giggled and laughed and sounded like the young girl he'd first met so many years ago before life had dealt them both terrible blows.

She twirled around in the rain in her nightdress her hair free and flowing down her back, a fairy princess dancing in the rain. Rain pelted her, plastering the wet material to her figure showing the outline of her curves. God she was beautiful.

Thoughts of Laura disappeared. Here was a woman who was strong, who took life by the horns and rode that cow until she tamed it. Here was a woman who he knew had a strong vibrant sexual nature, but wanted a man who deserved her.

He should have taken her that day so many years ago and married her. Maybe then Laura would be alive and Ruby wouldn't be risking it all searching for bounties.

With a sigh, he watched her run her hands down her body as she raised her face to the sky. He should go in before she found him watching her, before she realized he could see the curve of her breasts, the smoky aura of her nipples and the juncture between her thighs where her womanhood nestled. He should go in, before he did something really foolish like join her.

Standing, he motioned for the dog to go with him. The dog whined and Ruby turned towards the sound.

Their eyes met across the field where she stood, while the rain spilled from the sky. In the darkness, she walked towards him, her steps sure and confidant. His heart froze in his throat the closer she came, his shaft hardening at the sight of her beauty.

When she reached his side, her hand touched his cheek and pulled his head to hers, planting her lips over his. For a moment he was shocked, put then he pulled her into him and melded her wet body to his. His lips slanted over hers and he kissed her like a man who had lost everything and she'd rescued him. He kissed her like he'd never kissed Laura.

He released her lips and she stared at him questioning. "You better go up."

"What if I don't want to?"

"Dawn is going to arrive soon. That cold front is coming in and you're soaking wet. You don't want to catch your death of cold," he said his voice raspy. The urge to throw her on the ground and take her right there was uppermost in his mind, but that wasn't possible.

She glanced at the sky, sighed and looked him in the eye. "I know you think that you killed your wife, but sooner or later, we're going to satisfy this thing, whatever it is between us."

Her words had him groaning as he kissed her again. This time he took control and he wasn't gentle, but rough as his mouth closed over hers. His lips possessed hers as his tongue swept through her mouth, needing to be as close to her as possible. There was this attraction, this need to join with Ruby since the time he'd first met her. He'd wanted her all those years ago, but now he was a different man and she was a different woman. Yet still there was this need, this ache that demanded satisfaction.

She pushed back from him, separating them. They stared at each other. Her bosom rising and falling and he could feel his heart pounding inside his own chest, his blood pumping life, making him feel more alive than he'd felt in the last eighteen months of hell.

"You're right. I should go in."

He smiled. "Did you get scared? Decide that maybe this thing between us shouldn't be resolved?"

She licked her lips and grinned at him. "I didn't say that. But outside the hotel in an outlaw town, right before dawn, is not exactly where I'd pictured our first time."

"Just so you know. I swore never to marry again."

As soon as he said the words he hated them. They sounded cowardly, yet they were true. He'd killed one woman, he wasn't about to chance a second one.

"Who said anything about marriage?" she said staring at him. "I've got bounties to hunt and you, you're ready to quit the business. Nothing was said about forever, just about the right moment at the right time."

With that she turned and walked up the stairs. He watched her go, wondering what he'd gotten himself into. Maybe admitting to wanting each other had not been a good thing. If she wasn't in such a precarious position, he would ride away. But he couldn't leave her while she was working at the local saloon as a card dealer in a town where the only law that existed was vigilante law.

~

Late the next night, Ruby was dealing cards. She glanced over and saw Deke sitting at the bar, his back to the wall, turned to where he could watch her and drink.

Last night had answered so many questions about Deke.

Not only was the man a tough cowboy who had ridden with her father, he had a soft streak. He liked to heal horses, rescue puppies and women. Yes, he'd married, but it wasn't a love match, but rather a woman needing a husband. And because they'd been friends, he'd volunteered.

She dealt another hand of cards and glanced at the scurvy lot of men sitting at her table. There was no doubt in her mind that most of them were probably just one step ahead of the law or a bounty hunter. Maybe after she caught Rivera she'd return to Hide Town and clean the village up without the sheriff's help.

"Okay, gentlemen, who wants to open the bidding?"

"I'm in for a quarter," the man to her left said.

"I'll raise you a dime," another man said.

A surly man who had stared at her all night growled, "I just remembered who you are. It took me awhile, but you're one of those bounty hunting women."

Ruby sent the man a skeptical glance as the others at the table stared at her, their faces scowling. She threw her head back laughing. "What have you been drinking tonight? You need to share that loco juice with the rest of us. It's given you fanciful ideas."

Her heart was pounding like a train with a full load of coal and an empty car. Somehow she had to convince everyone that this man had no idea what he was talking about.

"No, I remember you. You and that redhead sister of yours brought a man into the Dyersville jail. I couldn't believe my eyes that you girls had brought in a hold-up man wanted for murder."

Ruby gave him her sternest look. "Place your bid sir. I don't know what you're trying to get at, but I don't have a redheaded sister. And do I look like the kind of woman who could bring a man to justice? Really?"

The men at the table chuckled and laughed at the idea. She leaned over and rested her chin in the palm of her hand, giving him a great view of her cleavage. She smiled and turned on her charm. "If I could be doing a man's job, do you think I'd be working in a saloon?"

He frowned. "Well, then you've got a twin sister out there, because I never forget a face."

"And this woman that brought in this criminal, what was she wearing?"

"She was wearing pants and you were wearing a skirt."

"Honey, did it look like this?" Ruby let her hand flow down her dress.

"No."

"Then it wasn't me. This dress is my working outfit. When I'm at home, I lounge around in my robe," she said trying to get their minds on the idea of what she was wearing rather than her being a bounty hunter. "Keep drinking, cowboy and maybe even share some of that loco juice of yours."

The men at the table all guffawed.

"Are you in or out?" she asked.

He frowned at her. "I'm out. Somehow I'm going to prove that you're a bounty hunter."

"You'd be better served to improve your card skills. You didn't do so well tonight."

The men laughed again and the man threw down his cards and slunk away. Ruby could feel her heart pounding in her chest like a stampede of cattle. She smiled at the men sitting at her table. So far they were buying her tale, but for how long? And how long before the man returned with proof of her existence?

"Gentlemen, where were we? This *bounty hunter*, wants to play cards."

As she dealt the next cards, she looked up and saw

Deke watching her. He glanced over to where the man went out the door and gave her a nod.

She turned back to the men at her table, just as Madam Hutchins cleared her throat.

"Ruby, George will relieve you after this hand. Meet me in the office."

Like a river, unease pumped through her veins at the idea of going to Mrs. Hutchins's office. The woman missed nothing that was going on in her saloon and obviously she'd overheard the conversation at Ruby's table.

"Thank goodness boys, I'm getting a break. George won't deal you as good a hand as I will. I have Lady Luck on my side. But don't worry, I'll be back soon."

She finished her hand and went in search of the madam. Time was not her friend and she needed to find Rivera and get out of here soon, before she was exposed as a bounty hunter. Before Mrs. Hutchins found some way of forcing her to work upstairs.

Mrs. Hutchins was waiting for her in the office.

"Come in, Ruby."

Her eyes were dark and not at all friendly. Ruby plopped down in the chair away from the woman. She relaxed. "It's been a busy night tonight."

"Yes, it has," the woman said staring at her. "What can you tell me about that conversation over at your table just now?"

Like a rain shower, trickles of fear spread through her limbs and yet she smiled and played dumb.

"What?" Ruby asked. "The man who thought I was a bounty hunter?"

"Yes, that one."

"What do you want me to say," Ruby said laughing. "Do you think I'd be dealing cards if I was a bounty hunter?"

"Maybe. Especially if you were after someone in my

saloon," the woman acknowledged.

Ruby rolled her eyes, playing the consummate actress. The woman wasn't dumb, but Ruby just needed to redirect her in a different direction, like towards the south end of a north bound animal.

"I'm after having a good time, earning enough money to keep me out of the streets and out of the brothel upstairs. I don't care what a man does as long as he plays cards at my table, treats me nice and isn't mean to me."

The woman leaned back in her chair and appeared untroubled. "Good. That's what I was hoping you'd say. But I want to warn you. I don't take kindly to women stirring up trouble amongst my girls if you know what I mean."

After the sheriff's arrival at lunch yesterday, Ruby knew that they were watching her and Hannah closely. And yet she wasn't afraid.

"Are you referring to Hannah?" Ruby asked.

"Yes."

"Look, the kid needed some encouragement. We went shopping, looked at cosmetics and then we had lunch over at the diner. Actually, I think I did you a favor. I told her that she needed to accept the life that had been dealt to her."

The girl would be dead by now if Ruby hadn't stepped in. How could someone take a young woman's life and throw it away. Yet that's what her step-father had done.

The madam smiled. "Let's hope so. But if I were you, I wouldn't associate with the girls. Men will think that you're just one of them and take advantage of you. Unless you've changed your mind and want to make more money."

"Like I said, I darn near killed the last man who tried to force me to have sex with him. This time, I wouldn't hesitate to kill any bastard that lays his hands on me."

~

Mrs. Hutchins watched Ruby as she laughed and talked with the men around her table. The house had doubled its take in the last week since she'd been dealing. They were earning more than ever before and now she was contemplating adding another female dealer to the mix. Maybe staring at a woman's breasts all night, especially ones that were off limits, enticed a man to gamble more.

It was definitely worth considering. But right now, she had concerns about her female dealer. A man had recognized her as a bounty hunter. Emily had never heard of female bounty hunters, but the man had seemed certain that she was this woman that had turned in a wanted man.

And then there was her lunch with Hannah. That girl had been nothing but trouble from the time she'd come into the house. The first night she'd screamed bloody murder until they'd had to gag and restrain her. She'd threatened to kill all of them if she ever got loose and Emily was beginning to believe her.

In the not too distant future, Hannah would be taking a ride with the sheriff, never to return.

Speaking of the lawman, he walked in the door and smiled at her. She waved him over and then took him by the arm.

"We need to talk."

The relationship she had with the sheriff was more than just scratching each other's backs. Oh no, he was her lover, her confidant, her best-friend and handled her dirty business. They'd been together for over four years. Quietly planning and running Hide Town.

"Oh dear, who do you want me to take care of now?" he asked.

"No one yet," she said. "Have you ever heard of female bounty hunters?"

He frowned. "I heard some rumors, but thought it was just gibberish. Why?"

"Tonight, at Ruby's table, a gentleman said she was one of those bounty hunter girls. He accused her of bringing in a wanted man to the Dyersville jail."

"That little sprite of a girl?" he asked in disbelief. He laughed. "I don't believe it."

"Said her sister and her did the job."

"If it's her, where is the sister?"

Emily frowned and stared at the woman who seemed very well adept at handling all sorts of controversies. Even now she was in full control of her table, shuffling the cards and handling the bets. In many ways, she reminded Emily of herself. Full of determination to succeed, fearless in the face of adversity. The girl had more spunk than any of her whores. And that worried her.

"I'm not certain. I don't know, but this man was throwing a fit at her table and she just laughed at him. Told him he needed to share what he'd been drinking."

The sheriff smiled. "That girl is nothing but trouble. I told you that when you hired her."

Oh, but what a hire that one had been.

"Yeah, but the house take has doubled in the week she's been here. Men love to look at her creamy breasts and lose. They can look all day long as far as I'm concerned as long as I make money."

He glanced out the door of the office. "Have you said anything to her?"

"I called her in and asked her about the discussion. She just laughed it off. I then warned her about being with Hannah."

"Good."

Emily wasn't certain she was buying the tale of the two of them looking at rouge pots at the store and then having lunch at the diner. Something didn't seem right about that story and yet her other girls had all gotten excited when they learned of Hannah's excursion. Maybe she needed to let them out more often.

"How could we find out about these so called bounty hunter women?"

The sheriff frowned and then slowly stood. "I'm going to contact the law offices at Dyersville and Zenith. Check out what they know about these women. See what they'll tell me. I'll send a telegraph in the morning and we should know something soon."

"Good," she said staring up at him.

"Are you coming to dinner Sunday night?" she asked.

"I wouldn't miss it."

She smiled. "Good we need to talk about Hannah. It may be time to end that problem."

"We'll talk about it after dinner," he said, patting her on the butt.

"See you then."

The sheriff walked out the door and she felt confident that they would soon learn if Ruby was up to something or if she was just another woman trying to make a living.

Chapter Nine

Deke wasn't waiting for Ruby outside the saloon. Diligently, he sat in his room, listening for her return back to the hotel. Tonight he'd felt certain he was going to have to stand up and protect her, but the woman was a darn good actress and could talk the spots off a cow.

The puppy sat in the corner and watched him pace the floor. Fear gripped his innards like he was busting a wild bronco. He was damn scared and after tonight, it was time to call this escapade to a halt. They'd not seen Rivera. Sure Hannah had told Ruby that he visited a soiled dove in the saloon, but where was he? Wherever the man was, he was laying low and they were sitting ducks in a lawless town filled with criminals.

After tonight, he didn't know how much longer their cover would hold before they were recognized and run out of town if they were lucky. Shot in the back if they weren't.

He heard someone outside and threw his hotel room door open. She looked over her shoulder at him and smiled. "Deke. I wondered where you were. I've gotten spoilt to you walking me back to the hotel at night."

Grabbing Ruby by the arm, he yanked her into his room. "You almost got caught tonight."

She waved her hand at him and shrugged her shoulders, her lips pinched together. "Oh that drunk was just trying to stir up trouble."

Deke had grown complacent, accepting that she was gathering information working as a dealer in a brothel. But suddenly the danger seemed to have escalated. The time had come for them to give up finding Rivera in this dirt hole town and move on, before the crooked law caught up with them.

"Well, he did a damn good job. Especially when Mrs.

Hutchins pulled you into the office. What did she say?"

Ruby shook her head, frowning, sending a shiver of caution through Deke. "It was nothing. She advised me to stay away from Hannah. Told me that the men would think I was fair game if they saw me with her."

He frowned. Would the men think she was a whore or would Mrs. Hutchins let them think that and give them the chance at her new girl, Ruby? It was time to leave town, before he had to rescue her from the brothel, before she joined the soiled doves working upstairs.

"What did she say about you being a bounty hunter?"

"I laughed and told her I wouldn't be dealing cards in a saloon if I was on the trail looking for criminals."

Frowning, Deke stared at Ruby. "Did she threaten you?"

"Kind of, but I'm not worried," Ruby said flinging back her blonde curls over her shoulder. "She can't prove it. Nobody knows Ruby Callahan."

"Well I'm plenty worried for both of us. Did you see the sheriff go in and talk to her after you left her office?"

"No," Ruby said pulling back her shoulders and lifting her chin defiantly. "He's already warned me one more incident and he's throwing me out of town. He's a strange one. "

Her voice conveyed no fear, but her eyes…her eyes belied the fact and he could see the apprehension reflected in her gaze. She'd never admit it, but even she was alarmed over raising the suspicions of the sheriff.

"We haven't gotten anything on Rivera. I think we should leave."

"No. Hannah said he normally comes in about once every two weeks. He's due. Let's just wait it out a little longer. If he doesn't come in after this Saturday night, we can leave, but I'm hoping he'll show up. If not we'll leave Sunday."

Deke wanted Rivera just as much as Ruby. The bastard had killed her father, he'd killed his mentor. But it wasn't worth them dying over. They'd catch Rivera a different way in another town.

"I'm getting a bad feeling about this, Ruby. In their eyes, you're suspicious. We should get out of town before they find out the truth."

"I'm staying." She lifted her blue eyes to him and stared him down.

He cursed. The woman was as stubborn as they came.

Deke shook his head. If he had his way, they would pack up tonight and hit the trail, before sunrise. Ruby took chances he'd never consider. She didn't feel fear and that scared him. In some ways she was worse than Laura. When Laura died, it hadn't been her choice, but Ruby didn't worry about dying and that scared him worst of all. For Ruby.

He reached out and touched her chin. "You're not invincible. You can get hurt and die doing this."

She stood. "I'm not afraid."

He didn't doubt her for a moment.

"I know and that's what frightens me most of all. Even smart men know when to be afraid. That's what keeps you alive."

Ruby shrugged and walked to the door. She glanced back at him. "I'm staying. You can leave if you want, but Rivera is due into the saloon any day now. I'm not quitting until he comes in and I capture him."

"And what if they find out the truth about who you are before Rivera shows up? What will you do then?"

Without a doubt, Deke knew they would both die. Because Deke couldn't walk out on Ruby, alone in the hands of a corrupt sheriff and a ruthless madam.

"They won't. "

"Damn it Ruby, you scare me."

"If you want to bail, there's the door. I don't need you. I don't need any man."

A trickle of ice cold terror skittered down his spine. Her careless attitude, her recklessness, her bold cockiness would someday get her killed and that spiked his anxiety to new levels. He didn't want to watch a woman he cared about die. He'd already experienced that once in his life and he'd sworn never again.

"I just may leave, because I don't want to watch you die." He knew it was a lie the moment the words spilled from his mouth, but still he wanted to frighten her, to make her see that they were in danger.

She stepped up beside him, running her finger down his cheek and across his lips, sending a shiver of desire, pulsing through his body, replacing the cold fear her words had triggered. "I'm tough. I can handle just about anything. Being rejected by the man that I cared about made me a stronger woman. Now, I'm not afraid."

It always came back to that day and he was sick of her doubting that he'd done what was right for her. He'd wanted to plunge into her body and claim it as his own, but had known that wouldn't be right. And she'd all but crucified him over doing what was right, instead of what she wanted.

He stepped in closer to her. "If I'd taken you that day, I wouldn't have been any better than the boy who tried to molest you. I would have been taking advantage of you. You would have hated me. As it was you still shot at me as I rode away."

Laughing she stepped out of his arms. "Oh I thought about putting a bullet in you, but then my Papa's words came back and he said never aim a gun at a man unless you mean to kill him. So I aimed above your head. Since the day you left me, I've overcome my fear. I'm not afraid of men. Guns. Snakes. Nothing. Because I know I'll find a way out of trouble. Somehow I'll survive."

Always, so cocky, so sure of herself. So invincible that it scared him.

She turned and walked back towards the door. "Go home if you want too, but I'm not leaving until I find Rivera."

She walked out the door. Deke shook his head and muttered to the empty room. "You're going to get us both killed."

~

Zach Gillespie stared at the telegram the operator had just handed him.

"How should I respond," the man asked.

Ruby was in trouble. The sheriff of Hide Town, Texas was asking if he knew of any female bounty hunters. And that town was known for the law being corrupt. While he didn't want to upset his wife, she had a right to know that her youngest sister might be in serious trouble.

"Wait until I get back to you. We don't want to respond too quickly."

With the telegram clutched in his hand, Zach walked the short distance to his wife's dress shop. When he pushed open the door, she looked up and smiled. She looked so different now in her fancy dress, her hair piled on top of her head, their baby just beginning to show beneath her skirts.

"Hi sweetie," she called. "Is it lunchtime?"

A shiver of anticipation trickled down his spine, straight to his groin. God, he was such a lucky man. Meg coming into his life was the best thing that had ever happened to this small town Texas sheriff. And he thanked God every day for Meg.

He stopped and admired the way she was measuring material for a new dress she was creating. "Isn't this fabric gorgeous? I just got it in and it will go wonderful for the dress I'm making Mrs. Daniel."

In the time they'd been married, Meg had changed and grown and become a woman that he loved more than his next breath. All the doubts he'd had regarding her being enough woman for him had vanished and now seemed so stupid. It didn't matter whether she wore a dress or pants, Meg, had always been a loving woman handling more responsibilities than a young girl should have to. When she'd been allowed to follow her dream, she'd blossomed into more woman than he could often handle and he was grateful to be her husband.

Meg was everything and more than he'd ever dreamed of.

"I fear Ruby may be in trouble," he said blurting out the words he didn't know how to say.

Her head jerked up and her hands came to a stop. "What kind of trouble?"

Fear etched across her face and he saw her reach down and smooth her hand across her belly, like she was protecting their unborn child.

He held up the slip of paper. "I have a telegram from the sheriff in Hide. He wants to know if I've ever heard of female bounty hunters."

"Oh no. Didn't you tell me that town was run by a corrupt sheriff?"

"Yes."

Meg frowned. "Should we tell Annabelle? I don't want to worry her at this point in her pregnancy."

Zach sighed. "How would she feel later if we weren't honest with her?"

"You're right," she said. "Let me close the shop and we'll ride out to the farm."

Zach had watched his wife try to protect her sister as much as possible in this last month. The sisters were close, but he'd never seen Meg so supportive, insulating Annabelle from as much as possible. Working even with her husband Beau, to keep the woman off her feet and resting, until the baby was born.

Thirty minutes later, Zach pulled the wagon up in the front yard of the McKenzie homestead. Beau Samuel came out of the barn. "Good to see you two."

After helping Meg alight, Zach approached the man. "We need to sit down and talk. I've gotten a telegraph about Ruby. She could be in trouble."

Beau's mouth twisted into a frown. "Annabelle's been feeling good today. I hate to give her bad news, but she'd be angry as a hornet in a bee hive, if she found out I was keeping information from her." He shook his head. "We better tell her."

They all hurried into the house. Annabelle glanced up from the pie she was making. The expressions on their face, must have alerted her. "What's wrong?"

She dried her hands on a dishtowel and hurried into the main parlor, her stomach looking like a rounded ball sitting at her waist.

"How are you feeling?" Meg asked.

"Pregnant," she said and sank down onto a nearby chair.

For a moment, Zach swallowed the nerves that rose up in his throat. In four months, Meg would look like Annabelle. It wasn't that the feared her swelling with his child, but more her health and well-being.

"Zach received a telegram from the sheriff in Hide Town. He wants to know if Zach has ever heard of any women bounty hunters," Meg said.

"I don't trust this sheriff," Zach said. "He's known for being corrupt."

They watched as Annabelle leaned back, rubbing her hand against her back, a frown marring her face. "But he didn't ask specifically about Ruby?"

"No," Zach said. "I have the telegraph here, if you want to read it."

Annabelle held out her hand. Together Meg and her scanned the troublesome document.

As sheriff of Zenith, Zach had sent similar telegrams trying to learn more information about someone before he arrested them. But he didn't want to tell that to Meg and Annabelle and worry them even more. As soon as his deputy returned and Annabelle had her baby, he'd go to Hide Town to see if he could find Ruby and Deke.

"You two could ride into town and help her," Meg said glancing between Zach and Beau.

"I care very much for Ruby, but I'm not leaving Annabelle until after our baby is born," Beau said gazing at his wife.

How could they blame the man? Annabelle looked like she could go into labor any moment. He wouldn't leave Meg when she was this far along. He wouldn't miss the birth of his own child for any reason.

"At the moment, I can't leave town," Zach responded. "But she's got Deke with her. She should be all right."

He hoped like hell he was right and that the two of them were not in any real danger. Just being in Hide Town was perilous for a law-abiding citizen, certain death for known bounty hunters and lawmen.

"If I wasn't pregnant, I'd go after her myself," Meg said twisting her hands.

"You've got our baby to think about," Zach informed her.

"I know. But this is the exact reason she needs to stop bounty hunting. It's dangerous."

Meg wanted Ruby to stop doing what she loved and while Zach agreed it was a hazardous profession, the girl was good at catching outlaws and bringing them to justice.

And because she was a woman, she got away with things men could never do. But she was his sister-in-law and he'd agree with his wife. But Ruby was a woman who'd always taken chances, even before Zach had come into their lives.

"So what are we going to do?" Annabelle asked glancing at the men.

"I'm going to respond to his telegram and say I've not heard of any women bounty hunters," Zach said.

Annabelle wiped away a tear. "That just seems wrong. I'm proud of what we've done and accomplished. I hate to deny that we even exist."

"Honey, it's the best we can do. By making the man think there are no female bounty hunters, then he can't connect that she's one. If she doesn't come home after the baby is born, I'll go after her," Beau said patting his wife on the arm.

"We could do more harm riding in there searching for her," Zach said.

Reaching out and gripping Meg's hand, Annabelle said, "I wish she would come home. But she's going after the man who killed our father. The one who put us on this journey."

"It needs to end," Meg said. "It's time to put this all behind us."

"Deke is with her. Let's just hope and pray she's okay," Beau said rubbing his wife's arm.

~

The next day, Ruby heard someone lightly knocking on her hotel door. Holding her breath, she swallowed nervously and opened the door her hand on her gun.

Hannah rushed into the room. "I'm sorry, but I have to tell you something and it couldn't be at the saloon."

"Come in," Ruby said though the girl had already pushed her way in. "Are you sure you weren't followed?"

"I made certain," she said.

Her face was flushed, her breathing quick. Ruby feared they were after her and she'd run to her hotel room to escape Mrs. Hutchins and her goons.

"I can't stay but a moment and then I have to get back," she said pacing the floor.

Ruby stared at the girl, her face was flush with excitement. "Today at lunch Clara said that James Rivera should be coming home in the next few days. She looks for him no later than Saturday. Since you asked me about him, I thought you might want to know."

Exhilaration zipped through Ruby and she smiled. Finally, maybe soon they would be done with this hell hole town and they could capture Rivera and get out of here, without the sheriff or Mrs. Hutchins realizing what they were doing. "That's great news. Thanks. I know it was risky for you to come over here."

The girl gazed around the room. "I should probably make my way back. They'll be looking for me, though things have been better. Since you talked to Mrs. Hutchins."

Ruby looked at the young girl, wondering what she was like before she'd been sold into prostitution. Wondering who could do such a terrible thing and live with them self?

"How did you know about my talk with Mrs. Hutchins?

Hannah laughed. "Oh believe me, the girls upstairs know everything that's going on down below. They've been talking about how they want to learn to deal cards and stop being whores."

"Are you doing okay?" Ruby asked Hannah knowing the waiting and hoping it was really true that she was escaping, couldn't be easy on her.

"I'm making it. Just don't forget your promise. I've been thinking. You've got something planned for Rivera, don't you?"

It was better for Hannah not to know what the plan was until they were riding out of town, escaping with her in tow, just in case something went wrong. Ruby prayed everything would go smoothly, but one never knew and she wasn't going to take a chance that somehow the sheriff would go after Hannah if she couldn't get her out Hide Town.

"The least you know, the safer you'll be. Thanks for giving me the information Hannah. Let me know if you hear anything else," Ruby said, ushering her to the door. They didn't need to get caught talking to one another again or they would both suffer the consequences. Ruby could lose her job and worse they would kill Hannah.

"Don't go off and leave me, Ruby," Hannah said, as she opened the door and peered out into the hallway.

"I won't Hannah. You'll know when it's time to go," Ruby promised her. "I'll send you a box of candy from an admirer – GR for get ready. The number of words in the message is the time we're leaving. At that time meet us behind the hotel. Be careful and try to get away without them following you."

"I can hardly wait. I'm so ready to get out of here," Hannah said hugging Ruby briefly, she opened the door and peered outside. There was no one around at this hour of the morning.

Hannah snuck out into the hall and hurried to the back staircase. Ruby watched until she was out of sight. So Rivera would be coming to town. Excitement spiraled through her and she almost felt giddy.

She needed to tell Deke, so that he'd realize they weren't wasting their time. And that he was right, it was time to leave, but with Rivera in tow.

Crossing the hall, Ruby knocked on Deke's door, there was no answer.

Could he have left town last night after she'd warned

him she wasn't leaving without Rivera? No, he would have said goodbye. Still, doubts lingered. She walked away missing him, wondering where he could be.

~

Ruby felt on edge. She hadn't seen or heard from Deke all day. She wondered if the bastard had up and left Hide Town without her. After everything they'd shared, surely he would have said something before he pulled up stakes and left town. But she wasn't certain and now here she was dealing cards in the Hide and Seek saloon once again. Alone and vulnerable.

Another night of men sitting at her table, counting on lady luck to make them rich or hang them out to dry.

"Miss Callahan, can I rub my cards against your chest?" an ole geezer asked her, his eyes almost falling out of his head.

Her first response was one that she was certain Madam Hutchins would not appreciate. So she tried to ease her rejection, wishing that Rivera would show up and they could put the dust of this lawless town behind them.

"Now old-timer, if I let you, then all these other men sitting at the table are going to want to do the same. The luck would be lost. I can't treat you any differently than I treat them."

The doors to the saloon swung open and in walked Deke. Her heart jumped and her pulse raced at the sight of the handsome man. He hadn't given up on her. He was still here. He glanced over at her and she smiled and gave him a wink. God, she was glad to see him.

And she needed to tell him about Rivera.

She loved the way he wore his hat, the sound of his boots on the wooden floor and the stretch of his shirt across his strong shoulders. Deke Culver was the real deal. A man with a heart of gold who had married a woman because she was his friend and needed help. A man who saved stranded puppies. A man who had rejected her…

She'd been young. She'd been angry and hurt and so full of conflicting emotions that day that she'd just wanted someone to sooth her. Make her feel better and he had up until she'd pressed him to take it even further. And he'd refused.

"Are you going to deal the cards tonight," a man seated in front of her asked. "Or keep staring off into space with that dreamy moony look you women occasionally get?"

"Sir, that dreamy look you're referring to is because someone at this table needs a bath and I suspect it's you," she said flinging a card at the man.

He laughed. "Excuse me. I just got into town and didn't stop at the bath house."

"The ladies upstairs always like a gentleman who smells good," she said flinging another card at him.

Maybe Deke had been right. If he'd taken her and ridden off, she would have looked back and thought he was just like Clay Mullens. Only instead of force, he'd persuaded her, though she'd been the one who was begging him to finish what they'd started.

That entire time had been confusing and one she tried not to think about. She'd been young, impressionable; wanting to understand life and be a woman, not the baby of the family who no one thought was capable.

So she'd become very capable. Fearless. Skilled. And get out of her way clever.

Deke walked to the bar and ordered a drink. A sense of satisfaction filled her. He was here. He hadn't left her behind.

"Come on gentlemen, is that all you're going to bet?" she asked her players.

"You've just about cleaned me out as it is," a man said. "What more do you want?"

The men put up more money and she dealt the next round of cards. Now if only Rivera would show up and they could go home.

"I want you to win and beat the house," she said smiling as she gave him a new card.

Business was slow tonight at both the tables and upstairs. The women were lounging around and some were even lingering on the stairs watching for any man who walked in the door.

After dealing the cards, she glanced up to see Clara, one of the whores, leaning all over Deke. The soiled dove had her hands wrapped around his shoulders, her body draped over him and she was whispering into his ear. The hussy was trying to convince Deke to come upstairs with her.

Jealousy slammed into Ruby's gut, twisting and stabbing like a knife. Deke was her man and no one touched him, but Ruby. Even if they weren't courting, he was still the man she considered hers. She'd believed he was her man since she was fifteen years old.

She paused at the realization that she considered him hers. He'd gotten married after leaving her behind, but that didn't mean she wanted to see another woman, especially a whore draping herself all over her man.

When the hand ended, she threw down her cards and motioned for the backup dealer.

George, the other dealer walked up. "Yes, Ruby?"

"Take over," she said, and stepped from behind the table. She walked towards Deke, each step determined, the swish, swish, swish of her petticoats letting everyone know she approached. She marched up to Deke, took the girl by the arm and pulled her off.

"He's mine," she said her voice low and threatening. "Don't touch."

"But…" Clara squealed.

Ruby didn't hesitate, she grabbed Deke by the hand and pulled him off the stool. Not only did she need to show everyone he belonged to her, but this would give them the opportunity to talk. She could tell him that Rivera was expected this weekend, just like she'd predicted.

"Ruby, everyone in the saloon is watching us, including Mrs. Hutchins," Deke said as he went with her.

"I don't care," she said. "I'm staking what's mine for these women. So they'll know hands off."

She turned and pulled him up the stairs. The men in the saloon cheered and the women clapped and giggled, and moved out of her way. At the top of the stairs she glanced around the parlor and then headed down a hall. The first room she came to was unoccupied. The bed had been freshly made, she pulled Deke inside and shut the door.

Inside the room, he glanced at her. "What was that all about?"

She swallowed, suddenly feeling nervous about her grand gesture that had gotten them time alone in a room where people had sex. "I thought you'd left town. I thought you didn't say goodbye. I needed some time alone with you and this was the only way I knew how."

He smiled. "Is that why you pulled Clara off of me?"

No, that wasn't the reason at all, but she wasn't about to admit that to Deke. How did Ruby tell Deke that as long as they were in the same place, that he belonged to no one else but her? Could she admit her jealousy?

She took a deep breath and huffed out her chest. "She had no business…trying to do…sell herself to you."

He took a step towards her. "You know that this kills the idea that we didn't know each other before we rode into town."

"No, we're just getting more acquainted now," she said walking backwards away from the door uneasiness prickling along her spine. The two of them were alone, in a bedroom, in a bordello.

Sounds were coming from the room next to them. Groaning and moaning and all kinds of noises that made her feel as out of place as a cow on a front porch. What was she thinking, dragging Deke upstairs?

She swallowed, her ears cringing, her face heating up, her breath getting raspy. A soiled dove was entertaining a man in the room right next door. *Oh my God, they were having sex, right next door.*

Ruby gazed at Deke to see if he understood what was happening.

His lips turned up in a grin and he took another step towards her. Oh yeah, he knew.

She hadn't really thought too much about what people would think they were doing up here in this room? She'd only seen one of those whores going after her man. Deke was hers, even if he didn't know it yet.

Deke advanced toward her. "Ruby we've been doing this dance for years."

"What dance?" she asked taking another step back, trying to squelch the nerves that were jumping like a Mexican bean at a convention.

"You know what dance. The one you wanted and I rejected you. Then I wanted and you rejected me. Now…now I have no objections. We're in a bedroom, alone, and people are going to assume we're consummating our desire for each other."

"All the more reason for us not too. Besides, we need to talk."

Deke shook his head. "No, all the more reason for us to take advantage of this time together. We've danced around this for years. The waltz ends now."

Anxiety just about leaped right out of her skin. "But…"

"What objections do you have now, Ruby? I'm not married. You're old enough, what's the excuse this time?"

Isn't this what she wanted? So why did it feel so scary and awkward and yet she didn't want to say no?

The back of her legs bumped into the bed. "I guess I don't have any."

Deke took one large step and was on top of her. "God, woman I have wanted and dreamed of you for so many years."

He had? She'd desired him since the first time she saw him.

He gripped her face in his hand and lowered his mouth to hers. He kissed her thoroughly leaving her hungry and aching in areas of her body she'd never considered feeling so sensitive before. Craving him she wrapped her arms around his chest, bringing him in close to her body.

Her hands trailed down his back and then returned to his head to seize him and hold his mouth in place. She didn't understand what was happening, but right now, he was kissing her in a way she'd only fantasized about.

She pushed back. "You're not going to back out are you?"

He frowned. "I hadn't planned on it."

"Good," she said with a sigh. "Kiss me like that again."

He chuckled. "I'd be more than happy to."

Chapter Ten

Deke stared into Ruby's eyes, all big and blue and innocent appearing and felt his blood rush to his groin like a locomotive out of control. The people in the room next to them were banging the bed frame against the wall, the sounds of their moaning ricocheting off the thin partitions and all he could think about was how they had chased this dance before. How many times had they gotten to the brink and then backed away.

Well no more. He wanted Ruby like he wanted his next breath. Like the sun needed the moon and the flowers the rain, he was tired of wanting and denying and wanting and denying and here they were.

His lips covered hers and he kissed her, needing to drink from her fountain and celebrate in her joy. This woman had intrigued him since the moment he'd met her. She was like sunshine radiating and touching him everywhere. The warm tendrils of her rays skimming across his soul, making him warm from the inside out.

No matter how much he tried to resist her in those early days, it had taken every ounce of willpower to keep from taking her that day. A woman whose father he would have disappointed if he'd been alive. The only thing that saved him from taking Ruby's virginity was his respect for Michael McKenzie.

Now, the girl was here, old enough, and no longer a virgin. The time had come for their bodies to do the waltz.

His tongue swept the inside of her mouth, raking her teeth, dancing, seducing and needing her. He pushed her and she toppled back onto the bed, their lips breaking apart. Her sapphire eyes opened and she stared at him, her gaze dark with desire.

Unbuttoning his shirt, she watched as he tugged the garment from his pants and slid it down his arms. He reached for the buckle on his belt and she rose up to sitting on the bed. Her hands quickly removed the belt, unbuttoned his pants, her fingers trailing down the length of his hardened shaft, feeling him through his clothing.

She glanced at him, her gaze filled with desire as she pulled his pants down to his knees, his penis springing out at her. With her hand, she gripped his manhood and he thought he was going to die. The feel of her soft skin stroking him had him reaching for her.

Together they fell onto the bed and he turned to remove his boots and socks and kicked his trousers the rest of the way to the floor. Naked, he wanted to feel her, see her naked body.

Reaching behind her, he unbuttoned her dress and then peeled the garment from her. The cleavage that other men had gazed upon fell into his hands and he caressed her gorgeous mounds. Her breasts were full and white and pert and so beautiful that he could get lost in them.

Placing his mouth on her bosom, he licked the luscious areolas of her breasts, plucking the nipple into his mouth. She tasted delicious and the moan that escaped her throat, sounded like sweet music to his ears.

He pushed the dress down her body, past her hips, where it pooled on the floor. His fingers touched the edge of her pantaloons and he shoved them down and she kicked them out of the way.

Stopping, he gazed at her naked, beautiful, white body and then into her sapphire eyes. Her eyes were glassy with passion and desire for him and it was all he could do to keep from crawling on top of her and shoving his way inside her. But he wanted her to enjoy this experience as much as he, because it could never happen again. He could never take the chance of being with her again and getting her pregnant. If he hadn't waited years for her, he would not be taking this chance, this risk even now. But he had to have Ruby. Now.

Pushing the troublesome thoughts away, he wanted only to concentrate on this moment in time. To concentrate on this beautiful woman and how she made him feel. How he couldn't wait to thrust himself inside her womanly sheath and bury himself inside her.

His fingers caressed her stomach sliding down to the curly folds of her center. When he touched her entrance she arched her back thrusting against his hand and whimpered, the sound filled with need. She was slick with desire for him as he thrust his fingers inside her, wanting to replace them with his shaft, but knowing he needed to make her ready to accept him.

She groaned and grasped his shaft in her hands gripping him tightly, hastening him to the edge. Unable to wait any longer, he crawled on top of her, placed his manhood at her entrance.

He stared into her sapphire eyes and she looked intently into his eyes, her gaze filled with passion and desire. She wanted him and he needed her to wipe away the memories of his dead wife.

Ruby should have been the woman he married. Now it was too late. But for just this moment he could dream of how it could have been if he'd not done the honorable thing. If he'd never wedded Laura.

He plunged inside her, staring at Ruby, their eyes connected as they joined. He met resistance. Shock froze his movements as, stunned, he stared into her eyes and she gasped. Surprise gripped him and he halted his movements.

"Don't stop."

He wanted to pull out, to back up and cease. *Ruby was a virgin*. She'd never been with a man before.

"But…"

She wrapped her arms around him, grasping him.

"Don't stop, "she demanded.

He couldn't have even if he'd wanted to. It was too late, he could no more stop, than he could stop breathing. He moved within her, slow at first. She was so tight and he was her first. The woman that flirted and teased with all of the men in the saloon every night had never copulated before. As the very first man she'd been with, he was determined to make tonight as memorable as he could in a room in a bordello, with the sounds of other people having sex all around them.

Thrusting into her body, his lips found hers once again as he poured all the longing he ached with into his kiss, melding her mouth to his, filling his soul with her essence.

Why did this woman intrigue him, thrill him like no other? If only he was a man who could give her forever. But he'd made a vow never to marry again, and not even Ruby McKenzie could shake him from his resolve.

"Deke," she cried and her body tensed around him, sending him over the edge. Like a bronco rider, he lurched from the saddle, filled with pleasure, such love and he couldn't return the emotion. Because he'd sworn after Laura's death never to love again. Never.

~

Ruby lay in Deke's arms, filled with wonderment, her heart racing, her body slowly cooling. She'd completely forgotten their surroundings though now moans could be heard coming from a room across the hall. Deke had been her only focus until now.

"Why didn't you tell me you were a virgin?" he asked his breathing still harsh sounding in the small room.

She shrugged. "It was none of your business."

His body tensed. "If you'd waited this long, don't you think you should have waited until you were married?"

What did it matter? Why was he making so much out of the fact that she'd never had sex with a man before?

"No," she said feeling irritated. "It was my decision."

Of course she hadn't planned on coming in here and fornicating with him tonight, but it'd been fun…it felt right, until he started fussing at her like she was twelve years old.

"You could have stopped if you didn't want to bed a virgin."

"No, I couldn't stop."

"Sure, you couldn't," she said. Sitting up, she glanced down at him. "What we just did was wonderful. Don't ruin it. This is what we should have done all those years ago."

She rose and started searching for her clothing, the intimate mood destroyed with the memory of the past and his harping on her virginity. He'd been her pick years ago and had run from the opportunity, now he'd done the deed and regretted it?

"And just like years ago, I'm not in any position to offer you a ring and a trip to the preacher man."

Good grief, she clenched her fists in frustration. Why did the man just assume she wanted a husband? Why did he assume she wanted to marry him? What if she was only using him to scratch an itch that had been there since they'd met years ago? Couldn't a woman use a man?

Shoving her legs into her pantaloons, she stared at him. "Why are you ruining what just happened between us? Why can't you let it be a wonderful experience that was destined to happen?"

"Because most women would expect a trip to the church. You know vows and promises of forever," he said almost yelling. "Especially when they're a virgin."

If he didn't shut up, he was going to spoil everything. What was his obsession with them marrying? Was it to appease her or was it his way of salvaging his guilt? She'd never said anything about a ring and promises of forever. She had no expectations, other than to catch Rivera.

"Would you keep your voice down," she said. "Do you think I want all the ladies to know you were my first? You're ruining my reputation."

All she needed was the women in this place to learn that she'd been a virgin. That would blow her tough image completely apart and leave her just as vulnerable as the soiled doves who worked upstairs.

He shook his head, sat up on the bed and located his pants on the floor. Standing he pulled them on.

"Ruby, confound it, every time I think I understand women, you shake me up and make me realize I know nothing," he said.

She pulled her petticoats on and then tugged the dress over her head and presented her back to him. "Would you please button me up?"

Slowly and methodically he buttoned her back into the dress. "I hate this dress. I can't wait for the time when you're no longer sharing your breasts with the men in this saloon."

Whirling around she faced him. "I'm covered. See?"

"Barely."

He stared at her and she could see the confusion and the frustration in his gaze. "I'm sorry. I didn't know you were a virgin. We wouldn't have done this if I'd known."

Clenching her fists to keep from smacking him, she could feel the rage, tightening her insides. Could the man be any more condescending? He'd just insulted her. "Oh so because you thought I'd already shared my body with several other cowboys, it was okay for you to take your turn?"

"No," he said, running his hand through his hair. "But if I'd known it was your first time, I wouldn't have chosen a bordello."

With these last few comments he'd completely sabotaged the evening. While she hadn't planned on having sex with him tonight, she'd risked a lot being here with him and now she just felt madder'n than a rained on rooster.

"And you didn't want to choose a bedroll on the trail and you didn't want to choose my home. Do you have to have the perfect spot to bed virgins? Is there a magical place where you take and deflower them?"

"Confound it woman, you are ornerier and harder to get along with any person I know."

"Oh, so it's all my fault," she said.

Shoving her boots on her feet, she checked her petticoats for her pistol and then let her skirt fall to the floor. She turned to him. She'd dreamed and waited for this night for years and now he was making it feel cheap.

"Tonight was wonderful right up until I expected you to turn to me and say, 'Ruby, that was so incredible' and I would have kissed you and said, 'yes, it was.' Not given me grief because I didn't tell you, I'd never had sex before."

Taking a deep breath to ease the anger from her face, she checked her expression in the mirror and wondered if anyone could tell she was no longer an innocent. But then again, Deke obviously had no idea she'd been a virgin.

Deke stood before her a sheepish look on his face. "Your first time ought to be special."

"And it would have been, if you'd just kept your mouth shut." She sighed. "Maybe I should have just let that whore have you. Now I've got to go down there and face a room full of men who are going to think I was up here having a grand old time. Which I was right up until you decided to lecture me on my virginity."

Going back to a bunch of rowdy men after having sex and everyone knowing you'd had sex, would be the height of embarrassment.

"Wait, I'll go with you."

Oh, no, that would only make it worse.

"No, I've let you do enough damage for tonight. I only came in here to tell you what Hannah told me about Rivera. He's going to be in town on Saturday. Now, I'm going down there and face those men on my own without your help."

"About damn time," he said. "Are you certain you can trust her?"

Ruby just shook her head. This conversation was over. She was done speaking to Deke.

With her heart near to bursting with disappointment, Ruby opened the door and stepped out into the hall, leaving a half-naked Deke behind. Tears filled her eyes, but the sight of the women, who were not currently occupied, all smiling and waiting for her, dried them up quicker than a ride through the desert.

Clapping their hands, they called, "Yay, you're one of us now."

Ruby bristled like a porcupine in heat. She shook her head. "No. No, I'm not. That was just a quick tumble to mark the man as mine."

Mrs. Hutchins walked out of the shadows. "My office now, Ruby."

~

Ruby knew this couldn't be good. In the short week she'd been working here, she'd quickly learned that a trip to the office with Mrs. Hutchins was not something you wanted.

After she'd shut the door, the woman took a seat behind her desk. "What the hell just happened? Do you want to work upstairs?"

As if this night couldn't get any worse, Ruby knew the woman had the right to be angry with her. She'd walked off the job for a romp with the man who had intrigued her since she was a young girl. Well now that itch was scratched and it was time to move on.

After all, he'd even said he couldn't offer her marriage, not that she was really searching for a husband, but she'd always been infatuated with Deke. Maybe it was time to move on.

The truth poured from Ruby's lips. At this moment she felt as helpless as a cow in quick sand. Yet she couldn't seem to stop the flow of words from her lips.

"No, I don't want to work upstairs. I'm sorry, I guess I lost my head there for a moment. Deke and I met riding into town and well, there has been something growing between us. When I saw Clara, draped all over him, trying to persuade him to come upstairs, I sort of lost it."

The woman laughed. "Get used to it honey. Men stray." She paused and carefully considered Ruby. "You're more innocent than I expected."

Men stray? More like they lied to get what they needed. This last week with Deke by her side, she'd begun to think that maybe there was something good between them. Maybe just maybe he was the man for her. But no more. Nope, she was a strong, independent woman who needed no one.

"Yeah, well men have wreaked havoc on my innocence. It's not like before."

The woman leaned over the desk. "I'm going to let this incident slide. But Deke will owe me for the room and for bedding you in my bordello. You understand? And another incident in the saloon like the one tonight and I'll expect you to work upstairs permanently. Understand?"

"Yes, Ma'am," Ruby said contrite. The woman was right, she'd risked everything on a quick tumble with Deke. She could be in so much more trouble and could have even possibly lost her job. The job she needed until she caught Rivera.

Taking a deep breath, she released it slowly. She had to

keep her focus on catching her man, her bounty, Rivera.

"Now get back to work at the tables. You're costing me money."

"Of course, Ma'am." Ruby rose to leave the room, ready to get out of this small office that felt so confined.

"I have to go collect from your gentleman friend."

Ruby felt her heart sink to her feet. "No, don't. Just take it out of what you owe me."

"Are you sure?"

The very idea that the madam would approach Deke about having to pay for the time they'd spent in the room, was embarrassing. She didn't need any more humiliation tonight. She'd suffered enough.

"Yes," Ruby said and walked out the door. Tonight had been special until right after their time together. And when Deke opened his mouth, he'd ruined everything.

~

That night when Ruby arrived back at the hotel, Hannah was sitting on the back steps waiting for her. The girl had changed out of her green saloon dress and wore a dark colored muslin dress, her red hair pulled up off her shoulders.

"Are you okay?" Ruby asked concerned that the girl had taken such a risk coming to see her.

Hannah stared at her in the darkness, her lips turned up in a smile. "I'm fine. I was worried about you. You were the talk of the upstairs this evening."

Ruby sank down on the steps. "I'm good. Tired, confused and disappointed, but other than that I'm good."

Hannah laughed. "So sex with that handsome man wasn't what you'd hoped for?"

"It's kind of complicated," Ruby admitted. "The sex was actually very good. It was afterwards that made me upset."

She couldn't complain to Hannah. The woman's life was way worse than hers and she didn't want to admit that she had been a virgin up until a few hours ago.

"Yeah, the girls said they heard raised voices. That's why I had to come check on you. I wanted to make sure you were all right and that you weren't packing to leave tonight."

"You're really not very trusting, are you?" Ruby told the girl.

Hannah shook her head. "No, would you be if you were sold?"

How could a woman trust any person, man or woman, after being sold into a brothel?

She watched the girl's gold-green eyes, gaze out at the pasture land that was behind the hotel. Ruby wanted more than anything to help her start her life over, but first they had to get out of town.

"You've got a point."

Crickets squeaked their lonesome sound and a hoot owl could be heard in the distance. Morning would soon be arriving.

"Is it difficult having sex with different men every night?" Ruby asked. "I don't have much experience in the bedroom and I can't imagine sharing yourself like that with men you don't even know."

Hannah hung her head and leaned back against the railing. When she raised her gaze there were tears in her eyes. "I hate it. I hate sex. When I leave here, I never want to sleep with a man again."

Though she'd been angry with Deke when she left the room, she had enjoyed them being together. She'd loved the way he made her body thrum like music, the melody building until the crescendo. But she was certain you didn't experience that being a whore.

"But Hannah, what if you meet someone you fall in

love with? What if a man treats you kind and falls in love with you? Don't you want children?"

"No decent man is going to want me," she cried. "I'm soiled. I'm scared that I'll catch some horrible disease or even worse, I'll get pregnant and have no idea who the father is."

Ruby could understand her hesitation, her fears. Would a good man consider her even though she'd never wanted to be a soiled dove? Sometimes life just wasn't fair.

The two women stared out into the darkness and Ruby confessed to Hannah what had really happened. "I'm sorry. Tonight was my first experience with sex and I enjoyed it."

"Yeah, I went into the room looking for you and saw the blood stained sheets. I hid them."

Fear and embarrassment surged through Ruby. She'd never even considered that she'd left signs of what had happened on the bed.

"Oh," Ruby said wanting to kick herself. She'd taken such a chance tonight and for what?

"I didn't want Mrs. Hutchins to learn you'd been a virgin."

"Thank you," Ruby said with a sigh. "I didn't even think about that."

"Do you care about this man?" Hannah asked.

Ruby stared out in the night, wishing she could be truthful with Hannah, but then again, her own emotions were like scrambled eggs all torn up. "Like I said, it's complicated. I've known him for awhile. Years ago, I wanted him, when I was just a young girl. But tonight was the first time we've ever lain together and while I thought it would make things easier between us, it's just entangled things even more. I don't know what to do."

"Do you love him?"

Ruby thought long and hard about Deke. Hadn't she always cared about him? But did she love him? No, she just couldn't. If she admitted to loving him, he would break her heart, again.

"I could. But he doesn't make it easy. One moment he's hotter than a firecracker and the next it feels like he's pushing me away. I don't know."

And if Ruby was honest with herself, one moment she wanted him and the next she was pushing him away as well. Ruby didn't want a man telling her what to do. She liked her independence. That's why she didn't want Deke to feel like he had to offer marriage. She wanted to live her life to the extremes with or without a man, it didn't matter. But she would never marry just to satisfy the dictates of society. If it wasn't love, she'd live her life on her own without a man.

"I have no need to worry about that. Some men may come in and ask for you by name, but most are just looking for a woman. Any vessel will do."

For this reason Ruby would help this woman escape this life and begin anew. No one should have to live doing something that was against their nature that they hated. No one.

Ruby sighed. "We've got to get you out of there."

"Yes," Hannah said. "I can't live like this any longer."

"Do you know what you're going to do once you leave?"

"I've dreamed about it for the last six months," she said with determination. "I'm going to find my step-father and kill him. And then I'm going to return and free all the other girls in the saloon."

Ruby turned in the darkness and stared at her. "You're going to need some help and some training. After we leave here, I'll teach you how to shoot and how to earn a living. Not to kill your step-father, but to hand him over to the law and let justice take care of him."

"Why are you helping me?" Hannah asked in the dark.

"Most women wouldn't care about a girl who was a whore. Most women look the other way, fearful this life will rub off on them."

How did she respond to Hannah? It was more than the fact that she'd been trapped into this situation. Ruby cherished her self-sufficiency so much that she couldn't imagine having it taken away from her. She couldn't be the woman who had to obey her husband and answer to his every whim. In fact, maybe she'd refuse to marry if this was how it would be with a man? She'd dreamed of so much more, but maybe she was better off without Deke or any man.

"Well maybe that's the problem with our society. If we all helped each other, maybe women would have more control. Have more say in how we were treated. I couldn't live without being in control of my destiny and I will do everything I can to help any woman obtain control of her own future. That's why I'm helping you."

Hannah reached out and wrapped her arm around Ruby. "Thank you. You will have my undying friendship and loyalty for the rest of your life. If ever you need help, I'll be there."

Ruby felt her eyes, prick with tears. She'd never had a friend like Hannah. Only her sisters. Somehow she felt like she'd just found another sister.

"Thanks, Hannah, that means a lot. Now, you better get back before they discover you're gone."

Chapter Eleven

The next day, Deke waited outside of Ruby's room. He'd known it was late when she came in, but he had to speak to her. But what was he going to say?

Sorry, I was shocked you were a virgin? Sorry, for not thinking that you could possibly still be innocent after all these years? Sorry, for not offering you forever?

What an awkward situation he found himself in and for the second time in days, he wanted to just get on his horse and ride. Yet, he couldn't go off and leave her in this town where she could disappear and no one would notice.

Finally, she opened her door and stepped outside.

"Good morning," he said gazing at her, noticing she wore her riding skirt. Was she planning on going somewhere?

She stared at him her blue eyes bright. "Good morning."

Oh, that look was one that said, you may think everything is just fine, but I'm so mad you'll be lured into thinking everything's fine and then I will take you down. Somehow he had to ward off disaster.

"Could I buy you a cup of coffee?"

"Sorry, but I've got errands to run. But thanks, maybe another time," she said and swept right on past him as if they were neighbors not lovers.

"Ruby," he said clearly frustrated.

She turned and gazed at him. "What?"

"Things can't be this way between us," he said.

Licking her lips, her eyes widened in that innocent, look that he wanted to kiss off her face. She was trying to act like this meant nothing. She was trying to pretend that what they'd done last night hadn't mattered. But it'd meant so much to him and he couldn't believe it hadn't to her.

"What are you referring to?" she asked shaking her head. "Last night?"

"Okay, I was wrong. I shouldn't have questioned your…"

She gave him a look that silenced him. Standing in the hall of the local hotel was not the place to talk about her virginity.

A smile spread across her beautiful face that didn't quite meet her eyes. "Oh, honey, you may have been my first, but it's okay, you won't be my last." She patted him on the cheek. "Now I've got to run. Maybe I'll see you later tonight at the saloon."

With a wave of her hand, she strolled down the hall of the hotel towards the stairs that led to outside. Her skirts swished back and forth, her cute little derriere twitching like a ship's beacon. The puppy whined at Deke and he glanced down at the dog at his feet. "Yeah, I know she was playing me," he said. "But don't worry, she's not going far. And sooner or later, we will talk."

~

Mrs. Hutchins sat in a hard wooden chair, in the sheriff's office. She glanced around at the wanted posters hanging on the walls. Many of the men were frequent visitors to the saloon, but they'd never be apprehended in her establishment. She wasn't stupid and knew her clientele did not sing in the church choir on Sunday morning.

They were lucky to still be walking on Sunday morning and not sprawled out in the street somewhere either drunk or dead. Many of her regulars were wanted by the law. But in this town the law was loose and mainly kept order in the town. As long as you didn't cause trouble, the sheriff left you alone.

Wyatt hurried into his office. "Emily, good to see you. What are you doing out and about today?"

She smiled at him. They'd been friends since she'd bought the saloon and she like to make sure that she kept him supplied with the best whiskey and finest cigars and personally, sex. It was the least she could do to help her establishment run smoothly. And if he took care of a problem for her, there was always a nice bonus for him. The arrangement worked well for both of them. She even enjoyed entertaining him once a week.

"What have you heard about Ruby? Any answers to your telegrams?"

There was something about this girl that just didn't make sense. She dealt cards in a saloon, but she seemed more like an innocent. Something about Ruby's story wasn't true and Emily meant to find out what.

"So far, just one. It was from a sheriff in Zenith. He said he'd never heard of any women bounty hunters before." The sheriff sat down in the chair behind his desk. "Has she caused more trouble?"

Emily laughed and shook her head. "Not exactly trouble, but last night she had the saloon in an uproar. She took that man named Deke upstairs."

The sheriff frowned. "They told me when they rode into town that they didn't know each other."

Shrugging she looked at Wyatt. "When one of the girls made moves on Deke, she hauled him upstairs and they used one of my rooms."

"For sex?"

"Yes. According to the girls not only did they have sex, but that there was an argument afterwards."

If that was their first time together, it could be their last and that would be just fine with her. She wanted Ruby working upstairs as it was and soon she'd come up with a plan to get the girl in the brothel. She'd quickly make even more money than she was now.

"Maybe instead of investigating her, I should be finding out about him," the sheriff said. "When he came into town, he said he was looking for his brother. Maybe I need to ask him how that search is coming along. And I'll do some checking to see if anyone recognizes his name."

"Once he leaves town, I'll be moving her upstairs." He smiled.

She nodded. Her gut instincts were telling her that these two were not who they said they were. They were up to something. She was going to find out and then deal with them appropriately. Emily had worked way too hard to have her business disrupted by a mere girl and a quiet talking man. She'd dealt with people like them before. Once she learned what they were up to, they would be taken care of. Ruby could fill Hannah's room as she would soon no longer occupy that space.

"Let me know what you find out. Mr. Culver hangs out at the saloon most nights. I've even seen him walk Miss Callahan over to the hotel. For a couple who didn't know each other, they've suddenly become the best of friends."

Why hadn't she realized this when she'd first hired Ruby. After this weekend, she intended to do some house cleaning, starting with Hannah. Even though the girl had settled down, she was more or a liability than an asset. It was time to rid herself of the danger.

"Don't worry about them. I'll see to it that we find out what they're up to."

~

Later that night, Ruby was at the tables dealing cards, wondering how long this could go on. She'd ridden out to the Rivera homestead today and spent the afternoon scouting around. Nothing. In fact, the place had looked empty. The brother was gone and there was no sign of life anywhere. If Rivera was coming into town this Friday or Saturday, there were no signs of him at the ranch.

Doubts were beginning to crowd her mind and make her question if she was risking too much in this hell hole of a town. Rivera could be anywhere. And could she trust Rivera's favorite whore, Clara?

Plus the time for Annabelle's baby to be born was fast approaching and as much as Ruby would like to catch their father's killer, she didn't want to miss out on the birth of her first niece or nephew. She worried about her sister, and didn't want to skip this important event in Annabelle and Beau's life.

"Ante up, gentlemen," she called.

"Ruby, when are you going to start working upstairs?" a young man asked her. "You know we'd all be lined up."

She stopped dealing the cards and gave him a stern glare. "Daniel, that day will never happen."

"Well, it did yesterday," he said innocently.

The men at the table all stared, their eyes focused on her. "Sometimes a girl has to lay claim to her man and that's what I did. Now lady luck does not talk about subjects that are personal. I'd suggest we get back to the card game."

"And if we don't?" Daniel said defiantly.

Since yesterday, the men were treating her different. Before she'd at least had a little respect, but not now. Now they were looking at her like she was honey and they were a swarm of bees.

"Sugar," she purred. "I'll have to call over Tom, Mrs. Hutchins henchman. The last time I had to do something like that they pulled down the poor man's pants before they tossed him in the street. I'd hate to see something like that happen to you."

Guffaws resounded at the table, but she could also tell she'd gained some new respect with them. But how long would it last? In the past two days, Deke's warnings were starting to corrode her resolve to wait for Rivera. She wanted to go home, now.

"Can we play cards?" she asked him. "Or do I need to motion the goon over?"

"Deal the damn cards."

Tossing out a card to each man, she watched their expressions and could pretty much tell who had the better hand.

The betting began and she had to pay attention as to who was the high bidder. Soon she dealt another round of cards. When she finished, she glanced up and saw that Deke had walked in the saloon. Their eyes met and she knew he was remembering last night.

Walking in here tonight had been difficult. Remembering what they'd done upstairs and how it had ended. She just wanted to kick and scream at him for being such an idiot. The dream of the two of them together had been so good and the reality had been even better, until he started talking. And then she'd wanted to hurt him.

Deke walked over to their table. He watched her as she dealt the cards. She turned to him. "Can I help you?"

"Darling, I just wanted to let you know that I'll be waiting for you tonight right over there in the corner," he said and smiled. "Gentlemen, treat the lady right."

He turned and sauntered back over to the bar where he turned and tipped his hat to her.

The man had some nerve. Yet, the men at the table suddenly were back to treating her with respect and a couple even shook their heads, when he walked away. As long as things were returning to normal, then she wouldn't worry about being treated with disrespect.

"Don't know if he's a lucky man or he's in for the heartache of his life. I guess you'll determine which one," a man said and picked up his cards.

"Women! Let's play cards," another man said.

"Ante up, gentlemen," she said and dealt the next hand.

Part of her wanted to say thanks and part of her wanted to tell Deke to keep from interfering; she could take care of herself. Yet there was a small part that warmed at how he'd called her darling and let everyone know he was there watching over her.

Just when she was ready to give up on Deke, he always seemed to find a way to soothe things over smooth as silk and come out ahead. What was it about the man that she couldn't seem to give up on? Why hadn't yesterday's tussle filled her need for him?

Because no matter what, she just seemed drawn to the man. Even in the worst of times.

Gunshots resounded right outside the saloon. The doors were flung open and a man yelled, "Clara."

Ruby glanced around the room at the men who had pulled their guns out and were pointing them at the cowboy.

Clara ran screaming down the stairs and launched herself into the arms of the man who had been firing the pistol, wrapping her legs around his body.

"James, you're back," Clara said.

Ruby felt her gut clench with hatred and her hands shook with the need to reach for her gun. James Rivera had just walked into the saloon.

"Came back just to see you," he said. Clara slid down his torso until her feet touched the ground.

Slowly the guns around her were shoved back into their holsters and Ruby breathed a sigh of relief. She'd still get her chance for revenge with Rivera.

"I missed you," Clara whined.

"I'm mighty happy to see you as well," the outlaw said and it was all Ruby could do to keep from pulling out her pistol and shooting the man right there. But she knew that would be murder for him and suicide for her.

Mrs. Hutchins frowned at the man. "James, how many times have I asked you not to fire your weapons right outside. It's a wonder someone doesn't kill you."

He grinned. "More times than I can count." Pulling out some money, he handed it to her. "That should fix whatever damages I've created and give me some alone time with Clara."

Nausea rose up in Ruby's throat at the idea of this man experiencing any sort of enjoyment tonight or any night. She had to fight the urge to kill him. She had to remember that she was just hauling him back for the law to serve justice. She had to remind herself of how he'd look swinging with a rope around his neck.

The woman hugged his arm into her side, holding onto the man like she feared he would disappear before her very eyes.

Ruby glanced over at Deke and he was frowning as he watched the happy couple, walk between the tables. He glanced up and caught Ruby's eyes, they stared at one another and she could almost feel him telling her that this was their man. This was the man who'd killed her father and his mentor. This was the man they were after.

Finally, he'd come into town. With his hat pulled low over his face, Deke made his way across the opposite side of the room and slipped out the door. He wasn't taking a chance that Rivera would recognize him.

Many hours later, Rivera finally made his way back downstairs to the gaming tables. Ruby worried that he wouldn't sit at her table, but late in the evening, just before the saloon was getting ready to shut down, Rivera took a seat at her table.

"Clara says you're the new card dealer. Deal me in," he said, staring at Ruby, his eyes dancing with alcohol and delight. "She told me Lady Luck has been bringing the house luck. I aim to change that tonight."

A forced smile spread across Ruby's face. Somehow she had to deal her father's killer a hand of cards and convince him she was his friend, not the enemy she wanted to reveal. "Sir, I just deal the cards."

"Well, Clara is going to give me luck tonight. Aren't you, sweetheart," he said rubbing his hand on Clara's leg.

"Of course, honey," she said drowsily. "If you earn enough, maybe we could get married."

"Maybe," he said.

Ruby had the distinct impression that he was just saying the words the woman needed to hear. He didn't have any intention of marrying the whore. But she wasn't about to say a word. Let Clara learn that on her own.

For the next hour, it was all Ruby could do to keep the cards flowing, her voice pleasant and not reach across the table and strangle Rivera. But she did what she had to, knowing that sooner or later she'd get her opportunity. Promising herself that patience was the key to obtaining her man.

"One last hand, gentlemen before we call it a night," she said. Glancing over she noticed that Clara had moved to another table and was fast asleep waiting for her man.

Dealing the cards she glanced over at the outlaw. "Mr. Rivera, please stay afterwards. I have a question for you."

"Anything for you honey," he said smiling.

Nausea roiled through her and she had to swallow to keep from throwing up. He thought she wanted sexual favors, but he'd soon find himself with a case of a stiff neck an' a short drop.

After the others had settled up the pot and walked away, Ruby turned to James Rivera and had to school the emotions she could feel surging through her. He couldn't see that she hated him and would like nothing better than to haul him out of town right this moment. But she had to wait.

"Several of our patrons are holding a special card game starting tomorrow afternoon. I thought you would be a great player to have in the mix. We're going to hold it in a special room of the hotel."

He frowned at her. "That's odd. Usually Mrs. Hutchins lets us use one of the rooms upstairs. Why aren't they holding it upstairs."

Ruby almost panicked. "She's renovating that room, adding more space, for more girls."

He shrugged. "I don't know. I haven't been home in quite awhile. My family is going to need my help."

"There's a special jackpot of five hundred dollars being offered to the winner."

"That's a lot of money," he said his eyes widening as he stared at her. "Where did you say it was?"

Oh, the jackpot was luring him like bait on a hook.

"The Hide Town hotel."

"And who is going to be playing," he asked.

She named off several of her regular players and he frowned.

"I've beaten all of them before. That money could be mine," he said running his hands through his hair.

"Okay, count me in. See you tomorrow afternoon," he said and walked out the door, leaving a sleeping Clara slumped over a table.

Ruby wanted to kick her and tell her he was gone, but decided it was none of her business and let her sleep on.

She turned to leave and there was Deke. "Oh," she said surprised that he was still there. It was late. "I thought you might be going after Rivera."

"Not tonight. The sheriff is hanging around and I don't want to draw his attention."

"Where's the dog?" Ruby asked glancing around.

"Waiting outside."

"This whole time?"

"Yes, we've been waiting, the two of us," he said.

"Exciting night."

"Yes, I'm ready to go home. We have things to discuss," he said leading her by the elbow towards the door.

"Whatever could that be?" she asked innocently.

If he brought up her virginity, he just might not live to see tomorrow. Yet, she couldn't wait to talk about Rivera and their plans to sneak him out of town before anyone noticed he was gone.

"You know exactly," he said and they stepped through the swinging doors to see the Wyatt Thomas, waiting on them.

"This your dog, Culver?"

"Yes, sir."

"You need to keep him off the street."

"I will sir," Deke said and Ruby could feel the tenseness seeping from his bones like minerals from a spring.

Fear clutched at Ruby and she put on her saloon girl persona. "Sheriff, so good to see you. I've been staying out of trouble."

The sheriff glanced at her. "That's not what I hear."

Ruby pouted her lips at the man and tried to act coy. "What do you mean? I haven't done anything wrong."

"Take a look to your left. What do you see?"

It took a conscious effort not to let the sheriff see how much she wanted to smack him upside the head.

"Deke?"

"Heard you and him went upstairs yesterday. That's asking for trouble."

A shiver of revulsion went through Ruby and she could see Deke was ready to pound the man into the Texas dirt.

Somehow she had to diffuse the situation before Deke killed the dirty lawman.

What a self-centered smartass that wore a badge. Only it was smudged from dirt that clung to this lawman.

"Won't happen again, Sheriff," she said ducking her head. She wanted to throw up, but knew that wouldn't really look to good right now, though it would make her feel better. She hated dirty lawmen and this one had so much scum on him, he'd never come clean.

"How's the hunt for your brother coming?" he asked Deke. "Any luck?"

"Not yet. I've been talking to the reverend when I can find him. Seems he likes to lay low."

"Most men in this town do," the sheriff said. "I'll give you two more days and then you're going to need to move on."

Deke shrugged like it meant nothing to him. "No worries."

"And take that mangy mutt you call a dog with you or I'll shoot him."

Ruby could almost feel the hair on the back of Deke's neck standing on end. The dog whimpered and gave a low growl.

"Not an animal lover, sheriff?" Deke asked.

"I have no use for them."

"Good," Deke said and tugged at Ruby's arm. "Good night."

Ruby had to resist the urge to turn around and make certain that the sheriff wasn't going to pull a gun on them and shoot them in the back. A creepy feeling slithered down her spine and made her want to run to the hotel.

She was so ready to go home. But knew the worst was yet to come.

Chapter Twelve

Deke would like nothing better than to see that stupid lawman face justice. He needed to somehow be brought before a judge and sentenced for being corrupt. And he hoped that before this was over the cavalry would ride in and arrest him. They weren't far from Fort Griffin and there were soldiers there who could clean this town up.

But right now he had to get himself and Ruby out of here safely with their bounty, Rivera. And right now, he'd ride out of here without the bounty, though he doubted that he could convince Ruby of leaving.

Creeping up the back stairs of the hotel they walked down the hall. When they reached Ruby's door, he waited while she opened it and then pushed her inside, following her into the darkened hotel room. He put the puppy on the floor, who curled up and went back to sleep. Deke waited while she lit a lamp.

"What are you doing?" she whispered in the dark, her voice like a caress across his tense body.

"We need to talk."

"Can't it wait until morning?" She finally got the coal lamp burning and in the light he glanced around the room at the clothes that were a mixture of the bounty hunter woman and the saloon girl.

"No, we need to make plans on getting out of town with Rivera and Hannah without half the gunslingers in this town following us," he said, breathing in the soft scents of her room. It smelled of roses and lilacs and lavender, the fragrance interrupting his flow of thoughts as he breathed in the sweet smell of Ruby.

"I just thought we'd gag Rivera, tie him up and then haul out of the hotel with him," she said brushing past him, her breasts rubbing against his chest.

Desire punched him in the gut like the kick of a bull. Standing here in this room, next to her, breathing in her womanly scent was enough to make him hard with wanting her.

"And you think that they're going to just let you ride down Main street with him all trussed up like a calf at branding time?"

"Look, I'm so ready to get out of this rat hole town that I'd try anything to get home."

Turning to walk away, he grabbed her arm and pulled her to him. "I'm ready to get out of here as well."

He hadn't meant to haul her into his arms, just to stop her from putting distance between them. In the glint of light, her pupils dilated and desire glowed from her gaze. She licked her lips and he almost groaned. This was not the time to have thoughts about what they could be doing on that bed.

"Thank you for what you did today," she said softly. "The men were testing me and then you came up and it ceased."

He lifted her chin to stare into her eyes. "I should have done something earlier. It was my fault. I didn't think about how they would react to you and me in the bordello."

She slipped out of his arms, stepping away from him. He could see her chest rising and falling with each breath, her creamy breasts all but spilling out of her dress.

"It's okay. I never thought of them thinking I would be available to…to…"

He smiled. She couldn't say the words and that filled with him with silly pride. All he wanted to do was lay her down on the bed and strip her clothes off slowly and methodically make sweet love to Ruby. Just one more time before they left this corrupt town and went their separate ways. Just one more time to explore her body. Because soon they would no longer spend each day together.

She had to go home to her sisters and he had to return to his empty life, in a house where the ghost of Laura lurked in every corner. Some days he thought about striking a match and burning down the homestead. But the property had belonged to her family for years. A dwelling that sat empty until he returned to rattle around in the cavernous building, lost and alone.

"So how do you want to handle getting out of town with Rivera," she asked facing him, the bed behind her beckoning to him like a sultry woman.

"I was thinking while you set up the card game, I could grab Hannah. The three of us nab Rivera. The horses are waiting in the back and then we do our best to get out of town before anyone notices."

She took a step towards him, laid her hand on his shoulder and ran it down his chest. He drew in a sharp breath. Scorching heat seared him with her touch.

"And once we get out of town, what are we going to do?" she asked, her hands still laying right below his heart. He took a deep breath and tried to concentrate.

"We're going to ride as far as we can until we run out of daylight. Then we're going to sleep under the stars without a fire, so we can get started bright and early the next morning. By supper of the second day, we should be close enough to Zenith that the sheriff will be afraid of the law."

Taking a step closer, Ruby was almost completely against him, the scent of roses swirling around the two of them like they were in a garden. Deke closed his eyes and tried to focus. He'd wanted to keep tonight strictly business and yet his body betrayed him.

She reached up and caressed the side of his face and he moaned, the sound loud in the stillness of her room.

"What if they follow us?" she asked her breathy voice sounding like a stroke down his body.

"That wouldn't be good. We'll need to ride along the edge of the river until we can cross over. Once we cross the Brazos, I'll feel safer."

"Then it'll be over," she said, her words having a ring of finality to them. Her lips mere inches from his.

As much as he knew it had to end, he didn't want this thing between them to stop. And as much as he wanted to he couldn't resist Ruby any more than he could stop breathing. Just one last time in her arms.

"Hopefully."

Greedily his lips covered hers with an urgency that he knew tonight would be their last. That tonight he would take one last risk and then never allow himself the sanctity of her arms again. His mouth plundered hers as he melded her sweet body to his. Need exploded through his body, rushing at him like a tornado on the prairie, sweeping everything from its path.

Her mouth opened like a flower and his tongue caressed the inside of her lip, then swept her mouth insistent and urgent. Wrapping her arms around his neck, she clung to him, pressing her body against his, letting him feel all of her womanly curves.

Slowly she ended their kiss and stepped from his arms, her chest still rising and falling. His chest clenched tightly as he watched her shaking her head. "I'm probably going to regret this, but not tonight. Tonight I want you."

She whirled around and presented her back to him. "Help me undress."

Relief surged through him and before she could ask twice, his fingers were reaching for her buttons. Hurriedly he unbuttoned her dress and let the gown fall to the floor. When she turned around to face him, she stood there in her corset, her breasts pushed up to almost spilling out of the garment. He'd never seen anything more beautiful.

Reaching out he ran his finger over the soft mounds and placed his lips along the tops, trailing his tongue over her exposed flesh. He reached behind her and pulled the ties that held her breasts confined and slowly released them.

She sighed and let the corset fall to the floor. Her breasts swayed in her chemise and with an urgent need he untied the bow and pushed the garment to the ground. Gripping the waistline of her pantaloons, she pulled them down, stepping gingerly from them.

Finally, she stood before him in all her naked glory. At the image of Ruby standing before him, thoughts of leaving town deserted him. He had to have her, now. One last time.

Blinded by her beauty, he let his fingers trail over her body, sliding from her shoulders, over her breasts, down to her waist, to the juncture between her thighs. Soft as satin and silk.

Their last joining had been frantic and hurried. This time he wanted to explore her body, linger over her curves, drive her to the brink of passion and relish in her ardor. This time had to last him a lifetime as he could not risk her life again. He couldn't watch another woman die.

Trembling fingers unbuttoned his shirt and pushed it past his shoulders. The touch of her warm hand as she glided over his chest, exploring him until he thought he would burst from wanting her. From needing to be inside her.

Her hands brushed the waistband of his pants and he yanked them away. "If you don't stop, I won't last much longer," he gasped. "I want this to be slow. To enjoy each other."

She smiled and the fire in her gaze scorched him with need. He doubted he could go any slower. Just her look was enough to push him over the edge.

Dropping down to the bed, he quickly removed his boots, his socks and lowered his pants to the floor. The touch of her fingers wrapping around his hardened shaft, caused his breath to leave his body in a gasp.

Gently he cupped her center, his fingers exploring her innermost folds, while his lips wrapped around her nipples, sampling her sweet flesh.

"Oh, Deke," she sighed as she tried to crawl onto his lap and tried to push herself down onto his member, but he wouldn't let her.

He held her in place as his fingers brushed her satiny folds, tempting and teasing while her breathing rose faster and faster as she arched her back against his hand wanting more. Ruby was as responsive as a forest to a fire, hot and frenzied beneath his fingers. He wreaked havoc with her senses until he felt her tense, her breathing stopped as she crumbled beneath his hand.

"I need you," she cried and his lips silenced her as he plundered her mouth once again. When she went limp in his arms, he released her mouth and she fell onto the bed.

"Deke," she said with a sigh.

This was his dream for tonight. That he could satisfy her every way possible and leave her sated and exhausted until morning.

Crawling up beside her, he felt her hand wrap around his manhood. Desire rushed through him at the touch of her fingers sliding around his hardened flesh, flicking the head with a gentle stroke. He lay back enjoying the feel of her ministrations, letting the fierce pounding of his blood overwhelm him as pleasure pulsated through him in wafting waves.

She leaned over him, her hand still caressing him as her lips covered his. Greedily devouring him, he let her take the lead in the kiss as she moved her mouth over his, her tongue tracing the edges of his lips, her hand sliding up and down his blood-engorged manhood.

Sensations ricocheted through him as he lay back and let her fingertips work magic on him stroking him ever closer to the edge. So imminent that he lifted her up and pushed her onto her back, covering her body with his.

"Now," he said as he plunged inside her, needing to bury himself deep within and feel her flesh surrounding him.

Wrapping her legs around him, she met him stroke for stroke, whimpering as he slowed the pace, trying to make it last. He clasped her hands in his, plunging deeper and deeper, her soul melding with his, their bodies joining.

His lips found hers again as they breathed in the breath of life together. Joined as one, he felt Ruby's very life essence flowing around him as he gasped for breath. At this moment, he'd never felt closer to another person. Like they were a part of each other, their hearts racing, their souls mingling.

And he didn't want it to end.

Ruby had shown her strength, her vulnerabilities, her laughter, her love, she'd shared everything with him, while he'd only shown her his loyalty. He needed to give her more. He wanted to open his heart to her, but could never let himself be that vulnerable ever again.

Unable to hold back any longer, he felt Ruby tensing around him. "Deke," she cried as her body stiffened, her eyelashes fluttering against her cheeks.

"Ruby," he groaned helpless to hold back another second, his body betrayed him and sent him spiraling to the moon and back. What was it about Ruby that he couldn't let go? Why did she affect him even more than Laura ever had? Why did she feel so right in his arms?

~

Ruby lay beside Deke, her breathing slowly returning to normal, wondering what had just happened. The first time they'd been together, it had been enjoyable, but this time there seem to be so much more. This time Deke had touched her soul and left his mark on her heart.

Deke curled around her on the bed, pulling her tight against him, his arms wrapped securely around her. And it felt like the most natural place for her to be in the world. Like she belonged beside him.

And yet, there had been no declarations of love or marriage or even next week. Nothing had been talked about. Just the urge to join, which they'd finally satisfied after all these years of dancing. But was their desire for each really quenched? Or had they just awakened the beast of longing?

"Was it this good between you and Laura," she asked out of the blue, wondering if this delicious gratification was only with Deke, unable to imagine she could feel this way with another man.

"No," Deke said, his body tensing. "Laura was special and sweet. But you…you're like jumping off a cliff, hoping there's water below to soften the blow and then plunging into warmth until you climb back to the surface. Being with you is nothing like Laura."

Ruby frowned, trying to understand what about his marriage to Laura had prompted him to never marry again. "She loved you very much, didn't she?"

"Yes," he said reluctantly. "She was happy and I did my best to keep her contented right up until the day she died."

"It wasn't your fault, she died in childbirth," Ruby said. "Lots of women die that way."

It was hard for Ruby to conceive that Deke would never marry again just because his first wife died in childbirth.

"You don't understand," he said. "It was *my* fault. A month before the baby was due, she asked me to stay home. I had one more bounty I wanted to catch. Then I wouldn't leave until the baby was a couple of months old. I promised I'd be home before the baby was born."

He sighed. "It took me a week longer than I planned to catch the criminal and then he was only worth a hundred dollars. When I got home, she'd been in labor for two days, alone."

Ruby tensed. "Why wasn't someone with her?"

This was Ruby's biggest fear of Annabelle somehow being left alone and going into labor. She'd been assured it could take hours, but what if Beau wasn't there? What if Ruby or Meg weren't there to help her? Ruby had promised Annabelle, she wouldn't miss the birth of her baby.

"We lived in her family home about a mile from town. Her mother and father had passed on and her brother was killed years earlier. My mother, who I asked to watch over her, was ill and didn't want to risk giving the illness to Laura. Why she didn't send someone else, I don't know. But Laura was alone for two days in labor. When I arrived she was weak, barely conscious and needing water. I was surprised she didn't die that night."

Ruby swallowed, she couldn't imagine trying to have a baby alone. No wonder Deke felt so much anguish about the death of his wife. No wonder he felt so much guilt.

He took a deep breath and released it slowly. "I just about killed my horse getting to the doctor. Then he took his sweet time getting back to the house. It was a mile. A mere mile out of town and it took him two hours to arrive."

A shiver of angst went rippling through Ruby. "Why?"

"He didn't believe me that her labor was as far along as it was. So he stopped by to deliver some medicine. By the time he got to the house, I'd delivered the baby. He was stillborn..." his voice cracked. "The cord was wrapped around his tiny throat. Laura held him and whatever strength she'd had left, seemed to seep out with her tears. Together we held our son and wept at his loss. Two hours later, I lost Laura as well. I lost my son and my wife because I chose one last bounty."

"The doctor not arriving didn't help," Ruby said.

"No, but I should have been there."

A tear trickled down Ruby's face and she quickly swiped it away. What could she say that would ease this man's pain? Tension radiated from his body like the rays of the sun, though they were colder than a Montana blizzard.

"I know you Deke Culver. You went on that last bounty to make certain you had earned enough money to take care of your family. You would never have knowingly left her alone."

"No," he said. "We didn't need the money. I went on that last bounty thinking that was my last chance to hunt before I became saddled with a family. I wanted the thrill one more time. And it cost me everything."

For a moment she was silent. She loved the hunt just as much if not more than he did. Yet now he wanted to raise horses and she wanted to continue hunting. He'd lost everything doing what he loved. Would she?

"I'm never getting married again because I'm not going to kill another woman with my selfishness. If I'd been home, Laura would be here today. This is my punishment."

How could she respond to his grief? How could she explain to someone that they weren't entirely at fault? Yes, he should have returned home sooner, but she might have died even with him there.

"You don't know that. You said yourself she was small boned. Maybe it was just her time to die," Ruby said.

"Maybe, but she would have had a better chance if I'd been there."

"You're right. If there is ever a woman again who is expecting your child, then you're there with her when it's her time. But even then there are no guarantees she'll survive," Ruby said, her heart aching. He'd made a terrible choice and paid a huge price.

A choice that would affect any hope of Ruby having a future with this man. Because she was realizing that until Deke forgave himself for the terrible choices he'd made, he'd never be with another woman, including Ruby.

"No. I promised myself after Laura that I would never get another woman pregnant."

"Excuse me. I could be expecting a child at this very moment," Ruby said.

He sighed. "You were the exception. I'm praying that we're safe. But I couldn't keep my hands off you."

"Just like I can't keep mine off of you," Ruby said snuggling deeper into him, feeling him harden once again.

"We can't," Deke muttered. "We just can't."

"And I say that we can," Ruby said, as she turned in his arms and covered his lips with hers. She poured her heart and soul into her mouth, hoping that she could heal Deke.

She wasn't sure what tomorrow would bring. She wasn't even certain that she would live past tomorrow, and Lord she had no idea what would happen between her and Deke, but she wanted this moment. She needed this time with this man. A chance to heal his wounds and satisfy the attraction she'd always felt for Deke.

He broke off the kiss. "I should go."

"No, stay the night. Stay because we could both die tomorrow. There's no guarantee that we'll get out of here alive."

By the light of the lantern she could see his frown as he relaxed against her. "Just tonight."

"That's all I'm asking for," she said and pulled his lips down to hers once again.

Chapter Thirteen

The next day, Hannah lounged in the living room of the bordello, knowing the night would be here before she was ready and she would have to spend the evening entertaining men in her room. If Ruby didn't take her when she left, Hannah already had the poison to kill herself.

She couldn't live this way any longer. She couldn't continue to be pawed by men and used like her body was a vessel for their exploitation. As a young girl she'd dreamed of a husband and a family and loving way of life. Now she awoke each morning with dreams of freedom.

And if possible, revenge against the man who'd sold her into this terrible life.

The whores in the house told her she'd come to accept her lot, but she didn't envision her life spent on her back satisfying unknown men. All she could think about was how to wound the man who'd done this to her. But if she couldn't escape, then poison would be her final retreat.

Though even then she hoped she could come back and haunt her stepfather.

She picked up a book determined to get lost in a story and no longer think about her situation. Right now she had to wait and give Ruby time. The other women were lounging in their robes, talking amongst themselves and just hanging out waiting.

A man was climbing the stairs and the women all instantly perked up waiting to see who he would choose to while away the afternoon with. Hannah shrunk deeper in her book hoping he wouldn't see her.

"Hannah Williams?"

She raised her eyes and gazed up at the man.

"Candy from an admirer," he said handing her the box. She gazed up at him in shock. No one had ever sent her candy before.

"Thank you," she whispered and watched him disappear.

The women crowded around her.

"Whose it from," Clara asked.

"I…I don't know," Hannah said. She opened the box timidly. She was afraid to let the girls see the note, but all it said was, *'Yours Truly, GR.'*

Oh my God, that meant they were leaving today. The GR stood for get ready. They were taking her away from here. A thrill of excitement scurried down her spine and she looked up at the women and smiled.

"Hannah has a sweetheart," Clara said.

"No. But he does like me," she said.

The women all laughed. "Wait until his wife finds out."

"He doesn't have one," she said leading them on, letting them think that there truly was a man in her life. Maybe that would help her to escape.

"Here have some candy," she said passing the box to each one of the ladies. "We don't get a treat very often."

"Oh, I get plenty of treats," Clara said laughing.

Hannah slowly walked to her room, needing some space and time away from the ladies. Time to pack up her meager supplies and prepare for a long hard journey out of hell.

Grabbing a satchel from under the bed, she filled the bag with the few things she'd collected that she wanted to save. A tintype of her mother. A nice dress, the poison, a book her father had given her when she was a young girl. Everything else in this prison could stay.

Two words meant two this afternoon. Now the hard part began. Waiting for two o'clock.

~

Tingles of nerves raced up and down Ruby's spine like a horse race sprinting at the sound of the shot. She'd checked out of the hotel and set-up the reserved room like she truly had a private poker game about to start.

Now all she needed was Rivera to show up and for her to get him out the back door of the hotel without being seen.

Deke would locate Hannah and then come back to the room to help her with Rivera. Last night she held Deke and comforted him while he'd told her about Laura. He'd suffered terrible consequences because of a bad decision. A bad decision anyone including Ruby could make. His tale had made her long to get home as soon as possible to Annabelle.

Wasn't her sister in the same situation? Hadn't she told Annabelle just one more hunt before the baby came? Though her husband Beau should be there with her, Ruby felt the need to be at her side.

As much as she loved being a bounty hunter, remembering family and loved ones came first was something Ruby struggled with. And Deke struggled as well.

The door to the room opened and James Rivera sauntered in, his spurs jangling in the empty room. He stopped in the doorway and let his eyes roam over her. She had to steel her nerves to keep from shuddering under his perusal. "Where is everyone?" he said grinning. "Am I the first to arrive?"

"Good afternoon, Mr. Rivera," she said schooling the features on her face not to show her hatred of the man who'd killed her father. "Why don't you have a seat at the table, while I pour you a drink?"

She needed to get the sleeping powder in him that she'd purchased over at the local mercantile.

"Oh honey, can't you do better than just liquor. I mean it looks like we've got some time before everyone arrives.

Why don't you sit on my lap and let's get to know one another?"

Revulsion, roared through Ruby like an angry tiger. The thought of this man touching her was enough for her stomach to sway like the bow of a ship, leaving her nauseous.

She smiled and pretended like she didn't have any idea what he wanted. She'd put a little sleeping powder in his drink and was hoping it was fast acting enough he'd soon feel the effects. "Let me get you that drink, first."

"To hell with the drink. Get your pretty little ass over here and let's play before everyone else arrives," he said pointing to his lap.

Ruby poured him a drink and took it to him. He pulled her onto his lap. Cringing inside, she schooled her expression into a smile, while she seethed. Soon enough she'd get even.

"Tell me who all is playing today." He grabbed the drink and tossed it down. She breathed a sigh of relief. He'd soon be drugged.

Saying the names of the biggest players in the saloon, he began to run his hand up under her skirt. Nausea rose inside her, threatening to spill as she halted his hand on her thigh.

A knock sounded on the door. Relief filled her and had her leaping from Rivera's lap, grateful to whoever was at the door. Opening the portal, Deke stood before her. She couldn't contain her smile, happiness washing over her like a gentle rain.

"You ready?" he asked.

"Let's do this together," she said.

"Okay, but try to block his view of me. I don't want him to recognize me until the last moment," Deke said pulling his gun out of his holster. He walked behind her, his head lowered, his hat pulled down low.

"Here's our second player," Ruby said, loud enough that Rivera sighed and straightened up. He stood and faced Deke.

"I don't think I've played against you…" Suddenly his eyes widened with recognition and he glanced at the gun pointed at his midsection. He jumped up to make a dash out of the room.

Deke moved to block his escape.

Ruby stepped over to the liquor, she lifted the whiskey bottle from the table and smashed the glass over the back of his head, knocking him unconscious. He slumped to the ground.

"Problem solved," she said with a grin.

Deke started laughing. "That's one way to get a man's attention."

"He wouldn't drink his whiskey fast enough. He just kept stalling and I was so glad to see you."

Quickly she hugged him to her. She felt almost light-headed with excitement at the idea of leaving this dirty town behind them.

"Let's get out of here and get you home," he said gazing at her his eyes so full of emotion. "The horses are behind the hotel and Hannah should be waiting."

She grabbed Deke's face and pulled him in for a quick kiss slanting her mouth over his. Elation flooded her. They had their bounty, the man who'd killed her father. They were going home. Releasing him, she smiled. "Let's go."

Picking up Rivera, the outlaw moaned as they placed his arms around their necks and helped him out the door. Walking into the main area of the hotel, several men checking in, glanced up. Rivera groaned and tried to open his eyes.

"Clara is going to be so upset with you for drinking too much," Ruby said, loud enough the men could hear. "She was expecting you tonight. Let's splash some water from the horse trough and maybe you'll wake up."

Ruby could feel her heart pounding with excitement. Nothing could beat this feeling of stealing a bounty right from beneath their very noses with the men not realizing there was a problem. It was the best aphrodisiac in the world.

The men went back to registering not bothering them or even acting suspicious. They stepped outside the back door and one of Mrs. Hutchin's goons came around the corner of the hotel.

"Is he hurt?" he asked.

"No, just drunk," Ruby said smiling hoping he would keep going and not ask any more questions.

Oh God, this was not what they needed at this moment. Hannah chose that moment to come around the corner of the hotel into the alley.

"Hey, what's going on? Where are you going?" he shouted noticing her suitcase.

She took her satchel and swung it at the man. It did very little to stop him. Turning around he ran towards Hannah but when he'd almost reached her, Ruby stuck out her foot, tripping the bouncer. He fell onto his face and slid into the building, hitting his head. He groaned, still moving.

Hannah ran to his side, reached under her skirt and ripped off pieces of her petticoat. Hurriedly, she began to tie him up with strips of the fabric. When she'd finished with his hands and feet, she took a piece and stuffed it in his mouth, tying the wad around his head.

"Sorry, but I'm not going back to the brothel," she said finishing up with a flourish, her breathing heavy, her hands shaking. "I'm not being left behind."

Ruby and Deke had been working to get Rivera tied up and on a horse. Together they lifted him onto the mare and tied his hands to the saddle horn. His head hung limp.

Finally it appeared they were ready to ride. Deke lifted the puppy and put him in the sling he had tied to his body. The dog nestled against his chest. "Let's go." Deke said.

"Thank God," Hannah said.

"Let's go home," Ruby said ready to see Rivera back behind bars where he belonged.

The women mounted their horses and he led the way out a side road behind the hotel. In less than ten minutes, they would be out of town and out of Hide Town, Texas hopefully forever.

~

As soon as she'd received his message that they needed to talk in private, Mrs. Hutchins had left the saloon and headed to the sheriff's office.

Walking through the town, she noticed how the shops were bustling with business, the restaurant had customers and even the mercantile.

Since she'd purchased the saloon almost three years ago, the town had changed and grown. Sure it was still a place where more outlaws than law-abiding folks resided, but at least the businesses prospered. She like to think she had something to do with that, since she'd been the one to bring in the sheriff making the outlaws know they were accepted as long as they behaved.

Outright anarchy only caused death and desperation.

The opening of the bordello had brought in more cowboys and less outlaws. Cowboys you could control. Outlaws had no control.

The sun beamed down on her and she knew that winter would soon be here, but today was warm, almost hot.

Opening the door to the sheriff's office, she strolled in. "Good afternoon, Sheriff."

"Emily. I'm glad you came as soon as you did. Have a seat," he said. He walked over to the chair she sat in and then leaned back against the desk. "Where is Miss Callahan?"

"She hadn't come in yet when I left. Why? What's going on?"

"I'm suspicious. I think she's really Ruby McKenzie. Look at the telegram I received from the sheriff in Mineral Wells" he said a frown gathering between his eyebrows.

She reached out and took the telegram. As she read the few lines, outrage pumped through her veins like a slow burn. She looked at the sheriff, her voice cool and refined. "This description fits her. Any idea who she's after?"

"No," he said. "And she hasn't made any arrests."

Though Emily had never had a run in with the law, she knew many of the men who frequented her saloon had bounties on them.

"And her friend Deke Culver I learned is also a bounty hunter. The two of them must be working together."

Emily thought of the man she'd seen almost every night in her saloon, the way one of her whores had tried to seduce him and Ruby's reaction. All the evidence had been right there in front of Emily and she'd let herself be duped by this girl. Until now. Ruby would soon find herself working upstairs or dead, her choice.

"What are you going to do?"

"I've already sent one of my deputies over to the hotel, to bring them both back. Seems they've broken several laws in our city and they'll be spending time in the calaboose."

Emily smiled. "I knew you would handle whatever problems we found on those two. After several days in jail, I'm sure Ruby will love to work off her fines in the bordello. Then once we've tired of her, you can dispose of the body."

The girls who worked for her knew better than to double cross her or the consequences they would face. Everyone obeyed except for Hannah…and even she had recently been following the rules.

He reached down and lifted her chin in his hands. "I don't know where you learned such shrewd business skills, but it makes me appreciate you all the more."

She smiled at him. "I'm glad you approve. I enjoy our arrangement."

"Sunday night?"

"Of course," she said knowing exactly what he expected and even looking forward to their time together. The man liked control and for one night a week, she let him have what he needed.

"What about our prisoners?" she asked wanting to make certain that the pair would not get away from the sheriff.

"Should be in the jail just any moment now," he said with a laugh. "I'm going to enjoy Miss McKenzie's visit and Deke Culver has captured his last bounty."

Emily stood and smiled. She laid her hand on his arm and gazed up at him. "I know I can always count on you, Sheriff. I would stay, but I've got other business to attend to. Let me know when you have them in custody."

He pulled her against his chest, his hand gripping her ass. "I'll send you a message."

With a caress of his cheek, she pulled out of his arms. "Thank you Sheriff."

Walking out the door, she sighed. She'd use the sheriff as long as she could. But now she had to get back to the saloon. Back to her business. And she would be talking to Hannah to learn if she knew Ruby was a bounty hunter.

Stepping off the wooden sidewalk to the street below, she glanced down a side street. There they were. There was Deke, Hannah, Ruby and Rivera riding away from the hotel.

"Sheriff," she yelled turning around and running back up the steps.

He came running out of the building. "What? What's wrong?"

"They're getting away. They have Rivera and Hannah. They're riding away."

"Damn it. We're going after them."

~

Deke heard the church bells ringing and knew they'd been detected. Even in outlaw towns, church bells were used for communication.

Rivera was barely hanging onto the saddle, still they had to ride fast.

"Come on, ladies, we've been discovered," he said. Reaching down he made sure the pup was secure and then kicked the sides of his horse.

After a few moments he'd not worried about Hannah on a horse. It was evident she knew how to ride and Ruby, certainly knew how to sit a horse. But Rivera was slowing them down, holding them up. The man barely knew what was going on and if they lost him, then everything they'd gone through would be for naught.

And Ruby wouldn't rest until he'd been captured. She'd be back in Hide Town before the sun sank, trying to locate and seize the outlaw again.

"Let's go," he yelled, urging them to ride faster. Hannah kicked the sides of her horse and led the way, but Ruby was not leaving Rivera's side.

Deke had prayed they would have more time before the sheriff realized they were gone and had taken Rivera with them, but somehow they'd been outed. In this part of Texas, the only thing standing between Indian Territory and the Brazos River were a few scrub bushes and some mesquite trees. Nothing else. Nowhere to hide, unless they rode along the river. At least on the river there were cliffs with a few trees. Cliffs where they could either hole up or a sharp shooter could take aim at them.

With sudden clarification, he knew they had only one chance. Get to Fort Griffin where soldiers were stationed. Where they could tell the law about Hide Town, where only corruption existed.

He rode up beside Ruby, their horses legs stretched at almost full gallop. "Change of plans. We're going to Fort Griffin."

"No," she screamed as they rode. "The soldiers are not in town. There's no law to protect us."

Deke nodded in understanding. There was no one to stop the sheriff and his men from coming into town and taking their prisoner and Hannah back to Hide Town.

"Okay, to the Brazos," he said and took off to lead the way with Hannah right beside him. The girl had a fierce look on her face like she would defy anyone who tried to take her back.

Ruby hung back riding alongside Rivera. Deke knew that soon, very soon they would see a posse and he just hoped they made it to the river before they caught up with them. That was their only hope of escape. Reach the other side and hopefully they'd give up or they'd have to shoot their way out of here.

A shot resounded. A bullet whizzed not far from his head, his nerves tingled with alarm. They'd run out of time and they'd yet to reach the river bank. He pulled his gun out and leaned over his horse, taking aim at the sheriff. Maybe if he shot the leader, the others would give up.

Bouncing in the saddle, he fired his weapon. The bullet went astray.

When he glanced back he could see the posse, but Ruby had slowed way down. She and Rivera were almost a quarter mile behind him.

He watched as she grabbed the reins of the man's horse and speeded up the galloping animal. Rivera swayed in the saddle and Deke feared he'd fall.

"Leave him," Deke yelled and she shook her head vehemently. He watched as she put more distance between her and the posse. His knuckles gripped the reins tightly, fearing for her safety. If they captured her, he'd have no choice but to go back. They weren't getting Ruby without a fight.

Hannah and him reached the river and begin to lead their horses down the steep bank to the water. Carefully they made their way down, letting their horses take the lead, bouncing in the saddle. He glanced back over his shoulder waiting for Ruby. If she didn't make it to the bank by the time he got Hannah down, he'd return for her.

Reaching the river's edge, Hannah looked at him anxiously, her eyes wide and for the first time fear shown from her eyes.

"Go ahead and cross."

"I can't swim."

"Your horse will get you across the river."

"I'll wait for you," Hannah said frightened. "I hate water."

"No," he glanced back behind him. He could hear horse's hooves pounding. The posse had to be close. With dread he went ahead and leading Hannah's horse, they began to cross the river. The water climbed up higher and higher on the horse reaching his waist, soaking each of them as they finally reached the other side.

Deke glanced behind him, knowing if Ruby wasn't making her way down the bank, he'd return across the river and drag her back with or without Rivera, he didn't care.

A horse screamed and he watched in horror as Rivera's horse buckled the animal's leg breaking. His heart wrenched with pain for the animal. Ruby stopped and climbed down off her animal.

She helped Rivera from the stricken horse. The outlaw swayed on his feet, the sleeping powder obviously making him drowsy.

"Leave him," Deke yelled. They would catch Rivera another time.

Ruby ignored him, she glanced behind her and even Deke could see the posse riding fast, closing in.

She slapped her horse on the rump, sending him down the embankment. Half dragging Rivera she walked to a cliff that hung out over the river. Suddenly Deke knew what she was going to do.

"No," he screamed, his heart pounding at the realization of what she intended on doing.

Ignoring his screams, he stared, realizing at this moment that he loved this woman. Had probably loved her since the first time they met and now he was going to witness her death. He was going to watch another woman he cared about die. Ruby was the fiercest, most loving woman he'd ever known. She challenged him, made him stronger and now he was going to lose her.

"No," he screamed again, wanting to stop her, paralyzed with fear. Knowing he couldn't stop her.

Backing up she ran dragging Rivera with her, pulling him along as she hurtled the two of them off the cliff. With a loud splash they landed in the middle of the river.

Another bullet landed in the dirt beside his feet and Deke stepped behind a large rock. The pup raised his head and licked his chin.

"Sorry girl," he said and pushed her back down into the sling. Now might not have been a great time to have a dog.

He searched the river trying to see where Ruby had come up. The skirt she was wearing would weigh her down, Rivera could choose that moment to hold her under the water and kill her if he wanted to.

The posse could shoot her in the water. His heart pounded in his chest. A body popped up out of the water. It was Rivera. He was unconscious or dead.

Ruby was nowhere in sight. Nowhere. Pain flooded his chest as his heart felt like someone had wrenched it from his chest. She was gone and he couldn't jump in to find her. He couldn't save her.

The posse sat on their horses watching Rivera's body float down the river. A petticoat drifted alongside the man, but there was no sign of Ruby. Tears filled his throat and he wanted to scream in anguish, yet he had to keep his wits about him. There were guns across the river that wanted him dead. That wanted Hannah dead.

A shot hit the rock in front of him. He stepped around and fired, hitting the sheriff in the arm. Quickly he stepped back behind the shield.

"Son of a bitch," the man screamed.

Another round of bullets echoed along the river embankment. When the firing stopped, Deke heard horses galloping away. He peaked out from behind the stone. They were riding away. They were leaving. After a moment, when he was certain they were gone, he hurried down the embankment, running along the river, searching for Ruby. He jumped into the river, looking everywhere, hoping he'd see her and find her in time to save her.

Walking knee high in the gurgling river, he searched, the rocks making walking difficult.

The body of Rivera floated down a ways.

With a splash she rose out of the water. She stood giggling, wiping the water from her face, her body drenched. "That was fun."

She was alive. She was breathing and she didn't appear harmed. And he loved her.

She bent over and laughed. "Flying off that cliff and landing in the water. I've never done that before. That was fun, hiding from them."

She stood in the river chuckling, like she'd had the best time.

He stared at her like he was seeing a crazy woman as anger surged threatening to choke him. He'd thought she was dead.

He thought she'd drowned.

He thought he'd lost her forever.

And yet she had probably played this perfectly. She'd hidden beneath Rivera's body, her nose out of the water just enough to breathe while she floated down the river with his body.

Deke felt the urge to scream at her. He was so angry and yet they didn't have time. They needed to get out of here just in case the posse had a change of heart and decided to return.

She smiled at him, noticing his silence for the first time. "Are you okay?"

"I'm fine." The words were curt and to the point. "Let's go."

She whistled and her mare that had been standing a ways down the river swam across to the bank. "Where's Hannah?"

"She's on the ridge waiting for us."

"Help me get him out of the water," she said, pulling Rivera's body to the edge.

Somehow she'd managed to hang onto Rivera under the toughest odds. Yet how many more times could she escape without someone putting a bullet in her? He couldn't watch her die.

"Is he dead?" Deke asked.

"I don't think so. I think he bumped his head when we jumped," she said. "I've never done anything like that before. It was fun until I felt like my petticoats were going to drown me. When I pulled it off, I could swim in the deeper parts of the river."

He'd thought she'd been dead. He feared he'd killed another woman. And she had enjoyed herself so much, she was laughing. Relief and rage filled him, but he bit back the retort that sprang to his lips. He lifted Rivera up and placed him on the back of Ruby's horse. He tied the man across the back, wrapping the ropes around the horse and his body.

"There that should hold him until we stop to make camp. Let's get out of here before that posse returns."

Chapter Fourteen

When the sun had completely sank behind the western sky and they could no longer see where they were going, Deke had let them stop for the evening. But there would be no fire tonight.

Ruby watched as Hannah took out their supplies from the saddle bags. She located the hardtack and placed it on a hot rock she'd found that had been sitting out in the sun all day.

"My Ma showed me how to do this," she said handing Ruby the warmed up hard biscuit.

Deke sat not far from where the girls were laid out on their bedrolls, his face hard, staring off into space. The puppy lay beside him and every little bit, he would throw her a piece of the hardtack biscuit and the dog would gaze at him with adoring eyes. Even in the darkness, she could see the bond that had developed between the man and his dog.

But something was wrong. Since this afternoon, he'd been quiet and surly and distant. Last night he'd cuddled and comforted her in ways she'd never imagined. Tonight he barely glanced in her direction.

"Here, Deke," Hannah said, handing him another biscuit. He took it and quickly ate the food. He stood and disappeared into the darkness with the dog trailing after him.

Ruby frowned. She didn't know what was amiss, but he wasn't acting himself. Even at his worst, Deke was always amicable. Tonight he'd withdrawn so far into himself she didn't know if she could reach him. She needed to check on him. Find out what was wrong.

"Hannah, can you watch Rivera? I need to talk to Deke," Ruby said standing.

Rivera had not awoken since the splash in the river. Maybe he'd hit his head somehow when they jumped. She didn't know if it was a temporary condition or permanent and frankly she didn't care.

"Sure, what do I need to do?" Hannah asked.

Ruby pulled out her extra six-shooter and handed it to Hannah. "He should continue sleeping, but just keep the gun trained on him. If he wakes up, give me a shout. I won't be gone long or far."

"Okay," Hannah said taking the gun from her. "I've never used one of these before."

"It's easy just point and shoot."

Hurrying out of the dark camp, she looked for Deke. Walking along the river, she saw him with the horses, his head resting on his mare's forehead as he rubbed her ears.

"Hey, you all right?" she asked.

He whirled around to face her. Grabbing her by the arm, he all but dragged her away from the animals. "No, I'm not all right."

This wasn't exactly the reception she'd expected. Once they were away from the horses, he released her. "Do you know what it was like for me today, to watch you jump off that cliff, not knowing if you were going to live or die? Do you have any idea how scared I was when I couldn't find you or even search the water because they were shooting at me?"

His voice was rising higher and higher in the darkness.

"No, but I was okay. Other than a few bruises, I'm fine." She'd never seen him so angry. Her fun-loving, caring man was red-faced, his eyes dark and his body tense. For a moment, her stomach leaped into her throat at the anger she could see on his face in the moonlight.

"Well I'm not fine. I probably lost twenty years watching you fly off that cliff and hit the water. I thought you were dead. I thought I'd lost you."

"I'm okay," she said staring at him trying to make him feel better. She touched his arm, the muscles rigid. She shrugged her shoulders. It was sweet he'd been worried, but she'd found the jump exhilarating. Suspended between the earth and the water, she'd felt like she was floating in the air. "I'm sorry you got frightened, but it was actually kind of fun."

In the darkness, she could feel him bristle and knew she'd just said the wrong thing. "Fun! You take reckless chances with your life, thinking you're going to live forever. Well my wife and child are dead. I had to bury them. Your father is dead. You had to bury him. Life is fragile. You're not invincible."

Silence filled the darkness as Deke seemed to finally run out of steam. Ruby didn't know what to say. Jumping that cliff had been scary, but the thrill of what she'd done had made it all worthwhile. She'd do it again, if she got the chance.

"I'm never going to be a woman who just sits at home and does needlepoint. Never."

Deke ran his hand through his hair. "You don't get it. I'm not asking you *not* to be who you are. I'm frightened I'm going to witness you dying. And that scares the hell out of me."

How could she respond? What she did was a dangerous occupation. He knew that first hand. But it gave her freedom, independence and a chance to do something different than most women. She wasn't just another pretty woman getting married and raising kids.

She was unique.

"I'm not going to watch you die," he said. "One day Ruby, you're going to run out of luck and it's going to kill you."

Ruby threw up her hands in the air. "Deke, you worry too much. I'm fine."

Shaking his head at her, he closed his eyes. "This time you're okay. But what about the next stunt where you take a foolish chance? When are you going to miss the water when you jump off a cliff? Or when will someone recognize you in a saloon and pull out a gun and shoot you right there? Or think you're a whore and take advantage of you? When will I get there too late to save your pretty little behind and find you dead?"

Apprehension trickled down her spine. She knew she was taking chances, but she would be okay

"Deke, stop. If you're trying to scare me, it's not working," she said though several times his words had worried her. It could happen if she didn't have a trustworthy partner.

"We make a good team. We could bounty hunt together and make lots of money," she said raising her voice excitedly. "This could be our first trip."

She knew with certainty this was what she yearned for. To work with Deke to bring in outlaws, until they tired of the hunt and then maybe they'd settle down and get married, but she wasn't in any hurry. Could he want the same things?

He shook his head empathically. "I'm not staying around to watch you die."

"I'll be more careful. I won't take as many chances," she said. This was her dream. For the two of them to hunt side by side.

"No. I'm quitting. As soon as we turn Rivera in, I'm getting out of the business and starting a horse farm. I'm giving up bounty hunting."

A sigh escaped her lips. "I thought we could find criminals together."

Closing his eyes, he sighed. "I can't. I can't take a chance on being a part of your death."

"Would you stop saying I'm going to die. I'm not going

to get killed," she said raising her voice, her hands on her hips.

They stood there, in the darkness, staring at each other, the puppy sitting beside Deke, watching them. Ruby didn't know what to say any more. She wanted being with Deke to continue, but he didn't seem interested and that wounded her pride. She was good at what she did and hungered for what she and Deke had to continue. She wasn't ready for them to end. She wasn't ready for him to leave her.

"Is Hannah watching Rivera?" he asked suddenly.

"He's still asleep. I gave her a gun and told her to yell at me if he woke up."

"Does she know how to use a gun?" Deke asked quickly striding towards the camp area. "After everything we've done to catch Rivera I can't believe you're taking a chance on him escaping."

Ruby hurried to catch up. "He's asleep."

Deke all but ran back into camp with Ruby and the pup following closely on his heels. When they approached where they had spread their bedrolls, they saw Rivera held the gun against Hannah's forehead.

"About time you guys got back. Now get me a horse. I'm not going back to jail."

Ruby's stomach tightened into a cramp at the sight of Rivera holding the gun on Hannah. She wanted to call herself nine times a fool. First with Deke and now with Rivera. All the work they'd done in the Hide Town was now going to be for naught. Hannah looked frightened and who could blame her. The man had her up against his chest with Ruby's gun being held against her temple. One wrong move and he would kill her.

"I'm sorry, Ruby," she said tears swimming in her eyes. "He tricked me."

"It's okay," she said wanting to kick herself for being such a fool. He must have been faking sleep this entire time.

"I'll get you a horse," Deke said.

"No, I want that bitch there that tricked me to get the horses. She's going with me," he demanded.

The dog growled a menacing sound.

"Keep that mutt away from me or I'll shoot it."

"Sh, girl," Deke said holding his hand down.

Fear spiraled through Ruby and she wished she could go back in time and never leave Hannah alone with the outlaw. This was all her fault. She should never have taken the risk. Now Deke and Hannah were in danger because of her.

"No, she's not," Deke responded.

Rivera cocked the hammer back on the gun and twisted the gun to point at Deke and then back to Hannah. "Do you want me to put a bullet in her head?"

"No. Just let the woman go. I'll ride back to town with you," Deke promised.

"Oh no, the women are going with me," he said.

Ruby knew in that instant that he intended to kill Deke. She wanted to get the horses and check to make sure that she still had her little petticoat pistol. She'd yanked off the heavy petticoat to keep from drowning and to make everyone think she'd died.

But had she gotten rid of her petticoat pistol? Even if she found the gun, would there have been time for the flint to have dried?

"It's okay Deke. Let me get the horses," she said and stepped into the darkness where the man couldn't see her. She yanked up her skirt praying she'd not lost the petticoat that held her gun and hoping if the pistol was there, it had dried enough to fire.

In the darkness, she sighed with relief when her fingers felt the steel barrel. Thank God. She untethered the horses and pulled them with her, carefully concealing the gun in her skirt.

When she walked back into camp, they were all waiting. Staring at Hannah, she hoped the girl could somehow get her message. Saying a quick prayer, she whipped the gun from its hiding place just as Deke dove towards Hannah.

Ruby's gun fired, flashing in the darkness, but so did Rivera's. She thought she'd feel a bullet slamming into her body any second, but nothing happened. Rivera fell to the ground a bullet wound to his head. Hannah kicked his gun away where he couldn't reach it any longer.

In slow motion, Ruby watched as Deke sank to the ground. Her chest exploded with pain as she realized he was hurt. A scream ripped from her throat. "No. Deke. No."

Oh my God, where was he hurt?

She rushed to his side and rolled him over. "Deke, talk to me. Deke, tell me where you're hurt."

Unconscious, he didn't respond.

The puppy whined and moved closer to Deke. The animal licked his hand and nudged him with her nose, but Deke didn't move. Tears filled Ruby's throat.

"Is he alive?" Hannah asked.

"I don't know."

Ruby's fingers touched the side of his neck, searching for a pulse. She could feel his heart racing, she could feel his breath on her fingers, but his eyes were shut and blood. Blood trickled from the edge of his forehead. She pulled him into her lap, and carefully examined the head wound.

Staring down into his face, her heart swelled with love and fear and longing. She loved this man. Had probably fallen in love with him when she was a young girl. He'd never left her heart and watching him fall to the ground fearing he was dead, she'd realized she loved Deke.

Rocking him in her arms, tears flowed unchecked down

her cheeks. He wasn't dead, she had to take care of him. She had to protect him.

"What's wrong?" Hannah asked.

"He's wounded. It's not deep. The bullet made a path across the top of his forehead and his head," she ripped a strip of her petticoat and held it against the wound, stemming the seeping blood.

Hannah knelt beside her. "Is he going to be okay?"

"I think so. I'm hoping the bullet just knocked him out," Ruby said holding his head in her lap, gazing at him. Was this how Deke had felt today when she'd jumped into the river?

This overwhelming sense of loss and pain and heart wrenching, gut seizing agony? What if he didn't wake up? What if she'd lost him forever? What if he died before she ever had the chance to tell him she loved him?

The dog lay as close to Deke as she could get, her head resting on his leg.

"What can I do to help?" Hannah said.

"Say a prayer that he's okay. I'm so scared."

~

The next morning, Deke woke feeling like he'd been kicked in the head by a bull. Groggy and weak, he felt his head. Touching the bandage, caused a whole new round of insistent, painful rat-a-tat-tat in his brain. The skin around his wound was swollen and tender. And then like the rising of the sun, he remembered.

Rivera had a gun against Hannah's forehead. He intended to kill Deke and Ruby firing her little pistol, the searing burning sensation in his forehead and then darkness. Deep, dark blankness filled his mind from last night until the lightening of the sky.

How long had he been out? He glanced around and noticed it was still their same camp, only now a dead body lay several feet away, his face covered, wrapped in a blanket and tied with ropes.

Rolling over he searched the bedrolls. Hannah lay curled up not far from Ruby's empty blankets.

When he moved, he awakened the dog that had been sleeping next to him. She jumped up and licked his face, covering him with dog slobber, whining and jumping excitedly, beside herself with happiness.

He rubbed the back of her ears and tried to settle her down, so as to keep his head from pounding even worse.

The sound of retching, of someone losing the contents of their stomach reached his ears and he glanced around. It had to be Ruby. He started to rise to check on her. Had the jump from the cliff somehow injured her internally? Had she been hurt after he'd been shot?

Slowly coming to his feet, he stood for a moment, swaying side to side trying to get his balance under control. Finally he felt steady and walked out of the immediate area searching for Ruby with the puppy close at his heels.

He found her sitting on a rock not far from the bedding.

"Deke," she said. "Oh my God! You scared me. You shouldn't be up."

"I bet I look better than you do. What's wrong? Are you hurt?"

She shook her head. "No."

"Then why are you over here vomiting?"

"It's the weirdest thing. I woke up this morning nauseous and feeling like nothing would sit on my stomach. As soon as I stood, I had to run to get out of camp before I threw up."

Deke stared at her, fear making his heart pound in his chest in time with his head. The memory of Laura throwing up every morning for the first two months she'd learned she was expecting sent tremors of fear spiraling down his spine. It had only been a week. It was way too early to know if Ruby was expecting, but still he'd heard of women being sick from the moment of conception.

No, not Ruby. She could die.

"When was the last time you had your monthly flow?" he asked.

"What kind of question is that? Is it any of your business?"

How could he have done this again? After everything he'd witnessed with Laura's death, he'd gotten another woman with child. He'd broken his vow to himself and now Ruby would pay the price for his lust.

"No, but what if you're pregnant? What if you're experiencing morning sickness?"

"No. I'm not having babies at this point in my life. I refuse. My independence is much more important."

"You may not have any say," he said. "If you're already expecting."

Part of him understood her reasoning and part of him was disappointed that she didn't want their child. But then again, he didn't want her expecting. How could he feel so confused? So torn? This was such a mess and it was all his fault.

She turned on him, her blue eyes flashing. "Let's get this straight. I'm not pregnant. I'd know it. I'd feel something. Besides it's only been a week since we..."

"You wouldn't know at first," Deke said quietly. "It hasn't been that long since we were together, but still you could be with child."

"No," she said her eyes suddenly worried. "Just no."

What more could he say? Fear clenched inside him at the idea of risking yet another woman's life to have his child. He wasn't going through another woman's labor and delivery of a child and lose them both in the end. He couldn't do it.

He couldn't lose Ruby.

"How are you feeling?"

"Lousy," he murmured.

All he could think about was the sound of Ruby retching and the consequences of them being together.

Never again. He'd sworn never again to get another woman pregnant and here he'd gone against his word. And if Ruby wasn't with child this time, if they kept on doing what felt so right between them, she'd soon find herself expecting.

And the girl would be very upset with him, not to mention he'd be devastated. He'd made a vow the night Laura died. He needed to remember that oath and get away from her before he impregnated Ruby.

She stood and they began the short walk back to camp. A sigh escaped her lips. "Are you feeling okay?"

"I'm better. We're still riding out of here today." The sooner he got Ruby home, the quicker he could ride away and put distance between the two of them. Unless she was expecting his child.

"What happened last night? How did you get shot?"

"If I knew, believe me I would have avoided that bullet," Deke said reaching up and touching the bandage. All he remembered was lunging for Hannah and then darkness.

She shook her head. "I was watching Rivera and the next thing I know you're on the ground and I've shot him."

"When I heard the explosion, I moved to knock Hannah out of the way. He fired at me and not at Hannah, but when I moved, I missed most of the bullet."

Ruby stopped and threw her hands around his neck. She pulled him to her and hugged him tightly. Her embrace was like a burst of energy, filling the empty places in his soul. But he couldn't enjoy the feel of her arms any longer. No more.

"Thank God, I didn't lose you or Hannah yesterday,"

she whispered against his neck.

"Rivera is dead," he said enjoying the feel of Ruby's body snug against his own. Soon, he had to put distance between them. Soon she'd be back in Zenith and he'd be down the road, separating them forever.

"We'll turn his dead body into the sheriff. But we're going to need to get back quickly. Are you able to ride?"

"I think so," he said. He stepped out of her arms. "We better wake Hannah and get going."

She tilted her head and gazed at him. "By tomorrow we'll be back in Zenith."

"Yes," he replied. He'd stay until he learned if Ruby was pregnant or not, but then he had to leave and he couldn't go near her again. He couldn't take the chance, though that was going to be harder than rounding up outlaws.

~

The next morning, Ruby knew she wasn't pregnant. This morning, her monthly flow had come to visit, leaving her achy and moodier than a bull next to a fenced pasture of heifers in heat. Sometime today they'd arrive home and she was quite ready for this adventure to end.

Since the shooting, Deke was acting different. She couldn't tell if he was hurting or if something was bothering him. Since the shooting she understood a little more about how he'd felt the day that she jumped off the cliff. Watching him lying there, blood trickling from his head wound, she'd felt more fear than she'd ever experienced in her life.

The thought of Deke dying had frightened her worse than Annabelle's disappearance. He'd been shot because of her and she felt bad enough about that. But if he'd died, she wouldn't have been able to live with herself. She could never tell him she loved him.

Holding him in her lap, while he didn't respond to her urgent cries for him to wake up, had been the worst moments of her life. And yet during that time, she realized she loved Deke. She loved him more than her next breath. She loved the way he made her feel. How he cared for her, how he was right. Someday there would be a bullet with her name on it, if she stayed in this business.

Yet, she didn't want a life like her sisters. She liked being independent. She liked earning her own money and doing something unique and different than most women. She liked the look of surprise on a criminal when they realized she was bringing him to justice.

How could she love Deke and keep doing what she enjoyed? How could she give up bounty hunting to be with Deke? But how could she live without him?

She didn't know. She didn't even know if he felt the same about her. For all she knew he would get her to Zenith and leave her with her memories of the two of them.

Half a mile out of Zenith she thought she should tell him the truth before they rode into town and her family descended upon them, giving them no time alone.

She rode her mustang close to his. He glanced over at her, his gaze not his usual warm and friendly look, but cautious. Withdrawn and moody the last couple of days, she felt like he was already riding away from her.

"I'm not pregnant," she said.

"We'll see."

"No, I know I'm not expecting a child."

His brows went up. "How?"

"Now that's a stupid question to ask a woman," she responded.

"Oh," he said suddenly understanding. "I'm glad."

Disappointment surged through Ruby. Tears clogged the back of her throat. She would not cry in front of him. No, she didn't want a baby. Her sisters were having babies.

She wanted to be a bounty hunter, didn't she? But the thought of having, Deke's baby…

No, she didn't want a baby. So why was she suddenly feeling sad that she wasn't pregnant? Why was she suddenly seeing images of their child?

"Anyway, I thought you would want to know."

"Thanks," he said. "We'll stop at the sheriff's office and drop off the body."

"Yeah," she said, suddenly unsure as to what would happen next. She didn't want Deke to leave, but why would he stay? What was keeping him here with her? And should she tell him that she loved him?

"What are you going to do next?" she asked.

He reached up and felt the bandage on his head. "I'm going home."

The dog poked her head out of the sling to make certain everything was okay. He stroked her ears and she went back to sleep.

Ruby bit her lip. She didn't want him to leave, but they had not talked about the two of them. The memory of him telling her he wasn't getting married returned and she swallowed. They didn't have to get married…but she knew her sisters would insist if they found out they had shared a bed.

"That makes two of us," she said quietly, wishing with all her heart that he would stay with her.

As they rode into town, she felt so uncertain about everything, except the fact that she didn't want Deke to leave. She didn't know what she wanted with the man, but she loved him, probably always had.

Thirty minutes after they arrived at the sheriff's office, they were on their way to the farm. The deputy had taken the body and recorded the bounty, but her brother-in-law Zach had taken Meg to the farm. Oh boy, that meant they were all gathered at the homestead and Ruby knew there would be hell to pay when they arrived for not returning with Caroline.

~

Deke knew he couldn't stay, yet he couldn't leave either. He couldn't ride off until he made certain that Ruby was safe. That she and Hannah were settled at the farm until after Annabelle had the baby. Then he would no longer be responsible for Ruby once he rode away. But until then, he had to make certain she was safe.

The woman was a walking disaster waiting to happen. And he didn't envy the sister's job of trying to keep her at home and out of trouble. It couldn't be easy.

When they rode up into the yard, the front door of the farmhouse flew open and both sisters came out. Annabelle was swollen with child and Deke knew her time would soon come. He said a small prayer that she'd be safe.

Meg was barely showing. Yet looking at both women, his heart wrenched with sorrow for Laura and his child. Could he ever look at a pregnant woman again, without his heart breaking in two?

"Ruby McKenzie, you are going to worry all of us into an early grave," Meg said beating Annabelle to her sister's side.

Ruby swung her leg over the saddle and jumped down and gave her older sister a hug. "Meg, you look so pretty. And the baby, oh my God you're showing."

Meg stopped and a glow came over her face and she smiled. "I felt her move the other day. We're so excited." Her brows drew together in a frown. "Don't change the subject. We've been worried sick about you."

Deke felt lonely as he watched the women. Sure he had a home, his mother and even an older brother, but nothing like what these women shared. Some families were close, some were not and his just happened to fall in the not so close category.

Annabelle waddled out and stared at her youngest sister. "If you didn't make it home before this baby was born, I was going to send out a search party." She glanced up at Deke. "Thank you so much for watching over her."

"I did a lousy job," he said. "She's a tough one to keep under control."

"That's why we like you Deke Culver, you tell it like it is," Meg said with a smile.

"Everyone this is Hannah. She's going to be staying with us for awhile," Ruby said.

"Just until I can find a decent job and get on my feet," the young woman said.

"Welcome," Meg said. "But don't be expecting much in the way of a job in Zenith. I'm surprised Ruby didn't warn you about how bad the jobs in Zenith."

"I'm going to help Hannah," Ruby said keeping her thoughts to herself about exactly how she intended to help the younger woman. No woman should be subjected to what Hannah had experienced in her life. Ruby would help her find a new way.

"Why don't you all climb down off your horses and come in," Annabelle said.

"Did you get Rivera?" Meg asked looking at Deke and then Ruby.

"Yes, he's dead," Ruby said. "I killed him."

Zach came out the door. "I hope it was in self-defense."

A zing of aggravation crawled up Deke's spine. He knew this was Ruby's brother-in-law the sheriff, but still the woman he loved would never intentionally kill someone who didn't deserve to die.

Deke took off his hat. "He was going to kill me. Ruby shot him."

Annabelle put a hand to her back. "I need to go sit down. Come in and tell us what happened. You too

Hannah. Come in and rest."

"I…are you sure? I could sleep in the barn," Hannah said quietly.

Ruby took Hannah by the arm. "Nonsense. You'll stay in my room with me. If I could sleep with Annabelle for all those years, I can sleep with you in there."

"But…" Hannah said and Ruby knew what she was thinking. The girl still thought of herself as a tainted woman, but that was pure hogwash. She'd done what she had to, to survive.

"Hannah, your new life begins today. Forget the past," Ruby said.

"Thanks Ruby, but I can't forget the past," Hannah said and walked with them into the house.

Chapter Fifteen

Deke sat through supper, his stomach churning, his nerves tense and knowing he had to get out of here. He couldn't stay another minute. He couldn't be there when Annabelle went into labor. He couldn't see her go through all the agony, the pain, the suffering. He couldn't take a chance he'd watch her die.

He walked out on the porch to get some air and stood staring up at the stars. If he could leave right now he would.

Ruby stepped outside. She linked her arm through his. "You seem restless. Is it seeing my pregnant sisters?"

She could read him so well, so why wasn't she asking about the two of them or had she just not gotten around to that question yet. How would she react when she learned he couldn't be with her? No matter how much he loved her, they couldn't be together. Any other woman would be pushing for forever, why not Ruby?

"It's hard," he said with a sigh. "I'm praying that with time it will get easier to look at women with child. I know that not all pregnancies end badly, but right now it's still painful to see."

Every time he saw a woman with child he remembered Laura's happiness over expecting. Her anticipation of the coming baby and then the painful memory of her death. Holding his dead, infant son was something he struggled with every day. He'd been such a fool.

Ruby was silent as she gazed up at the stars. "I didn't know Laura, but I'd think that she'd want the best for you."

Their friendship had grown into a comfortable companionship, but he'd never loved her, like he loved Ruby.

"She would have," he said without hesitation. "She had a sweet, gentle soul."

"Completely unlike me," Ruby said wistfully. "I wish I could be more like her."

Deke grabbed Ruby by the arms. "No," he said vehemently. "You're who you are for a reason. I love the way you're adventurous, outgoing, dangerous and fun. I love everything about you just the way you are. Except you take reckless chances that frightens me."

The words were out in the open. Those three little words he'd promised he would never say that he'd blurted out. He hadn't meant to tell her his feelings. It could go nowhere and yet they'd felt so natural coming from between his lips.

There were so many things he loved about Ruby and he didn't want to compare her and Laura. It wouldn't be fair to either woman. They were different and yet he cared about both women. Ruby had secured his heart when she was just a young girl, only he'd buried those feelings for years. Like the first rattle out of the box, she'd touched his heart and soul in ways that brought back the yearning he'd felt for that pretty young girl.

Silence filled the air. Ruby lifted her hand and caressed the side of his face. "I love you, Deke. I think I've been in love with you from the moment I first laid my eyes on you. I even tried not to love you this time."

His heart swelled with emotion and sweetness flowed through his veins. If only he could return the feelings, but he declined the notion to let himself even consider the emotion. Yes, he loved Ruby, but he didn't deserve to love again. One woman was buried because of his reckless selfishness, he refused to endanger another woman.

Pulling her into his arms, his hands came around her. "I should have married you all those years ago before I tied the knot with Laura."

Ruby shook her head. "No, we weren't ready. You had to marry Laura and I had to go bounty hunting with my sisters. We both had things in life to accomplish before we found each other again."

Deke felt his chest ache like someone had reached in, grabbed his heart and was trying to yank it from his body. Ruby deserved so much more than Deke. He was a broken man who'd made a mistake and left his pregnant wife alone, to catch one more bounty. One last criminal before the baby was born. His selfishness caused the death of his wife. Happiness was something he didn't deserve. He certainly could never marry again without risking getting his wife with child.

And Ruby…good lord the woman was danger walking with a target strapped to her back. Sooner or later, some angry outlaw would send a bullet her direction.

"Deke, I wasn't certain how you felt" Ruby trailed her hand down his face, pulling his lips to hers. "I love you."

His mouth covered hers and with his kiss he poured his heart and soul into his caress. Plundering her mouth he took possession, kissing her with all the passion he felt for Ruby. He loved her. He'd loved her for years, but he couldn't be with her. He couldn't take the chance of killing her like he'd killed Laura.

He kissed Ruby like he'd never kiss her again, needing and wanting her, quivering with the need to carry her away to the barn, but refusing. They weren't taking another chance of her getting pregnant. They'd gotten lucky the first two times, he wasn't risking a third time.

He broke off the kiss. His breathing heavy and restrictive. "You better go back inside. I'm going to bed down in the barn tonight."

She gazed at him the moonlight. "I'll see you in the morning."

"Good night, Ruby," he said and opened the door, pushing her inside before his willpower was completely devoid of strength. As he closed the door, he felt his chest shatter with pain. He'd never see the woman he loved again.

No he wouldn't be here in the morning. He'd be traveling, searching for his next bounty. Chances are that there's a bullet with his name on it.

~

The next morning, Ruby awakened to the house being quiet. Annabelle was normally the first one out of bed. She'd collect the eggs and often have breakfast on the table by the time everyone had risen.

"Ruby," Hannah said.

"Go back to sleep. You can sleep in," Ruby said.

Hannah sat up in bed. "No, I need to talk to you."

She glanced over at the young girl, her auburn hair flowing around her shoulders. She looked so innocent and young and how she'd survived living in a brothel, Ruby could only guess. Now she was free to choose her own life.

"Okay, what's wrong?" Ruby asked, pulling her boots on.

"Nothing is wrong. I appreciate everything you've done for me. But I don't think your sisters would approve of me being here if they knew I was a soiled dove."

If Hannah went searching for another job in a saloon, taking risky chances with cowboys, then Ruby knew she'd be right. But Hannah had not chosen the life that was thrust upon her and Ruby's sisters were open-minded enough that they would do everything they could to help the girl.

"Well, Meg no longer lives here and Annabelle is about the kindest person I know if you don't say anything negative about her husband or her sisters. I can tell them if it will make you feel better, but they're not going to care. They're going to be glad we got you out of that saloon."

Hannah sighed. "I just don't want to upset them."

Ruby placed her hands on her hips and stared at

Hannah. "Meg tied her husband up naked in the middle of Main street and left him. It's going to take a lot to hurt their sensibilities. You just need to concentrate on you. No hurry. Just think about what you're going to do with your life."

Meg was the fiery redhead and once she learned Hannah's story, it would be a wonder she didn't ride out and find the stepfather and turn him in herself. No, her sisters would not care about Hannah's past. They would be concentrating on her future.

Hannah smiled. "That's the other thing I wanted to talk to you about. I want you to teach me how to shoot. I want to become a bounty hunter."

Ruby starred at the young woman. "You're not planning on going back to Hide Town are you? You wouldn't be thinking about revenge, would you?"

Returning to the ruthless outlaw town would be the worst thing Hannah could do. They would love the opportunity to kill her. They wanted her silenced.

"Not unless they cross my path," Hannah said. "Then I could be tempted to kill my step-father."

"Hannah, I'll do everything I can to train you to become a bounty hunter, but I can't condone you going after someone to kill them. A good bounty hunter does not take the law into their own hands."

"Isn't that how you felt about Rivera?"

Ruby stopped as pain gripped her middle and squeezed her heart. The memory of her father's killer was an ugly remembrance of agony that had almost cost Deke's life was well as her father's. "Yes, but I would have brought him into the law if he hadn't put a gun to your head and tried to shoot Deke. I would never shoot someone with the idea that I wanted to kill them."

When they'd first started hunting, Meg had drilled into her the importance of letting the law do their job. Not seeking retribution, but allowing the law to render the punishment so that real criminals were put behind bars.

"That's the way I feel about my step-father."

"Promise me you'll stay away from Hide Town," Ruby said with a frown. She felt concerns that the girl would return and get herself either killed or be taken back into prostitution until they could dispose of her. She didn't want that for Hannah.

"I promise to be the best student you've had. I want to learn how to shoot and hunt for criminals like you. I promise not to kill unless I'm forced to, to defend my life."

"You're the only student I have for now." Ruby stood and gazed at the young woman. It wasn't exactly what she'd asked for, but maybe she was just excited. "Okay, we'll get started later today. But now I'm going to go collect the eggs before Annabelle this morning."

"Thanks Ruby. I owe you so much," Hannah said.

"Get some rest," Ruby said walking out the door.

Ruby hurried through the quiet house, eager to collect the eggs and see Deke. She still hated the chickens, but at least she was no longer afraid of the silly birds. She shoved them out of the way and they had finally learned to respect her.

Besides sneaking out early, she could kiss Deke good morning and maybe even talk to him about their plans. She wanted to continue bounty hunting, but would he? There were so many small details to work out…including marriage. He'd said he was never marrying again, but that was before they fell in love.

Shooing them out of their roost, Ruby collected the eggs from the hens. Once she'd finished, she opened the barn doors wondering why Deke had yet to come out. Usually he was an early riser.

When she entered the barn, she saw that his horse was missing from the stall and realized Deke was gone.

Sometime during the night, he'd fled.

"You bastard!" she said sinking down to the ground, her heart wrenched with pain, her chest feeling like someone had hit her smack in the ribs, knocking the air from her lungs.

Deke had said he loved her and then he'd left like a thief in the middle of the night. Not once but twice had he made a complete fool of her. Not once but twice he'd spurned her love. There wouldn't be a third time.

~

Hannah picked up the pistol that Ruby handed her. "Okay, Ladies, we're going to start off just learning how your body should be lined up before you fire."

A thrill of excitement went through Ruby. She was teaching two young women how to protect themselves. How to earn a living without depending on a man and giving them both self-respect. She couldn't help but smile. This could be the start of a great opportunity for Ruby to pass on the knowledge she'd learned hunting criminals.

Ruby twisted Hannah into the stance she wanted her in and then lifted her arm to point the pistol. "Don't close your eyes when you line up the sight of the gun with the target or squeeze the trigger. Line up the pistol, take a deep breath, hold it and slowly squeeze the trigger."

Wrapping her arms around Hannah's body, she lined her up and then squeezed the trigger. The bullet slammed into the dirt. "Okay, that's not a bad first attempt. Now we're going to repeat that process at least twenty times today. When you finally hit the tin can sitting on the fence, we'll stop for the day."

"Okay, Caroline it's your turn. You've had practice firing before, but your shots are not very precise. I want you to knock as many cans off the fence as you can. And don't close your eyes. Aim, hold your breath and look down the gun barrel to your target."

Caroline frowned and turned towards Ruby and Hannah, her gun in her hand, pointed at them. They both hit the ground.

"Confound it Caroline, watch where you're pointing that thing. I want to live to see my new niece or nephew," Ruby said standing and moving her arm away from the women.

The woman's eyes widened and she put her hand to her mouth. "Oops! Sorry, I didn't mean to."

"Just watch where you're pointing the gun. You know how dangerous a misfire can be. Now aim, take a deep breath and hold it while you fire."

The gun boomed and Caroline knocked a can off the fence. She turned her wide big brown eyes towards Ruby. "I did it. I hit the can."

Ruby smiled, wishing the happiness would reach her heart, but nothing seemed to affect her right now. Absolutely nothing. She felt dead inside like whatever spark of life was there before had been completely snuffed.

"Good, do it again."

How long had it taken her to hit the cans on the fence when she'd first started firing her guns? She couldn't remember it was so long ago. And she'd been a young girl. An innocent at the time.

"How will I know I've got the hang of firing a gun?" Hannah asked.

"When you can do this," Ruby said whipping her pistol out of the holster and knocking down all five cans on the fence.

Ruby didn't do it to impress Hannah or Caroline. She knocked down the cans to give the women a goal. Once the young women could knock off all he cans on the fence in a row, she'd graduate from Ruby's training.

"How long did it take you?" Caroline asked.

"Awhile. Practice is all that it takes."

People expected to just pick up a pistol aim it and hit the target. But it wasn't that simple and it took time and practice to become accurate. In this line of business, shooting was what kept a person alive.

Annabelle waddled down to the fence. "Who are you shooting at?"

"Just tin cans," Hannah said.

Ruby chuckled. "Annabelle, Meg and I use to draw faces on the cans and then we'd shoot the can's down."

Right now Ruby knew exactly whose face she'd draw on a can. His dark hair and emerald eyes would stand out on the rusted tin.

"Caroline, I didn't know you were here," Annabelle said.

"Good to see, Cousin. That baby's coming any day now."

"Yes and I'm ready."

A cool breeze blew, sending a chill through Ruby. Winter would soon be upon them and there would be no hunting until spring with just her memories.

The days of the three of them firing their guns to ease their frustrations seemed so long ago, but had only been a couple of years. So much had changed in that time. And now both her sisters would soon be teaching their children how to fire a gun.

"Oh, I bet you got better much quicker that way. I can think of two faces, I'll be putting on my cans," Hannah said.

"I don't know about getting quicker, but we took out a lot of frustration," Annabelle said. "And at that time we had lots to be angry about, didn't we."

The memory of the three of them losing their jobs and taking out frustrations putting bullets in poor defenseless cans was now a sweet recollection. The times had been hard, but it made them strong women.

"We did." Ruby hugged her sister. "I probably should do some target practice now to ease my displeasure."

Caroline patted her on the arm. "I'm sorry about Deke."

"Don't be. He obviously didn't want me badly enough to stay. I'll get over him."

Ruby had loved Deke since she was fifteen, but if he could ride away, then maybe it was time to let the feelings go.

Hannah picked up her pistol, aimed and fired a shot, hitting the wooden fence. She smiled. "If he doesn't want you, then he's a crazy man. Be strong Ruby. You deserve a man who loves you, for who you are."

"We all do Hannah, even you," Ruby said and fired her gun at a can sitting on the fence, knocking it to the ground. That one was for Deke.

~

Annabelle knew her time was close, but yet she'd watched Ruby moping around for the last two days since she'd discovered Deke had ridden off without saying goodbye.

She'd had enough. She didn't need to worry about anything but the birth of this baby, so today when Meg came out to check on her, they were going to have a family meeting. Enough pining for what Ruby didn't have, Annabelle needed action.

Besides her back had been killing her for near two days. She couldn't see her feet and her breasts were big and heavy and her waist didn't exist any longer.

Meg arrived right on schedule. She walked in and gave Annabelle a hug. "How are you?"

"I'm pregnant. And the new has worn off. I'm ready for this baby to arrive, so I don't feel like I'm hauling around a sack of feed all the time. I'm tired and mean enough that my husband has been fond of working out in the garden every day. And my back is aching bad enough that I'm thinking this may be the only child we have."

Meg laughed. "Lord help Zach when I reach the stage you're at. You're a lot more patient than me."

"And Lord help me from killing Ruby."

The girl's heart was breaking. She could see it on her face, but she refused to talk about the problems between her and Deke.

"What's wrong?"

"She's moping around here like her best friend died. Deke left night before last in the middle of the night without saying goodbye."

"That man has broken her heart more than once."

"Yes and this time I think more happened than she's letting on, if you get my drift. I mean they were alone without a chaperone and they've always been attracted to one another."

Ruby had loved Deke since she was fifteen, so Annabelle didn't doubt for a moment that they had been intimate.

"Oh dear. How is she taking it?"

"Not good. Twice I caught her crying. Ruby doesn't cry."

Annabelle knew it was serious when she witnessed Ruby wiping away tears and struggling to keep from sobbing. This time Deke's leaving had broken her heart. And there was nothing Annabelle could do but hope she got over him or they found a way to be together.

Meg shook her head. "You remember how it was, Annabelle. You cried pretty much every day. You two were so stubborn."

"And you and Zach were at odds as well," Annabelle said staring at her sister.

The months since they'd both married had been good

for them. And their husbands loved and treated them like queens. Yet both couples almost ended before they'd begun. Now it appeared Ruby and Deke were facing the same dilemma.

"How can we help them?" Meg asked.

"Until Ruby tells us the problem, we can't," Annabelle said.

"Where is the girl?"

Just then Ruby came in from collecting the eggs. Her face was drawn and tired and she looked sad. She hung her bonnet up on a nail. "I swear that one hen is not going to live to see another day. If she pecks me one more time she's going in the pot."

Ruby glanced up and noticed both of her sisters staring at her. "What?"

"Sit down. We need to talk."

The young woman made her way to the table, her face changing from frustration to a blank expressionless stare. She knew what was coming.

They all sat down around the table where they had made their families decisions together for many years.

"Annabelle told me about Deke. I'm sorry Ruby."

The girl shrugged her shoulders. "Nothing to be sorry for. The man said he loved me and the next morning he got on his horse and rode away. That's a fine way for a man to show you he cares about you. He's not worth my time or my trouble."

The bravado in her words was to hide the pain Annabelle could see on her face. This time Deke may have killed the love between them. This time, Ruby may have given up on the two of them.

Meg shook her head. "Do you love him?"

"Now, that's not a fair question to ask."

"Why not?" Annabelle asked knowing how her sister felt about Deke, but wanting her to confess her feelings.

"Because the two of you know I've cared for that man for years. Maybe not grown-up love, but still you know it's always been Deke."

Annabelle shook her head. "I do not believe you."

"What do you mean? You and I fought over him," Ruby said.

"We were both young and stupid. We were both too young to go there. But you were only fifteen at the time."

At the time Ruby had been a brash, flirtatious woman who was used to enticing men to do her biding. She wasn't ready for a man like Deke.

"If you love him, then why aren't you fighting for him?" Meg asked. "Why haven't you ridden after him?"

Ruby's eyes widened. "Have you taken a good look at Annabelle lately? She looks like she's going to explode at any moment and a baby's going to walk out of her belly partially grown. If I didn't know better, I'd think she was going to have twins."

"Sh! I don't want twins. Don't jinx me."

The thought of taking care of one baby was overwhelming, but two…how did people cope with two of them? And sure she had her sister's help, but they had their own lives and learning to take care of one baby was all Annabelle wanted.

"I'm not going to go off and leave her while she can't see her feet. I'm just not," Ruby said.

Leaning over Annabelle patted her on the arm. "Thank you. But your heart is not here. Why can't you and Deke be together? Why did he leave?"

Annabelle knew that there was something that she wasn't telling her sisters. Something that was keeping the lovers apart and was the reason that Deke rode away. Ruby loved him, so what problem was keeping them apart?

Ruby glanced down at the table. "It's you Annabelle."

"Me? What did I do?"

"You're pregnant," Ruby said.

Annabelle listened while Ruby told them about Deke marrying Laura and how she'd died during childbirth. How at the sight of Annabelle, Deke had recoiled and withdrawn.

"I know it's seeing the rounded belly of a woman with child," Ruby said.

"That's not what made Deke leave the woman he loves behind," Meg said. "Or he doesn't love my sister enough to make her his wife."

The thought of losing this baby after carrying it for almost nine months would devastate Annabelle. In some ways, she could understand Deke's plight, but she couldn't change his situation and frankly she didn't want to. This baby meant everything to her and Beau.

Annabelle shook her head. "I'm sorry, but the world is not going to stop having babies, just because Deke Culver gets upset at the sight of a woman with child."

"I know. And I think he'll get over it, it's just going to take some time. But in the meantime he's refusing to get married again because he doesn't want to get another woman pregnant. He fears watching another woman die."

The three women sat back and frowned. Annabelle knew that women died in childbirth, but she was more afraid of the baby dying than her own death. That thought kept her awake at night.

"Men can be impossible," Meg said.

"How do you help someone get over this?"

Time was the great healer. Annabelle missed her papa so much, but life had gone on. Deke would eventually heal, but right now it was painful.

"You go after him, you tie him up and you tell him how done you are with him. That he's left you twice now and that there will not be a third opportunity," Annabelle said. "Then if he comes after you, you know it's going to be okay."

"But if he doesn't," Meg said looking directly at Ruby. "You ride away. You're done."

When you love someone with all your heart and soul, riding away was not as easy as it sounded. Annabelle knew. She'd walked away from Beau. Thank God, he'd found her.

"That's not going to cure him. He said he would never marry again or get a woman pregnant or have children. And he wanted me to quit bounty hunting. Maybe we aren't supposed to be together," Ruby said swiping a tear from her eye.

"Love means sacrificing your happiness for the good of the person you love. Do you love Deke or are you just infatuated with the idea of love?" Annabelle asked.

If Ruby loved Deke, she would give up bounty hunting for him and Annabelle would be so relieved that her sister was no longer in danger.

"How do you know?" Ruby asked. "How did you know with Beau? With Zach?"

"I knew with Beau when we reached Fort Worth," Annabelle said.

"And I knew Zach had to prove to me he was a good man who was worthy of my love," Meg said.

Would Ruby give up bounty hunting for Deke if that's what he required?

"Is Deke worthy of your affection?"

"I think the question should be, am I worthy of Deke's devotion. I'm wondering if I'm worthy of that man's love? I know this is a huge thing for him and I don't want to let him down. He's a good man. Am I capable of being the kind of wife he deserves?"

Annabelle resisted the urge to smile. Yes, Ruby was in love with Deke. She was already thinking like a woman in love.

"There's no way of finding out until you find him."

"But Annabelle…I can't go off and leave you."

"Hannah is here and I'll be out every day, until you get back."

Ruby stared at her hands and then she looked up at Annabelle. "Are you okay with me leaving?"

Annabelle loved her sister for thinking of her welfare, but she needed to work things out with Deke. "I want you to be happy. This baby is going to come when it's good and ready and not before."

Ruby smiled for the first time in days and Annabelle knew they'd made the right decision. "I'll hurry. I don't know where I'm going to find him, but I'll head in the direction of Dyersville, where he said he was going back and hopefully he'll be along the trail. You're certain Annabelle?"

"I'm certain," she said with a smile. "Just hurry or you'll miss the birth of your first nephew or niece."

"I won't be gone a moment longer than necessary."

"I know," Annabelle said and prayed that she'd return before the baby was born.

Chapter Sixteen

Deke Culver sat around his campfire, drinking. Already he'd emptied one bottle and had a second bottle just in case this one didn't dull the pain. Whatever it took to vanquish the image of Ruby from his mind and his heart and his soul. That girl had imprinted herself onto his very essence and he couldn't get her out of his mind.

Every time he closed his eyes she appeared. Every time he laid down his head to sleep, she invaded his dreams. And every time he thought of what he wanted to do next in his life, Ruby's image emerged.

It was almost like his soul was crying out that he'd lost his guiding force. Like he had lost his way in the wilderness and now he wandered aimlessly. So lost, he did what he had only done a few times in his life. He got drunk.

Tonight he'd saturated his body with liquor. Hard liquor that he hoped would wipe the slate clean of images of Ruby in that risqué dress dealing poker. Of Ruby dancing in the rain. Of Ruby, her head thrown back in passion as she came apart in his arms.

God, he loved her. He knew he did. But because he loved her, he couldn't be with her. She couldn't die in his arms, like Laura. He couldn't face another tragedy of that realm. He would shoot himself rather than watch someone else he loved die.

That was why he couldn't be with Ruby. If childbirth didn't kill her, she'd kill herself by taking a risk. A needless chance. And he wasn't going to watch her get shot by an outlaw she was chasing. Or take a chance and jump off another cliff into the river. If the fall didn't kill her hitting a rock could.

There were so many things he loved about her, that she frightened him. Losing Laura had almost killed him and he hadn't loved her like he did Ruby. If Ruby was to die, how could he handle the pain?

Finally, he'd drank himself into a stupor and he sunk down onto his bedroll, numb from the alcohol and passed out.

~

Ruby found his tracks and it didn't take long to catch him. She'd spotted him right after dark and sat in stunned silence watching him drink himself until he obviously could no longer function.

She'd never seen Deke drunk. In fact, she'd only tasted the alcohol on him once. The night he'd caught her dancing in the rain.

The sight of him inebriated out of his mind, taking a risk on the trail to anyone who happened by when he was besotted, just made her even angrier. The man thought she took chances, he needed to look inward.

Well she was going to fix him right up. If he thought she took risks, she was going to show him what a fool he was for jeopardizing his life, drunk.

An hour before dawn, she snuck into his camp. The puppy looked up at her with sleepy eyes, its tail thumping in recognition and gave a quick bark of hello. Quickly she wrapped the rope around his feet and tied it securely. Throwing the rope over a tree branch, she tied one end to her saddle horn and then talked her mustang into moving forward. The horse lifted Deke's body up off the ground.

When he was swinging upside down wildly from the tree, he opened his eyes. "What the hell?"

Ruby bit her lip to keep from smiling. The fool was certainly not expecting this early morning wake up call.

"Good morning, Deke."

"What the hell?"

"I'm showing you how you take reckless chances that

could get you killed. You drank so much last night that I was able to ride into your camp, this morning, tie you up and hoist you into a tree. You didn't even move when your dog barked hello."

The pit in her stomach that had been coiled into a knot suddenly released and calmness settled over Ruby. Whatever doubts that remained about the two of them vanished. He deserved this little retribution for forgetting how good they were together. For forgetting the attraction that existed between them since she was a young girl. For forgetting about the love that flowed between them like a river, connecting them. But he wouldn't forget after today.

"Let me down. My head is throbbing and this doesn't help. I'm going to puke if you don't get me down."

"That's what happens when you drink too much."

"I had things to forget."

"Things? You mean me? Alcohol will not wipe me out."

He swung there glaring at her.

"Twice now you've turned me down. You tell me you love me and then you ride away."

She watched him trying to reach his feet, his hands flaying wildly in the air, causing him to swing even more. Part of her felt bad for hurting him, yet her heart kept telling her, this was right. This shaking up was exactly what Deke needed.

He stopped flailing and stared at her upside down. "You should be glad I left you. I refuse to watch you get yourself killed."

"Coward."

"The hell I am."

"That's not why you left me."

Deke's fear of getting her pregnant and seeing her sisters with child was what had him moving faster than a squirrel in a cage.

His body swung in the tree as he bent to reach up unsuccessfully to get loose. Finally he stopped again and glared at her. "You know I can't be with you. I'm not killing another woman."

She crossed her arms across her chest and stared at him. How do you reach a man who is hurt like Deke?

"Don't you think women die every day from childbirth? Do you think you're the only man who's lost a wife? Has the world stopped having babies because Deke Culver's wife died?"

"Cut me loose," he demanded trying to reach the ropes around his ankles. "I know babies are born every day. But it's my fault Laura is dead."

Ruby shook her head at him. "Did you do everything you could to save her life?"

"Yes."

Sure Deke had made mistakes with Laura's pregnancy. He'd gone off bounty hunting leaving her alone. That one would ride his conscious to the end of his days, but even when you make mistakes, you get a second chance. A chance to do better.

"Then how is it your fault? You can either continue living in the past, blaming yourself for something you had no control over or you can stop being a coward and get on with life. Your choice."

Deke looked like if he could reach her, he'd smack her, but she wasn't worried. He might want to throttle her, but would never hit a woman. The knots would hold for awhile longer. But right now she had to help him see reason.

"Cut me loose," he yelled at her.

She shook her head. "I loved you. I loved you enough that I had even considered giving up bounty hunting because you wanted to get out of the business. I was willing to make sacrifices and you weren't."

"The hell I wasn't. And you never told me you would

give up bounty hunting."

"That's because you ran like a coward during the night."

"Well, I wasn't going to stick around and watch your sister…"

Somehow he had to realize that not every pregnancy resulted in death.

"My sister is doing just fine and I'm confident that Annabelle will have that baby and live to watch the child becomes an adult."

"I hope so. I really do," Deke said still trying to reach his ankles. "Now get me down before I start throwing up."

Maybe next time he wouldn't drink quite so much. Maybe next time he'd realize that he had been foolish to get besotted and left himself vulnerable on the trail.

"Why should I?"

"Because, you love me."

"But you don't love me enough to spend the rest of your life with me. I could get killed riding home today. You could get killed watching the grass grow. We only have whatever time God has given us to be together. And you're wasting it."

Ruby threw a knife and it landed in the dirt, just out of Deke's reach. "Have a great day, Deke. I'm going home to my sisters. I'm doing chasing you."

She tied the rope around a tree, being sure there was no slack. She climbed up on her horse and turned to stare at him, tears streaming down her cheeks.

"I never suspected that you were a coward, but damn it Deke, you're the worst kind of yellow belly. A man who can't admit his feelings."

She rode out of the clearing. It was time to go home to her sisters. She'd given it one last try and he hadn't budged.

~

Deke Culver was the biggest damn fool. And now he was going to have to do some major apologizing to Ruby for her to agree to marry him.

The last week he'd been miserable without her. All he could do was remember and think about her and wonder what she was doing. And when she'd ridden into his camp, he'd felt so much relief at seeing her, until she'd left him hung over and tied up.

Somewhere along the trail he'd realized that it wasn't just the childbirth thing, but it was dying. Any time anyone loved this much the risk of having his heart ripped out was there, leaving you vulnerable. Laura had been a really good friend, but Ruby was everything.

Ruby made him into a better man, she was strong and tough and more woman than he'd ever dreamed of loving. He wanted as much time as possible with this woman he'd fallen madly in love with.

He rode up into the yard of the McKenzie farm. No one greeted him. No one came to the door. As he stepped on the porch he could hear a woman screaming.

The sound sent a shiver of fear scurrying down his spine. What if that was Annabelle?

"Beau Samuel what have you done?"

"Honey, take a deep breath. Sugar, you know I mean well. We're all learning here."

"Where is the doctor?"

"He should be on his way," Beau said.

Maybe Deke should ride away and come back later after the baby was born. He didn't want to witness the birth. The remembrance of Ruby calling him a coward settled on his chest like an anvil. The time for running away was over. He needed to face his fears. And it sounded like the biggest one was happening now.

He knocked on the door. Hannah answered.

"Oh dear," she said.

"I need to see Ruby," he said, holding his hat in shaking hands.

He was running out of time to walk away.

"Who is it Hannah," Ruby called.

"Deke," he called.

"Get in here."

He walked into the house and through the door of the bedroom. He stared at the group around the bed. Beau was white as snow, Ruby gazed at him anxiously and Annabelle appeared worn out.

"What's wrong?" Deke said not even saying hello.

"It's been a difficult birth," Ruby said. "Annabelle is worn out and the doctor has yet to arrive."

Just like what happened with Laura. He clenched his fists, his breath swooshing from his lungs as he resisted the urge to turn and run away. He wanted nothing to do with watching Annabelle struggle to birth a baby and then the two of them die. He had to leave.

Ruby watched him and he could see the need for his help in her eyes, but he wanted to run. He couldn't help her, he just couldn't.

She'd called him a coward and she was right. He was frightened out of his mind and this was exactly what had happened to Laura. He couldn't relive this with Annabelle.

"I can't stay."

Ruby bathed Annabelle's face with a cool cloth. Her voice was tired and full of fear. "Get out and don't come back."

That was all that he needed to hear. "Wait, Ruby."

He swallowed and tried to control his shaking hands. What had he done that helped Laura? What had happened those final moments before they delivered the baby?

Glancing at Beau because he needed to know that he

was okay with him helping his wife. He asked, "How long has she been in labor?"

"Twelve hours. Meg's gone to find the mid-wife."

"How far apart are the pains?"

Laura's pains had sapped her strength at the end. She'd been almost limp after the last one that had delivered their child.

Annabelle turned her tired eyes on him. "They're coming faster and faster."

That meant the end was not far off.

"Do you mind if I take a look?" he asked glancing between Annabelle and Beau. "When I delivered my son, he arrived when the pains were almost on top of one another."

The couple exchanged glances and Beau said, "Go ahead."

Deke lifted up the sheet and he could see that Annabelle was almost ready. "Good news. I can see the top of the baby's head."

He took a deep breath. Somehow he had to help this couple keep from experiencing what had happened to him. But what if they died? He couldn't live with himself if another mother and child died because of him.

Quickly he pushed the thought away and remembered what he had to do. Keep the mother calm and help her push through the pains.

"Annabelle, I need you to calm down and remember women have been having babies for hundreds of years."

Ruby's mouth dropped open and he smiled at her. Hadn't she reminded him that the world would continue to have babies without him?

"Oh my God, I can feel him," Annabelle said.

Ruby rushed to her sister's feet and gazed at the head. "Come on Annabelle, the baby is almost here. Give us one more push and I think the baby will be born."

Annabelle gazed up at Beau. "I'm too tired. I can't."

"Come on honey, you want to see our baby girl, don't you?"

"It's a boy," she argued. "Oh no, here comes another pain. I can't do this…"

Deke ran his hand through his hair, his nerves tightening inside him, fear pushing him to save Ruby's sister. "Beau, crawl up in the bed with Annabelle and place her in between your legs. You're going to lift Annabelle during the next pain. Ruby you're going to push down her stomach, like you're trying to push the baby out."

"Okay," Ruby said getting into position.

"Let's hope this works," Deke said. "Push, Annabelle. You're almost there. Breathe and push."

"Come on, let's do this together. Push honey, push," Beau said coaching his wife.

Annabelle strained and screamed as she was pushing, her face glowing a bright red while her husband lifted her. Ruby made hard stroking motions with her hands on Annabelle's extended belly like she was shoving the child out.

"Almost there," Deke said placing his hands to catch the baby's head. With a mighty swoosh, the baby's head came through and then Deke gently pulled the rest of her body out.

"Hand me a wet rag," he said.

Ruby handed him the wash cloth and he gently wiped the baby's face and mouth clean, so she could breathe. The baby girl opened her eyes and glanced at him. She was alive.

The infant started to cry and Annabelle held out her arms. "Let me have him."

"Hang on Mom, we need to cut the umbilical cord. Beau would you do the honor of cutting the cord on your baby girl."

"It's a girl," Annabelle said laughing.

Beau reached down and cut the cord that tied the infant to Annabelle. Tears rolled down his cheeks and he lifted the infant from Deke's hands and laid it up on Annabelle's stomach. Through her tears, she smiled down at Deke.

"Thank you," she said. "I don't know how much longer I could have gone on."

His heart nearly burst with pride, and love, and joy. "No, thank you for letting me be a part of this joyful occasion."

"I know your past, Deke. I'm sorry about your son, but you saved me and our daughter. Thank you," Annabelle said weeping.

Tears welled up in his eyes and he glanced over at Ruby. She was openly crying. "If you hadn't come today, I don't know what would have happened. Thank you."

She fell into his arms and he held onto her. He owed this family so much. While the death of his own infant son and Laura would always be painful, today was the first step to healing that hurt. He'd delivered Annabelle's baby.

"Maybe we should let the new family get to know each other," he said.

They walked out of the room, holding onto each other.

"You were right," he said. "I'm the biggest coward that probably walked this earth. I'm afraid of seeing you hurt. I'm afraid watching you take chances. I'm afraid of pain – the pain of losing you. Yet somehow during the last week it's hurt more to know that I hurt you by leaving after saying I love you and missing you."

She glanced up at him staring him in the eye. The pain of leaving her rushed at him and he knew he couldn't live without her.

"I'm a weak, spineless man who doesn't like to see the people I love hurt. When I care about someone, I give them everything and so when they hurt, I hurt. When they feel pain, I feel pain and when they die…I want to die."

He took a deep breath and released. "But right now I'm in the worst sort of pain, because I knew when you left, that you weren't coming back. That there would not be another chance to prove that I love you. That no matter what you were done. And that scared me worse than anything I've ever felt."

He got down on one knee and she gasped.

His heart was overflowing with love for this woman and no matter what, her dangerous activities, her recklessness, her need for adventure, none of that would stop him from loving her. From wanting to spend his life with her.

"I know I said I would never marry again. I would never take a chance of endangering your life, but you make my life fun and exciting and I can't imagine you not being by my side. I love you, Ruby. Please say you'll marry me."

She licked her lips. "You're not going to back out again, Deke, are you?"

"Never. You make my life richer and happier than I've ever been. I need you."

Ruby flew into his arms, sending him backwards onto the ground. He wrapped his arms around her. "Yes, I'll marry you. But I have a few conditions."

"And they are?" he asked suddenly worried.

"I am a strong, independent woman. You will not boss me around and tell me what to do."

"Can we make our decisions together?" he asked.

She thought about it for a moment. "Yes. I can agree to that."

"Okay, what else."

Taking a deep breath, she released it slowly. "I want to train young women to be independent. To become bounty hunters if they choose. Or simply to learn how to shoot. I've got to have something to keep me busy and needlepoint is not going to do it."

Relief flowed through Deke and a joyous laugh came from within. "As long as you're careful. And by careful, I mean you teach them to hit a target and not you."

She smiled. "Deke it took you long enough to come around."

He held her in his arms. "Like I said, you scare me Ruby, but I love you more than the fear you incite in me."

"Every time I scare you, we'll make love," she said.

"I'll take you up on that offer," he whispered. "You know proposing is kind of scary."

Ruby's eyes widened. "What can I do to help you through your fear?"

"Well…" His lips claimed hers and for the first time in years, Deke felt like he'd come home to where his heart belonged.

Thank you for reading!

Dear Reader,

I hope you enjoyed Ruby and Deke's story, *Daring*. I'm having so much fun writing this series that I've decided to add three more women. Next up will be the young girl who was sold into prostitution, Hannah in Determined. That story should be available in July. Caroline's story is after hers and I'm hoping to have that one out in September.

Plus look for a new series I'm starting this summer called *Scandalous Suffragette Brides*. This series will be about young women who wanted the right to own a business, own property and vote in a small town where women are to be seen and not heard. Look for that in mid-summer.

I have one small request. If you're inclined, please leave a review. Whether or not you loved the book or hated, it I'd enjoy your feedback. Reviews are difficult to obtain and have the power to make or break a book.

Reading one of my books is like spending time with me, and I just want to say thank you from the bottom of my heart.

Yours in Drama, Divas, Bad Boys and Romance!
Sincerely,

Sylvia McDaniel

Books by Sylvia McDaniel

Contemporary Romance

Standalones
The Reluctant Santa
My Sister's Boyfriend
The Wanted Bride
The Relationship Coach
Her Christmas Lie
Secrets, Lies, and Online Dating
Paying for the Past
Cupid's Revenge

Anthologies
Kisses, Laughter & Love
Christmas with you

Collaborative Series

Magic, New Mexico
Touch of Decadence

Western Historicals

Standalones
A Hero's Heart
A Scarlet Bride
Second Chance Cowboy

The Cuvier Women
Wronged
Betrayed
Beguiled

Lipstick and Lead
Desperate
Deadly
Dangerous
Daring
Determined
Deceived

Scandalous Suffragettes
Abigail
Bella
Callie
Faith

The Burnett Brides
The Rancher Takes a Bride
The Outlaw Takes a Bride
The Marshal Takes a Bride
The Christmas Bride

Anthologies
Wild Western Women
Courting the West
Wild Western Women Ride Again

Collaborative Series

The Surprise Brides
Ethan

American Mail Order Brides
Katie

About the Author

Sylvia McDaniel is a best-selling, award-winning author of historical romance and contemporary romance novels. Known for her sweet, funny, family-oriented romances, Sylvia is the author of The Burnett Brides, a western historical western series, The Cuvier Widows, a Louisiana historical series, and several short contemporary romances.

She is the former President of the Dallas Area Romance Authors, a member of the Romance Writers of America®, and a member of Novelists Inc. Her novel, A Hero's Heart, was a 1996 Golden Heart Finalist. Several other books have placed or won in the San Antonio Romance Authors Contest and the LERA Contest, and she was a Golden Network Finalist.

Married for nearly twenty years to her best friend, they have two dachshunds that are beyond spoiled and a good-looking, grown son who thinks there's no place like home.

She loves gardening, shopping, knitting, and football (Cowboys and Bronco's fan), but not necessarily in that order.

Look for her the first Tuesday of every month at the Plotting Princesses blogspot, and be sure to sign up for her newsletter to learn about new releases and contests. Every month a new subscriber is entered into a drawing for a free book!

She can be found online at: www.sylviamcdaniel.com or on Facebook. You can write to Sylvia at P.O. Box 2542, Coppell, TX 75019.

Looking for a new book to read?
Check out Determined!

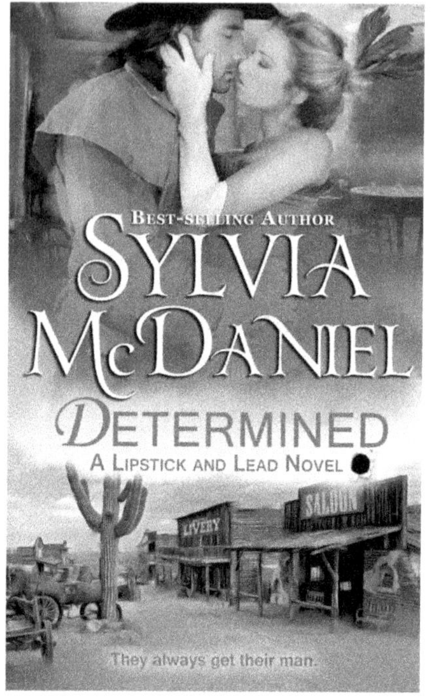

Hannah Williams' first goal after becoming a bounty hunter is to return to Hide Town, Texas to seek revenge on the man who sold her into prostitution. While searching for her stepfather, she stumbles across a man brutally beaten and takes him to her hideout. There, she is horrified to discover she has rescued the very man who turned his back on her during her blackest moment.

Preacher Jackson Colster never imagined the girl he refused to help would one day return to town and save his life. Now he must save Hannah from her destructive path of retribution while resisting the lure of her determined spirit. Or in mending her damaged past, will she help him confront his own haunting nightmares?

Can Hannah and Jackson heal their wounds, silence the past, and let love guide their future?

Sneak Peek into Determined

Hannah Williams knew life was hard. This past year had shown her she could never let her guard down, or she'd suffer the consequences. That very guard was firmly in place as she watched a man beaten while she hid in the bushes on the outskirts of Hide Town, Texas.

In this town, the bad guys were in control, and she'd returned to get revenge on the people who'd changed her life forever—to reclaim her good name and kill the man responsible for her misfortune and the woman who'd helped him.

From the shadows, she watched the madam's three goons beat the man who hung limply between them, no longer fighting. His face was bloodied, his eyes already swelling shut, his lip cracked and bleeding.

Oh, how she wanted to scurry away, leave him and the goons, and mind her own business. But what if Ruby hadn't rescued her? What if six months ago she'd ridden away, leaving Hannah behind?

"Enough," one of the men said. "I think he's damn near dead."

"Let's go," the ringleader said. "It's getting close to dark, and I've got things to do besides beat a stupid man."

"What about the girl?"

Hannah sank back deeper into the shadows. What girl were they talking about? While she'd returned to town seeking retribution, she wasn't ready to show herself just yet.

"She's not here. He must have gotten her out of town."

"Damn, she was a pretty one. I was looking forward to getting me a piece of that young'un."

Alarm spiraled through Hannah, yet she wasn't afraid. Her resolve strengthened, and she reached down and felt the gun at her side. Lovingly, she touched the revolver, knowing she didn't fear using it on any man who would harm her.

"If you think she's so gorgeous, you chase her into a town where the sheriff doesn't look the other way. You'll be looking down her father's rifle in no time with a village full of people ready to string you up for hurting one of their own."

Another young girl must have been captured, and they'd tried to force her into prostitution.

Dropping the man's arms, they let him fall to the ground. "Let's leave him for the coyotes."

One of the men gave the senseless man a swift kick in the ribs. The body on the ground moved but didn't make a sound. She wondered if he was dead.

The outlaws climbed on their horses. Hannah watched as they spurred them and rode off in the semi-darkness. Now what did she do?

Creeping out of the shadows, she hurried to the man on the ground and rolled him over. He groaned, letting her know he lived. There was little time in case the goons returned. The beaten man had one chance to get on her horse, or she was leaving him behind.

She shook him. Slowly, he opened his swollen eyelids and tried to gaze at her.

"Do you want to live?" she asked, knowing they needed to get out of here before the outlaws circled back to finish the job they'd started and found them both.

He groaned.

"If you want to live, you've got to help me get you on my horse. I can't do this alone."

There was no way she could get him in the saddle without his help, and there was no way he could walk. And there was no way she was staying here on the prairie tonight without a fire.

"Leave me. Let me die," he groaned. "I'll be in a better

place."

Shaking her head, she started to walk away and then went back, unable to do as he requested. "Better hope the coyotes don't find you before you die. Because there are a lot of those critters around here, and they're hungry. They like to play with their food for a while before they rip into the carcass. You'll taste pretty yummy to them."

"All right, you made your point."

She watched as the man crawled to his knees, shaking his head. Rushing to his side, she helped him to his feet. Placing her arms beneath his armpits, she supported him as he hobbled to her horse. "What did you do that angered the madam's goons?"

"You're in danger," he managed to mumble between swollen lips. "Leave me."

"I live with danger," she spat out. She had only one goal left worth living for. After that, she didn't care what happened to her. But she wasn't dying until her revenge was complete. If it took her fighting from the pit of hell, she'd settle the score for losing her innocence and the killing of her mother.

Helping him crawl up on her horse, she climbed up behind him. He leaned forward, hugging the animal's neck, barely able to ride, and she feared he would fall before they could reach the abandoned shack she'd claimed as her own.

"What's your name?" she asked.

"Jackson Colster," he muttered through swollen lips.

At the name, anger rushed through her like a strong wind. This ugly man was the damn preacher who had turned his back on her when she'd tried to escape, the very man who her mother had gone to and told she feared her husband. His only response was to tell her that marriage was forever.

This preacher man? Hannah hadn't cared whether he lived or died so why was she now helping him to live?

The urge to push him off her horse and leave him behind was strong, but Hannah was not going to be a hypocrite like the one she had riding on her horse. She'd give him shelter, doctor his wounds, and send him on his way.

While she prepared for the coming battle.

~

Jackson slipped in and out of consciousness as they rode through the darkness. He knew he was lucky to be alive, though at this second, he wished he would die. There wasn't a spot on his body that didn't throb, even his big toe felt like they'd taken a hammer to the digit. For a moment, he'd thought an angel had arrived to take him to heaven, but when she said she was leaving him for the coyotes, he knew he was still here on earth.

Someone had rescued him, and that didn't feel right.

The horse stopped, and the girl slipped over the side. "Come on, we're here."

He had no idea where *here* was, but at least his sore body wouldn't be bouncing on the back of a slow moving horse. Gingerly, he slid his leg over the side and let his torso slide down the animal. When his feet touched the ground, he would have fallen, except there were two small strong hands there steadying him.

"Where are we?"

"An abandoned shack," she said. "I'm sorry, but there are no fires and no lights."

"Why not?" he asked, not really caring, but wondering just the same.

"Don't need any unwanted company," she said, vague in her response.

There was no way he could survive another beating, so he was fine hiding out.

They took a step toward the cabin, and he wanted to

groan with the smallest movement, but he bit his lip to hold in his response.

"Just a little further, and then we'll get you settled for the night."

"Thank you," he said softly, knowing he owed this woman for saving his life.

"Don't thank me," she said, her voice tense in the darkness. "I didn't save you because I like you. I saved you because someone else rescued me. I'm just paying back the universe for sending someone who had the courage to get me out of that hellhole."

Like a bolt of lightning striking the ground in front of him, he recognized the young woman.

The whore who had begged him to liberate her from the madam. At the time, he'd been new to town and believed she'd willingly chosen her lifestyle. Now, he knew different. Now, he knew the ugly truth surrounding the way the madam acquired her new girls.

Hannah Williams was the girl he'd refused to help, the one he'd always regretted turning his back on. "Hannah, why did you return?"

"Only one reason, preacher man. Revenge. You're just lucky I'm not interested in killing you for your lack of compassion."

Preacher man came out sounding like an insult, a slur to his profession. She had every right to be angry with him, but right now he just couldn't feel any worse than he already did. And he'd stolen the last young girl from the madam.

"I didn't save you, but you rescued me."

"I damn sure did. Shows I have more compassion than you do."

He sighed. Being a man of God was never easy, and Hannah had been one of his many failings. "I wish you hadn't come back."

www.ingramcontent.com/pod-product-compliance
Lightning Source LLC
Chambersburg PA
CBHW070923190726
48292CB00004B/1087